THUNDER AT DAWN

'Open fire!'

He heard that last passed to Garrick.
Seconds later the after 9.2 recoiled, spat
flame and smoke and the *crack*! racketed
through them, the shudder ran through the
ship.

Thunder closed the wreck of the *Elizabeth
Bell* slowing.

A salvo burst and Wakely said
behind him, 'Short!' And: 'That one was
short, sir!'

They had dawdled only minutes but that
was too long, far too long.

The *Elizabeth Bell* went down as the 9.2
shook their ringing ears. She stood on
her head with her rusty stern and idle
screw perpendicular, slid down with a roar of
escaping steam and dull thumping internal
explosions.

Thunder At Dawn

Alan Evans

CORONET BOOKS
Hodder and Stoughton

Copyright © 1978 by Alan Stokes

First published in Great Britain
1978 by Hodder and Stoughton Limited

Coronet edition 1980

British Library C.I.P.
Evans, Alan
    Thunder at dawn.
    I. Title
    823'.9'1F   PR6055.V13T/

    ISBN 0–340–24511–5

Printed and bound in Great Britain for
Hodder and Stoughton Paperbacks, a
division of Hodder and Stoughton Ltd.,
Mill Road, Dunton Green, Sevenoaks,
Kent (Editorial Office : 47 Bedford
Square, London, WC1 3DP) by
Richard Clay (The Chaucer Press) Ltd.,
Bungay, Suffolk

To my father,

who was 'old Navy'

My thanks are due to many people who helped me with this book and in particular David Lyon of the National Maritime Museum, Derek Pilley and Lieutenant Michael Pilley, R.N. But any mistakes are mine!

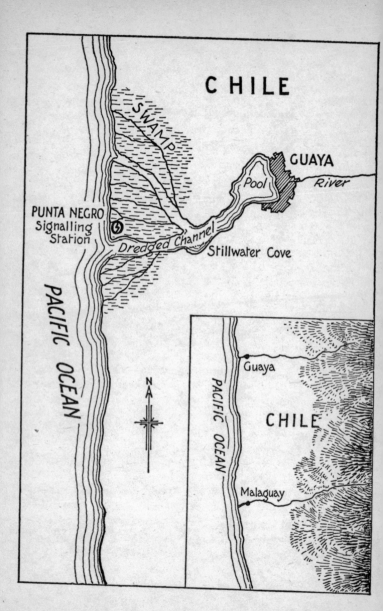

I

BLACK AS THE hob of hell.

First of June 1916.

Off Jutland.

A wheeling darkness cut by the white wings of *Sabre*'s bow-wave. The Coxswain seemed to float like a wraith on the little open bridge as he shouted wide-mouthed at Smith. "Black as the hob o' hell, sir! But there's summat out there!"

Smith grinned at him, cool. Cold. They were not good enough at this night-fighting and a destroyer was a fragile craft. They'd had a taste of it an hour before, been hit and hurt and fired all their torpedoes. They raced on through the night, trailing the pin-point of red that marked *Swordsman* ahead, and ahead of her was the flotilla leader, *Sentinel*. While outside in the darkness ...

Young Gillies, the Sub, yelled, "Ship! Red four-five! Challenge, sir?"

Smith heard himself answer, "No!" He saw the looming black bulk of two big cruisers and just from that glimpse he knew them. But *Sentinel* challenged, signal-lamp blinking, only to be washed in the converging cones of searchlight beams and smashed as the cruisers' guns opened up. The little ships, *Swordsman* and *Sentinel*, exploded in flame.

Sabre could try to run, or she could draw the fire.

Smith heard his voice crack as he yelled at the gun's crew forward. "Fire at the lights!" The quickfirer broke into its barking. It was the only weapon they had. "Hard aport!" *Sabre* swerved and plunged at the cruisers and the lights burst on him, blinding him, revealing all of them on the little bridge as in the light of day, their sole protection the canvas dodger that barely kept off the spray. They were under fire from both cruisers so that *Sabre* ran through a forest of water-spouts like towering, white-topped trees.

The near-misses hurled the sea inboard, the hit aft heeled *Sabre* over. The blast from another threw Smith to the deck and the gun had gone, leaving a crater that belched flame. *Sabre* rolled under him and Gillies fell on him, his serious young face blank and eyes wide.

The lights snuffed out, *Sabre* capsized and Smith fell into the reaching dark, the sea wrapping cold around him.

He woke, sweat cold on his skin, threshing in the big bed. The woman, still sleeping, mumbled and reached out for him but he slid away from the hand, out of the bed. He stumbled, groping, across the dark room to the window, twitched back one curtain and stared out at the day. It was barely light, a winter's dawn come grey under the hanging pall of London's smoke. The street lay quiet between the high, handsome faces of the houses of the wealthy. Only one old man shuffled along, shoving a barrow, collecting the piles of horse manure with brush and shovel.

Smith shivered, standing naked at the window, the body seeming frail, ribs standing out under the taut-stretched skin, scarred. The dream came only rarely now but still real as the real nightmare had been. He wondered if he would ever be quit of it. He stared out at the street. It was a strange place and he was still a stranger here. He turned from the window, restless, found his clothes and dressed quickly. He spared one glance for the bed, the room in half-light now from the crack he had left in the curtains. The woman sprawled, full body loose, breasts spilling from the silk of the nightgown, the lips slack in exhausted sleep.

Last night, last week, last —

It was time he was gone.

He moved quietly down through the house, silent but for the slow-ticking clock in the hall and let himself out into the morning.

He must see the doctors again, and surely they would pass him fit this time.

He walked quickly, a middle-sized, slight figure in the dark blue of the Royal Navy with the three gold rings of a Commander. A very young man for that rank. A thin face, sharp-featured under the cap, with pale blue eyes. Not handsome. He walked quickly and it was not because of the cold. There was an urgency about him.

Time he was gone.

Later that day they talked of him at the Admiralty. It was close to noon but London was still shrouded in that dirty, grey light. In the Admiralty the lights burned yellow and a fire crackled in the grate.

The Captain read from the folder: "David Cochrane Smith." He paused, then: "Unusual background." He looked across at the Admiral curiously.

Who answered shortly, "A village boy from a village shop. For an officer it's extraordinary." He stared coldly at the Captain. "Take the advice that was given to me: Mind your own business."

The Captain flinched, swallowed then returned to the folder. "The doctors think he went back to sea too soon after that sinking at Jutland. Then to be carted ashore *again* with a wound — " He shook his head. "They say they will pass him fit but he must not return to the Grand Fleet; it's too early for active duty of that kind."

11

The Admiral snapped irritably, "*Active* duty? That's the trouble. He's been too damned active."

"And she'd follow him to Scapa Flow."

"She'd find it damned uncomfortable."

"She's a very wealthy woman. She could make it comfortable."

"I doubt it. But she could make a nuisance of herself. *Blast* the woman! She's like a bitch in heat!"

"Yes." The Captain thought the simile apt. "But she's an extraordinarily attractive woman to be panting over him. I wonder what she sees in him? And she's not the first."

The Admiral muttered under his breath, glaring into the fire.

"Sir?"

"I said," the Admiral repeated distinctly, "what a bloody mess. On top of the woman there's this rumour. He has to open his mouth at one of her parties and who does he open it to? A gas-bag! Who tells his tale all around town. 'Enough men killed. The Navy ought to stay at home.' Good *God!*" The near-bellow rumbled away and after a moment he went on, "They've labelled him as a defeatist. The story has even gone around the Fleet. Did you know that? I got a signal from Scapa asking me if it was true! We can't send him back even if the doctors would allow it, not with that label around his neck. And there'd be questions in the House if we tried it. But I want him out of this, well clear of her and the newspapers. I don't want him away for ever; just long enough for this to blow over, for the truth to be told and accepted; and quick enough to avoid another scandal with *her*. He's a good officer."

"He has a wild reputation."

"That's not the same as being wild. He's a man who seizes action when the opportunity offers and he's had plenty of offers. He's a good officer."

"But not indispensable?"

12

"No one is indispensable." He added with grim sincerity, "Thank God."

There was silence in the room while they mentally reviewed alternatives. The Admiral broke it. "I have it. A ship that returns to home waters in the summer at the end of her commission, and far enough away now. *And* she's short-handed."

"Where? Which ship?"

The Admiral reached for his pen. "On the West coast of America. *Thunder*."

2

MARCH 1917.

The night was dark under an overcast sky. H.M.S. *Thunder*, a darkened ship, was a black speck on the black immensity of the Pacific. Her crew were tensed at their action stations and Commander David Cochrane Smith stood on her bridge gratings, peering with his hands clenched tight on the rail. Look-outs strained their eyes against the darkness. Somewhere to the east lay the coast of Peru but the enemy was close.

A look-out shouted, "Ship bearing green four-oh." There was a rumble as the guns trained around and the searchlights on the wings of the bridge and up in the tops twisted in their mountings. They crackled into life, their beams stabbed out across the dark sea to light up the target on which the guns were lined. They lit up *Thunder*'s forty-foot steam pinnace with its stubby funnel, young Midshipman Manton at the wheel. Buckley, Mantor's leading hand, lifted one arm, waving, the pinnace spun away into the sheltering dark, the searchlights snapped out. The exercise went on.

The exercises were almost a nightly event. Smith had started them as soon as he joined *Thunder* so they called them Smith's game and referred to him as the Bat. They groused about the exercises as a matter of principle but secretly found the game a break in the deadly routine of work and drills. They had become expert.

Smith stood aloof on the bridge, his face grim. He had reason. He had come to *Thunder* certain that he was banished, his career virtually at an end. He had known other officers who had faded into obscurity after some minor scandal ashore. He joined her at Esquimalt in British Columbia where she had just had a refit. In the first hour, through a chance-heard conversation he learned his reputation had preceded him: he was a pacifist, his nerve gone; his affaires were the scandal of London and the Grand Fleet. He knew the crew were wary of him and pride would not let him explain.

He could have said that a drunken armchair tactician had been critical of the Navy's inability to destroy an enemy who refused to come out to be destroyed. Smith had boiled over and replied that he had seen enough men killed at Jutland and *that if the rest of the country were like the drunk* the Navy would do well to stay at home. The story had been repeated but not the words in italics. He would not explain that and he could not explain the women.

But he had been in the Navy since he was twelve and lonely often enough. As a cadet at *Britannia* he had been an outsider, accepted but different. An orphan brought up by a retired Chief Petty Officer and his wife, his home a village shop; he had been different enough. They wondered how he had got into *Britannia* and so did Smith. Before he was old enough to try to find out the C.P.O. and his wife were dead and the Navy was his home and his family. But he wondered still.

Now he paced restlessly out to the wing of the bridge, aware of them watching him and stared out at *Thunder*'s shadowy bulk. He had found a ship run by Garrick, the First Lieutenant because the Captain, embittered at his backwater command, kept to his cabin and his gin. He looked now at that bulk, impressive in the darkness with the bristling guns and thought it was as well this man of war was a ship of peace. The nearest enemy was ten thousand miles away.

Thunder was a four-funnelled armoured cruiser of twelve thousand tons. She had served on the Pacific seaboard, based at Esquimalt and cruising off the coast of South America, for two-and-a-half years since the outbreak of war, the sole representative of a Navy stretched thin by the concentration in European waters. Before the war she had been a unit of the Third Fleet, which meant she was laid up with a tiny caretaker crew. Her crew admitted the dockyard at Esquimalt sent her back to sea as nearly new as hard work and ingenuity could contrive, but it was only a relative term.

She was too old. Laid down when Victoria reigned, her designed speed had been lower than the later more modern cruisers and it was doubtful if she could attain that speed now, let alone maintain it for any length of time. Davies, her Chief Engineer, Lieutenant-Commander R.N.R. and recalled from the Merchant Service, swore that she could. But he always evaded putting it to the test and nobody believed him. She was slow. So on the mess-decks they said, "Had to call her *Thunder*, didn't they? 'Cause it's a bleeding certainty you couldn't call her *Lightning!*"

Joke.

She had been built with some abortive idea of using her in the rivers and shallows of the China Station. It came to naught, but thus designed to cruise in shallow waters, in any kind of sea she was an uncomfortable ship. So they said, "Called her *Thunder* 'cause she's one long roll!"

Joke.

Plenty of jokes. In the wardroom that first night Aitkyne, the navigator, tall and elegant and watchful said, "We wondered if you'd arrive in time for resurrection day, sir."

Smith, sweating coldly and stomach rebelling on what was also the first night at sea, clutching a glass of sherry he wanted like the plague, asked blankly, "Resurrection day?"

"Bringing the old girl back to life again, sir. Taking her to sea." Laughter. Then Aitkyne added, "If she was a house, you'd expect to find bats and ghosts."

Smith replied, "One carries one's own ghosts around." And told himself he had still to learn to keep his mouth shut. He had spoiled the joke and they looked at him oddly. The spectre at the feast, or rather the party. It was a party given to welcome Smith aboard but he had sensed the self-consciousness behind that welcome and knew the cause. They were all wary of him and that was a pity because he liked the look of them.

And *Thunder*'s wardroom was comfortable with a long table at which the officers ate, two sideboards, easy chairs, carpet on the deck and even a piano and a gramophone, though the last belonged to young Wakely, one of the midshipmen, and had been borrowed from the gunroom for the occasion. After two-and-a-half uneventful years on that station it was hardly surprising that they had discarded the spartan surroundings familiar to the Grand Fleet. Any fool could be uncomfortable.

But on the surface they made Smith welcome. A new face in the wardroom, a new face aboard *Thunder*, was an event. Her crew had served in her since the war started. The midshipmen had joined her not long ago as fifteen-year-old cadets to fill the gaps created by aging officers invalided out and one lost at sea in a gale. A score of young seamen and boys had accompanied the cadets. That had been *Thunder*'s first and only draft.

The crew of the fore-turret was a fair sample of *Thunder*'s crew, which consisted largely of reservists with that sprinkling of young seamen and boys. Farmer Bates was a grandfather, one of seven aboard. Gibb at seventeen was far and away the youngest in the turret but he had settled in. *Thunder*'s slowness and rolling, her old guns and short-handed crew did not worry him because she was his ship. His *first* ship. And because here in these waters those things did not matter anyway.

Thunder carried a 9.2-inch gun in a turret forward and

another aft. Of her twelve six-inch guns, in casemates like armoured steel pods bulging out from her hull, four were on the upper deck, one at each corner so to speak. The other eight were on the main deck below, four to a side. The guns were elderly and it was a notorious fact that in her class of ship the eight guns on the main deck could not be fired in bad weather because opening their ports would let in the sea. That did not matter in the case of *Thunder* because she sailed with a reduced complement. That is to say that, as she was not expected to fight in a Fleet action nor anything like it, she was not manned for the purpose. Half her crew of 600 were engineers or stokers because at her most economical speed she burned 100 tons of coal a day, every piece of which had to be shovelled from bunkers to fires. There were barely enough gunners for the turrets and the four upper deck six-inch.

Garrick was Gunnery Officer. The ship had engaged in practice firing shortly after leaving Esquimalt and the gunnery had been startlingly good, but Garrick was a gunnery fanatic and had trained and drilled these men for two-and-a-half years. The men were all right, but there weren't enough of them and the ship and her guns were too old.

Smith shrugged; these things did not matter. *Thunder* would drag out her last days beating up and down this coast then return to home waters to become a depot-ship – back to the dockyard wall. What mattered was that he had his duty and he would do it. He heard a scrape of a boot on the ladder and saw the clinging figure scrambling unsteadily up to the bridge and thought these last days and weeks would be long ones. It was his sentence and there would be no reprieve.

He stepped forward as the Captain stumbled on to the bridge and fetched up against the rail. Before Smith could speak he growled, "Get on with it!"

"Aye, aye, sir."

Now instead of tension there was an unease on the bridge.

18

Smith saw Aitkyne's mouth twisted with disgust and saw the navigator turning away to hide it. A look-out yelled, the guns trained, the lights blazed out at the pinnace then died and the darkness returned.

The Captain turned slowly on Smith and said thickly, "Waste of time." And added an obscenity. Smith did not answer. The Captain pushed past him to the head of the ladder and fell head first to the deck below.

It sounded like a sack of coal hitting the deck.

Smith shouted, "The Captain's fallen!" He dropped down the ladder and knelt by the Captain. The Captain's cap still rolled on the deck till Smith set his hand on it. Aitkyne leaned over him. "I shouldn't touch him, sir. Doctor's on his way."

Smith shook his head and fumbled in the pocket of his bridge coat for a torch.

Albrecht the surgeon came, breathing heavily and dropped to his knees beside the Captain. His examination was swift. When he gently and carefully lifted the Captain's head in the light of Smith's torch they all saw the terrible wound at the back of the skull where it hit the deck. A party gently carried the Captain down to the sick-bay and Smith waited there until Albrecht made his report. "Massive concussion. God knows what damage may have been done to the brain."

"He has a chance of recovery?"

"I wouldn't have been surprised if an injury like that had killed him instantly. Add to that the effects of shock and . . ." He did not need to finish; the gin reeked.

Smith went to his cabin. He managed to sleep only once and only then to jerk awake, running with sweat. He had not dreamed of the Captain, the fall and the sickening end of that falling. It was the old dream again of the two great ships growing huge out of the dark to hurl the fires of hell at him. He made his way forward through the sleeping ship to the sick-bay, and found Albrecht alone. Smith raised his eyebrows in enquiry and the Doctor shook his head. "No change."

19

They stood in silence watching the Captain until Smith asked, it was more question than statement, "An unusual name, Albrecht."

Albrecht's lips twitched sardonically. "In this Navy, yes. My grandfather came over from Germany in 'forty-eight. He became British; I was born British. When this war started and the mobs threw bricks at shops with German names I thought I might change my name. But I didn't *want* to. I wasn't ashamed of it. And then it seemed if I had called myself Atkins they would still have chased me but with white feathers because I wasn't in uniform. So I decided they could all go to hell and joined the Navy for the duration." He smiled faintly. "The lower deck call me the 'orrible 'un." The smile faded. "But I didn't want anything to do with the war. I didn't want to join the Navy, I just ran away to it. I think the war is stupid and ought to be stopped – " He broke off.

Smith said, "That's a view that takes some courage with a name like Albrecht."

The Doctor shrugged. "No. When you're a ministering angel it's different. If I was a sea-officer – " Again he stopped but now embarrassed for Smith.

Who smiled coldly. "If you were and you had any sense you would keep your mouth shut."

Albrecht stared at him. "You are not a pacifist?"

Smith said deliberately, "I think wars are better won than lost, better avoided than won. They're not an excuse for stupidity and carelessness."

Albrecht blinked. "That's scarcely the philosophy of a fire-eater."

Fire-eater. Smith knew he was not that. Someone must have described him thus to Albrecht, though God knew why.

"It's the philosophy of a man who has been shot over."

"More than once."

"Yes."

"And likely to be again." Albrecht shook his head, baffled, intrigued.

"If you see a risk that has to be taken, *you*, Doctor, take it and cut away. So do I."

Albrecht grinned. "But my patients don't cut back."

Mention of patients sent his gaze back to the Captain. His feeble hold on life was slipping away with the night.

He died at daybreak.

They buried him at sea. Afterwards Smith confirmed the course he had ordered the previous night when the Captain fell. Then it had been an attempt to get the Captain to a hospital ashore but now it was to reach a telegraph office and inform the British Consul in Chile. *Thunder* had radio but the Navy's signalling stations did not cover South American waters. Admiralty kept in touch with her by cables and she entered ports at intervals to collect them. The Consul had to be informed of the Captain's death and that Smith had assumed command; he would advise Admiralty.

Now it came to him. The Captain was dead and he was in command. He was conscious of a lightening of the atmosphere in the ship but that, he believed, was not because he had assumed command but because the bitter presence aft had gone.

As if in mourning the weather was breaking and the wind rising. When they raised the coast of Chile in the early evening a bright sun still shone but astern the clouds were breeding black.

The sun had no warmth in it. Smith shivered. The Captain's death was a bad start to a command and Smith was still not accepted, nor likely to be, he was certain.

The Signal Yeoman shattered his mood of introspection. "Signal from shore, sir! S.O.S.! Bearing red three-oh!"

Smith swung around and raised his glasses, berating himself for not having seen that winking light, for day-dreaming. Night was falling, the setting sun sending *Thunder*'s shadow stretching long towards the shore that was still bathed in that last light.

"T – H – D – R." The Yeoman spelt out the slow flashes of the point of light. "Think they mean *us*, sir."

What else could it mean? But who would know this ship?

The Yeoman: "S.O.S. again, sir. An' it's a light from a motor car. Front light."

"Hard to see but I think it's a 24/30 Buick tourer." Midshipman Somers was on the bridge for some reason and had a telescope clapped to his eye. Excitement had wrung the comment from him. Now he realised his temerity and said meekly, "Sorry, sir."

Smith scowled. He could barely make out that it was a motor car. "Don't see that it matters, but what makes you so sure?"

"My father had one before the war, sir. But of course, when the war started he gave it to the Army with most of the others."

Somers was undoubtedly the richest, or potentially richest man aboard. His father probably did have half-a-dozen motor cars including a Rolls-Royce. He was a tall, handsome boy, a fine athlete with a good brain. In spite of all these reasons for envy he was well-liked.

Smith ordered, "Port ten." *Thunder* began to close the shore. Dusk had swept over them and now reached the blinking light that seemed to flicker in that dusk more brightly before it died.

Smith snapped, "Ask nature of emergency."

Thunder's signal-lamp clattered out but there was no answer.

The Yeoman grumbled, "Stopped now, sir. Can't see much of anything. Thought I saw a flash, though."

Garrick had pounded up on to the bridge and stood panting, too late to see the signal but he'd found out what had happened. He panted, "Damn funny business. S.O.S. from the *shore*! And *naming* us?"

Smith said laconically, "Yes." He tried to hide his own curiosity. The obvious answer was to send – No, he would not! "Fires lit in the pinnace?"

"Yes, sir." Somers answered. "And steam up."

"Bit early, weren't you?"

Somers replied straight-faced, "Mr. Knight said we had to be ready, sir."

Knight was the Signals Officer and also drew an interpreter's pay for his labouring Spanish so he went ashore to send and collect telegrams. He was stout and when the ship held a concert he did a knock-about turn with Lieutenant Day of the Royal Marine Artillery as a coster and his missus. It was vulgar, obscene and funny. He would be eager not to miss a moment of that run ashore in Castillo.

Smith grunted, "Then we'll go and see what it's all about." And to Garrick: "I'll go myself. Tell the doctor to come along ready to do his stuff."

Thunder hove to, the winch hammered and the derrick swung the pinnace over the side and down to the water. Her crew boarded her and cast off. Smoke belched from her stubby funnel and they could hear the rapid scrape and clang as the stoker below hurled coal on the fire. They ran in to the shore, Somers at the wheel straining his eyes against the gathering dusk, steering for a stretch of beach. The engines stopped, thrashed briefly astern, stopped again and they ran in to the shallows.

The shore was quiet, peaceful, empty. Smith wondered uneasily if he was the victim of some practical joke, if he would return to the ship having made a fool of himself. He snapped, "Come on, Doctor. You too, Buckley." He jumped over the bow and up to his waist in water and waded ashore, followed by Albrecht and the burly leading hand of the picket-boat. Beyond the beach the ground rose steeply. They could not see the motor car nor any sign of life. There was silence but for the crashing of the surf.

As they climbed up from the beach Albrecht panted,

"Wonder what it can be? You can have nasty accidents with motor cars, though. Once had a fracture of the wrist – some chap not cranking the damn thing properly. And – "

Smith rasped, "I won't be sorry for any fool who sends an S.O.S. to my ship because he's fractured a wrist."

They climbed over the crest, crossed a little plateau and looked into a shallow depression that twisted away inland. They could see the big Buick Tourer, a dull gleam of metal in the dusk, a score of yards to their right. They halted, peering. Albrecht said, "There's a body, at the front of the car." Smith saw it, lying crumpled untidily under the dead carbide lamps, one arm thrown out. Albrecht took a pace forward and a shot cracked out.

There was the spit of flame to their left, from further inland up the depression and then the crack of the shot. Immediately it was answered by a shot from the car. In the flash Smith saw the head lifted briefly from behind the car, then the darkness closed in and his night vision was destroyed. "Get down!" He shoved Albrecht down. "Buckley! Back to the pinnace and bring back two men, rifles for all of you!"

"Aye, aye, sir!" Buckley plunged away. Smith thought Buckley was under the impression they were going to fight a little war here but he was very wrong. This was a neutral coast, Smith and his men were belligerents and any action of that kind would be a flagrant breach of neutrality. But they had to be ready to defend themselves.

And that wasn't all. Smith was here; that was a fact. If anyone was killed or injured, *anyone*, while Smith meekly stood by and looked on it would not make pleasant reading in his report. He thought bitterly, What a bloody mess!

To rub it in, the shots came again, from left, from right. A slug clanged against the motor car and howled off into the night.

Albrecht whispered, "Somebody's going to get hurt if this goes on, besides that chap lying there already."

Smith ground out, "Keep still." He rose to his feet. He

was a score of yards at least from either of those firing, they had pistols and he knew it was very long odds against anyone hitting him with a pistol at that range in this light. He swallowed just the same before he shouted: "Cease firing! I am a naval officer!" He spoke in English because he had no Spanish. "Show yourselves and put up your hands!"

It worked. A moment of silence then a man rose from behind a rock to the left, his hands lifted above his shoulders. He started to walk towards Smith. As he approached, he spoke. "Ah sir. I'm very glad to see you –"

But Smith's eyes were on the girl. A *girl*! He stared dumbfounded as she stepped around the motor car and walked towards him, holding herself stiffly erect, hands at her sides in the folds of her skirt, that ended just above her buttoned boots. He saw her face, pale under a mass of dark hair and the lips were a tight line and the eyes glared past Smith.

They were close now, the man's hands coming down, one sliding inside his jacket. "I have my papers which will –"

The girl's arm lifted from her side, straight, the barrel of the pistol like a pointing finger. She shot him.

The flame seemed to burn past Smith's face as he started forward. He was momentarily blinded but his outstretched hand clamped on hers and tore the pistol from her. Sight returned and he saw her face again and it was rigid, without any emotion at all.

Smith swung away from her. The shot at point-blank range had kicked the man on to his back. He lay spreadeagled, eyes wide, a huge stain across his chest. Albrecht came running and dropped to his knees. When he arose he shook his head and started towards the man who lay by the motor car.

The girl said, "Luis is dead!" Her voice was flat, without emotion and Smith wondered was this really a *woman*?

Light glowed inland along the depression and they heard the sound of an engine. Albrecht stood up again and came back to Smith. He said softly, "He's dead too, sir."

25

The glow had grown and another motor car lurched around a bend in the depression and its lights swept the dark, wavered on the little group and the motor car halted. Smith held up his hand against the glare. The girl tried to run but Albrecht grabbed her. She fought him. "It's the rest of them!"

Before the words could sink in the firing started. One shot, then a fusillade and Smith heard the air whisper around his head. He thrust Albrecht towards the beach. "Run for it!" He saw Albrecht running, the girl ahead of him, then dropped to one knee and lifted the pistol. He fired twice towards the lights and the shooting, aiming high but he heard a yell and the firing stopped. It was only for a few seconds but it gave him time to run up and across the plateau. As the firing started again he stopped and knelt and fired again, just one shot then the pistol was empty. He threw it away and started towards the beach, skidding down the slope in a shower of sand and pebbles.

Halfway down he met Buckley and two seamen, all three of them with rifles at the high port. Smith panted, "We're being fired on and they may be following. Return the fire to keep their heads down but *aim high*! I don't know who they are." It was certain they had more right on this coast than he, even possible they were justified. Suppose they were police or troops? What a *bloody* mess!

They fell back towards the beach. Buckley jerked out, "There's one." A shadow lifted above the crest and spurted flame and sand kicked up a yard away. But then Buckley and the seamen fired a volley and the shadow ducked from sight.

They retired to the beach in good order, waded out to the pinnace and scrambled aboard. Smith gasped, "Return to the ship."

"Aye, aye, sir." The engines thumped slowly then gathered speed. The pinnace went astern then spun on her heel and headed out to sea. Smith watched the shore but he saw no one, there was no firing. It was still and silent, empty as they had found it, as if nothing had happened.

But it had.

The clouds humped black overhead now. Lightning flickered and thunder rumbled distantly. A flurry of rain blew in their faces. The sea was getting up and the pinnace pitched through it.

Smith asked, "Where's the Doctor and – and – "

Somers answered, "He took the young lady into the cabin, sir." He was intent on conning the pinnace but Smith could feel his curiosity and knew the seamen were watching him, too. They weren't the only ones who were curious but Smith *had* to have answers to a number of questions and would probably have to be careful in finding some answers himself when he wrote his report.

He moved to the cabin but just then the girl blundered from it, staggered and almost fell then lurched to the side and hung over it, very sick. Smith stood beside her but did not touch her. When she raised her head he said, "I would like an explanation." He said it stiffly, formally because this was a formal business; a man had been killed in front of him.

The girl said, "I'll tell the Captain." There was a trace of cockney in the accent.

"The Captain is dead. I am in command."

Her face turned up to him, eyes searching. The lips trembled but the voice was still steady, tightly controlled. "What's your name?"

"Smith. Commander David Smith."

"You're new."

"I came aboard two weeks ago." Then, realising: "But how do you know – "

"I know the names of most of them. Garrick, Aitkyne, Kennedy – " She shook her head as if to clear it. "My name is Sarah Benson. I suppose you could call me a spy." She caught Smith's stare and her lips twitched in bitter amusement. "Cherry, the Consul at Guaya, will vouch for me." Guaya lay a hundred-odd miles to the south.

She paused but when Smith only nodded guardedly she went on, "The German Intelligence agents are thick as fleas on a dog's back all up and down this coast. The last three months I've *been* all up and down it. I dug up a little bit here and a little bit there and maybe I dug too much because yesterday some fellers came looking for me. We had to run for it. Luis, the chap with me, a sort of chauffeur and handyman, he got shot. I had to drive the Buick. We were trying to reach Castillo so I could send a telegram to Cherry but they got word ahead of us somehow and headed us off.

"They drove us down the coast, trapped us. Then I saw the ship. I knew her. I've seen the old *Thunder* many a time since 1914. Luis used his jacket across one of the lamps to flash a message but then they shot him again. Killed him. Poor Luis."

Was there a catch in the voice then?

But she went on steadily. "The point is this: In this business you can sometimes find out what they know though you don't go round stealing the plans and all that nonsense. More often you can find out what they *want* to know and that's very important. I told you I'd been all up and down this coast the last three months. Well, everywhere it was the same. They wanted to know about *Thunder*. Where and when she made port. Where she headed. They have contacts of one sort or another in the telegraph offices and the shore wireless stations who pass them the information. If any ship at sea reports sighting you, the information goes to them."

She paused again, her shoulders slumped as if the resolution was draining out of her now. She finished, "That's all. What it was all about. They're tracking you."

Smith was aware again of the pinnace plunging and soaring, that they were close to the great black loom of the ship. Smoke from the four funnels rolled down to them on the wind. He believed her. More than that, he felt the prickling apprehension and the excitement building inside him as always before impending action. But action? Here? He asked, "Why?"

Her head moved negatively. "I don't know. I don't *know* for God's sake!"

Lightning flashed again, close now and he saw Albrecht moving towards them. He saw the girl's face, drawn, the mouth bitter. But he remembered her face as she shot the man who stood before her empty-handed, remembered the flash, the slam of the shot.

And she saw his reaction and turned from him. She had told him all he needed to know, she thought. She had not really told him about the wild ride on the bad roads with Luis sprawled on the floor of the Buick, his head on her knee and his blood on her hands. Nor of huddled behind the car while Luis exposed himself to send the signal, risked his life until they tore it from him. Of crouching and firing and sobbing with fear as the bullets smashed into the car. She had done enough; she was finished. She had been through a very bad time and she craved comforting and affection but Smith stood remote and stiff-faced.

Memory stirred. She said, "Smith. David – David C. Smith?"

Smith blinked. "That's right. How – "

But then she crumpled and Albrecht caught her and she clung to him.

The pinnace tossed in the shadow of the steel wall of *Thunder*'s side until the big boat derrick swung out, the winch hammered and she was whipped up from the sea and swayed inboard. Sarah Benson, covered in blankets, was passed down to the deck and hurriedly aft to the Captain's cabin in the stern. There were already two men in the sick-bay and Smith had not moved into the Captain's cabin that was in fact a suite. The main cabin stretched the width of the ship with its long highly-polished table but a twelve-pounder crouched at each side as a grim reminder that this was a ship of war. The sleeping cabin lay to one side, further aft still was the day-cabin and this gave access to a stern walk that curved around the stern of the ship. A Captain – the Captain – could cut himself off from the rest of the ship and live in isolation. And so could Sarah Benson. Smith did not know what to do with her but she would not stay aboard his ship a moment longer than necessary.

He paced the bridge restlessly in the slanting rain that came in on the wind, swaying as *Thunder* rolled in the swell, acting the old bitch she always was in any bad weather. On the main-deck, where the crews of the guns lived and slept in the casemates, the sea would be coming in and swilling across the deck and the men would be cursing. Smith went over the girl's story but it boiled down to that one phrase: They're watching you.

Why? *Why?*

It was important, Smith knew it. He paused in his pacing to stare back along *Thunder*'s length, at her funnels that poured out smoke and soot and the big ventilator cowls that sprouted from her deck and marked her age like a woman's grey hairs. He was uneasy.

They hove to again off Castillo and Knight came to him. "Any further orders, sir?"

But Smith shook his head. Behind him Garrick glanced at Aitkyne, concerned. The story was all over the ship that there had been shooting ashore and men killed. So Smith should make a report to the authorities here.

He knew it. But there was the girl and her story. He was fishing in strange waters. He would take her back to her master – Cherry? That was it – at Guaya. After he'd talked to Cherry he would decide on his report and to whom to make it.

The pinnace crashed out of the night in bursting spray and Knight reported to the bridge. "Telegram sent, sir. An' there was one for us, in code."

Smith nodded. "Get on with it."

Knight went off to decode the telegram and Smith ordered a course for Guaya and went to his sea-cabin below the bridge. As he dragged off his jacket he caught the whiff of cordite that still clung from Sarah Benson's shot and he saw it all

30

again, the man kicked back, the spattering blood and her face and he shivered.

Sarah Benson lay awake. Exhaustion claimed her but memory hinted then eluded her. Purkiss, the sick-berth attendant, brought her a cup of tea. He was twenty years old, nearly three years out from home and soft-hearted. He looked at her and was smitten. It was obvious and too good a chance to waste and she did not waste chances even when her eyelids dragged and her stomach rebelled. She pumped him. He talked to her about Gabriel, the sick-berth P.O., Albrecht the 'orrible 'un, Garrick and the others. And Smith. "Real mystery man. They shipped him out in a hurry – practically shanghaied him. There's talk of a lady, a real Lady. They say he's a reglar divil with – "

Albrecht came then but it was enough. Memory functioned and the pieces clicked into place.

Her sister, Alice, was a governess in London and wrote her long weekly letters in copperplate about the War and Society and The Town. Sarah read them fascinated by an alien world. And one small item concerned a Commander David C. Smith, "a handsome, charming young gentleman they say . . ."

Sarah had looked to find a man in command of this ship because she felt *Thunder* might soon need a man. Instead there was this poodle-faking, social climber who had stared at her with horror as she shot the renegade Englishman. Oh, she knew the man and that he carried a pistol in a shoulder holster and his empty hands meant nothing. She had never before fired a shot in anger and the memory would haunt her the rest of her days. It haunted her now but she would not explain to Smith. He could think what he liked.

She was frightened, fear coming late to shake her, miserable. She was lonely, curled small in the bed and she cried herself to sleep.

Knight brought the decoded telegram to Smith. It came from the Consul in Guaya, Chile: "Request urgently your presence this port. Extreme importance." Cherry would not know *Thunder*'s whereabouts. This telegram would be one of several sent to ports along the coast where she might call for news or orders. Smith handed it back to Knight without comment, grunted "Goodnight," trying to sound like a man who wanted his sleep and was unmoved by the adventures of the day or this telegram. But when Knight had gone he lay awake. "Extreme importance." "Request urgently." Cherry could only request but Smith would need to have a good reason to ignore that request. In the event it did not matter. He had to be rid of the girl and that meant Guaya and Cherry. *Thunder* had a rendezvous with a collier to the north but that was two days hence and she held coal now for eight days' cruising.

Cherry's telegram had come on the heels of the girl's message but each carried its own warning. Of the same danger? What danger? The girl knew of no danger. Cherry spoke of none. But Smith was certain that danger was there. He lay wide-eyed, staring sightlessly at the deckhead above him with its slick of condensation and rust breaking through the white enamel in a red rash.

He slept, to wake sweating as the big ships roared down on him out of the night and a white-faced girl shot a man again and again.

3

In the morning Horsfall woke Smith with a cup of coffee. Smith had inherited him. Tall and thin and lantern-jawed, he was obviously sometimes called Horse-Face but usually it was Daddy.

Now he fussed around the cabin like an old hen.

Daddy was a reservist, not a grandfather like Davies, the Engineer, or some of the others but he *looked* the oldest man aboard. He had been one of *Thunder's* caretaker crew; the only one of that ancient little band who had somehow wangled his way to sea and they said he had been scraped off the dockyard wall along with the ship. He shuffled about in an old pair of plimsolls by express permission of the Doctor because his feet troubled him greatly. They also served him and a lot of the crew as a barometer because he claimed he could predict the weather by the feel of them.

"Lovely morning, sir. Sky's cleared beautiful but I reckon it won't last. I can tell. Me feet, you know, sir."

"Yes, I know." Smith sipped at the coffee and thought about Sarah Benson and Cherry.

"Gabriel, that's the Doctor's mate, sir, he says that young

lady woke up and ate a breakfast near fit for a horse and turned over again."

"Good." He would be rid of her.

"Funny her coming aboard like that, sir."

There was nothing funny about it. Two dead men. Smith might have been another.

"All the lads are wondering about her, sir, keep asking me they do, what about that young lady? 'Course I can't tell them anything."

"Of course not."

"No, sir."

"Well, when they ask you again you can tell them – " Smith paused, thinking.

"Yes, sir?"

"You can tell them I've sworn you to secrecy."

Daddy looked at him blankly and Smith went on, "Well, it's better to be sworn *to* than *at*."

Daddy took the point and the empty cup philosophically. "Aye, aye, sir."

Smith grinned wryly at his departing back.

They raised Guaya at noon. The port itself lay two miles up-river on a big basin. They first entered what appeared to be an estuary but was really one channel of several of the river's delta mouth. The coast was hills dropping green forest down steeply to the sea and the river. The river ran wide from the basin for a mile then on approaching the sea split into channels that threaded through a tangle of tree-clothed islets, most of the channels so shallow as to be swamp. *Thunder* steamed up the most direct channel that had for that reason been cleared, and was kept clear, by dredging.

They passed the signalling station to port where it stood on a low hill, Punta Negro. Past it another channel wound away between forest walls. The delta in that direction, north, was a huge swamp that bred a yellow fog with each dawn. The telephone line that linked the signalling station to the port looped sagging across that channel to the mainland. A small launch was moored against a little jetty from which a narrow track led up to the signalling station. The launch was the only other link between station and port; there was no road. To starboard a cove was bitten out of the forest: Stillwater Cove.

Smith thought that Cherry would have known of *Thunder*'s arrival since the station saw her lift over the horizon. So he could expect Cherry and his explanation soon. He shifted restlessly on the bridge.

Thunder rode rock-steady in this sheltered water, only the slightest nodding of her bow as she butted into the current, steaming slowly with the engines thump-thumping over, slipping through the water of the river that was brown with mud. On either hand the hills rose up from the river and climbed to the sky. A bend in the river lay ahead. They hauled slowly up on it, rounded it and opened up the basin and Guaya. There were a score of ships in the basin and room for them. Most lay out at anchor but three lay at a long wharf taking on copper ore. Guaya was a mushroom town. Twenty years before it had been a village, but then the copper mines opened inland and it had boomed.

Smith took in the town, white buildings against the green of the hills behind. He also took in the ships in the basin and one of them in particular. As *Thunder*'s three-pounder saluting gun began its metronomic popping, saluting the port, Smith stared at the ship.

Garrick, telescope to his eye, said quickly, "U.S.S. *Kansas*, sir. She was reported in these waters. Brand new, her first cruise. Rear-Admiral Donoghue."

America was still neutral.

Smith grunted. "He rates a salute. See to it."

Aitkyne said softly, "By God, what a ship. Twenty-one knots and thirty-odd thousand tons." (*Thunder* was twelve thousand.) "Twelve fourteen-inch guns and twenty-two five-inch."

"And one of those fourteen-inch shells weighs half-a-ton." Smith grinned at him. "So if they look our way, smile."

The salutes rolled flatly across the basin, *Thunder* rode to her anchor, the port medical officer came and went and Cherry came aboard. He was short and dapper, dabbing at his round face with a handkerchief.

He held out his hand. "Cherry. Delighted to meet you, Commander. Only wish in the circumstances – your Captain – " He shook his head then fished an envelope from his pocket. "Telegram for you, coded." And as Smith passed it to Knight: "Can we talk?"

Smith led the way to his cabin on the upper deck but not before he growled an aside to the plump and pink-cheeked Midshipman Wakely. "Ask Miss Benson if she'll be good enough to join us in my cabin."

"Aye, aye, sir!" Wakely shot away.

Cherry asked, "Did you say Benson? Would that be Sarah Benson?"

"It would." Smith's tone was neutral. Once in his cabin he told Cherry how he had brought the girl aboard. "You understand, I must make a report. I should have reported to the authorities ashore immediately after the incident but in view of Miss Benson's position – I thought it best to see you first."

Cherry nodded. "I've been worried about that girl. Had no word from her for a week. I recruited her when the war started and she's the best agent I have but I feel a special responsibility for her. I've known her a long time. Her father came out to South America from Wapping ten years ago. He works on building harbours, a foreman. He started in Argentina and later moved over to this coast. So Sarah speaks Spanish and Portuguese like a native and she learnt German from a ganger who boarded with the family for two years. On top of that she's clever and brave, sometimes too brave for her own good and my peace of mind." He thought for a moment then shook his head. "Say nothing. Report to the Admiralty, of course. I will do the same in confirmation. But say nothing to the Chileans and I'll lay the Germans will keep their mouths shut. They can't make things awkward for us without exposing their own involvement and they don't want the Chileans lifting any rocks." He grinned. "Any more than we do." The grin slipped away and he pulled at his chin. "So they won't say anything about that business. But one thing they have done already is to lodge a complaint with the Chileans about Sarah and now the Chileans want to ask her about her activities and possible involvement in espionage. We can't have that so she can't go ashore."

Smith protested, "But this is a warship not a liner! If she can't go ashore then she must be put aboard a British merchantman."

Cherry said apologetically, "That would be a good idea. Unfortunately, for once there isn't a British ship in this port."

Smith glared at him. This coast swarmed with British shipping but it was his bad luck to find a port without a British vessel. Cherry scribbled in a notebook with a pencil and tore out the page. "If this could be given to my boatman, Francis, to give to my wife urgently."

There was a rap at the door and Sarah Benson entered. Smith scowled past her: "Here, Mr. Wakely." He passed him Cherry's note. "For Mrs. Cherry and it's urgent"

Sarah Benson said emphaticaly, "Damn!" as Cherry explained why she could not go ashore.

Smith said stiffly, "A warship is no place for a lady but we'll try to make your stay as pleasant as circumstances permit." He swore at himself for being pompous but this girl forced him to it.

She thought he could not understand the life she'd led these past three years. Besides, she was not a society hostess, not a Lady. She laid the cockney on thick. "Well, it's not my fault I'm a woman. What do you want me to do? Swim ashore in me shift and give meself up to keep your ship a virgin?"

"Sarah! Please!" Cherry was embarrassed and annoyed. He had sensed the atmosphere of hostility and was baffled. What had got into the girl? "The Captain is right. He should not have to accept responsibility for you in this ship. And I'm certain you were glad enough to come aboard her."

Sarah was silent a moment, then: "That I was." It came quietly. She looked up at Smith. "I'm sorry. I'll try not to be a nuisance." It was an apology, no more, justice being done.

Smith inclined his head. He saw she wore a medallion, a large gold piece that hung on her breast from a fine chain around her neck. Her hand went to it. "It's very old. My father found it and gave it to me. For luck."

Smith thought it was barbaric.

She said bitterly, "I'm not sure if it works."

But Smith looked at Cherry. They had wasted enough time. "You sent for me."

Cherry glanced from one to the other then got down to business. "I believe we have a contraband runner in this port. When Miss Benson passed through on her way north she remarked on a ship that had just arrived. She was Argentinian, a seemingly ordinary tramp of three thousand tons *but fitted with modern wireless.*" He paused for effect and Smith's eyebrows rose. Fitting wireless was expensive, and unusual in that class of ship to say the least. Cherry went on, "I asked our people in Argentina about her, the *Gerda* she's called. She was one of a pair bought by an Argentinian firm only three months ago and fitted with wireless. This is their first cruise. Their skippers and crews, every manjack are of German birth or extraction and the money for the ships came from German funds in the Argentine. That last can't be proved but it's known."

He paused for breath and Sarah Benson beat Smith to the question. "You said a pair?"

Cherry nodded. "The other is the *Maria.* I made enquiries and found she was at Malaguay." A port a hundred and fifty miles to the south of Guaya. "The *Gerda* has laid here for

38

nine days. She hasn't discharged her cargo and she claims to have engine trouble which her own engineers are working on. I asked Thackeray and he confirmed that the *Maria* is telling the same story there."

Smith asked, "Thackeray?"

"Consul in Malaguay."

Sarah Benson said caustically, "You'd have to ask him to confirm. He'd do nothing on his own. He doesn't want anybody stirring up the water in his little pool."

Cherry said, "It's my belief they're just waiting while a cargo of nitrates is arranged for each of them. Then they'll discharge and mend their engines quickly enough."

Smith asked, "What are they carrying now?"

"Welsh steam coal, both of them. But it's nitrates they're after, I'm sure of it."

It could well be. Munitions needed nitrates and Germany needed munitions.

Cherry said, "I've protested to the Chileans, of course, but there is a large German element in the population and they have a deal of influence. The Chileans say that I'm only voicing suspicions and have no evidence that the ships are really German. They said there were unusual aspects, particularly that there were a pair of ships but that these probably had a simple explanation. Like coincidence. *Coincidence!*"

Smith said, "It would seem to have a long arm in these parts. So they won't intern them nor send them on their way."

Cherry grumbled, "Correct. They will do nothing. That's why we need you outside of here or Malaguay when they sail, to stop and search them. They're certain to have *some* evidence aboard." He stopped and dabbed at his face. He looked relieved and Smith knew the reason: the decisions were out of Cherry's hands now and instead in those of Smith.

Smith shifted impatiently. "I want to see her."

They walked forward of the bridge until they stood under the muzzle of the 9.2 and Cherry pointed at the collier. *Gerda* lay at anchor near the northern shore which was almost deserted, the buildings of the town being spread in a half-moon around the eastern and southern shores of the pool so it was not surprising there was no other ship near her. She was rusty and grimy but the wireless aerials strung from her masts were easily seen.

Smith said, "Engine trouble or no, she has fires." A thread of smoke twisted from *Gerda*'s funnel. He stood lost in thought but he was still aware of Cherry telling Sarah, "I sent a note ashore to Mrs. Cherry asking for that suitcase of yours."

Smith said absently, "Fortunate that you have some clothes at the consulate."

"I have suitcases spread over a couple of thousand miles. I travel a lot and I often have to travel light."

Smith nodded. "I noticed."

He chewed it over. Two ships. German crews, German money. Wireless. Nitrates. He was ready to accept Cherry's reasoning, to act on it, only . . .

Sarah Benson said slowly, "I don't know. There's something – not *right* about it."

Cherry asked, "What?"

Sarah said again, "I don't *know*. It all fits but – " She shook her head.

Cherry chuckled. "Woman's intuition?" He glanced, amused, at Smith.

But Smith was not laughing. He stared at the *Gerda*. And then at Sarah Benson. The wind had brought some colour to her cheeks. It all fitted but – she was right, there was a piece missing. He had come to this port with that unease, that excitement that always came to him before an action and this was not that action. There was something else. He took off his cap and ran a hand through the fair hair sweat-plastered to his skull.

Cherry thought he looked very young.

Aitkyne's eye was on Sarah, hungry, but Smith caught it, and the navigator quickly crossed the deck. "Ah, Mr. Aitkyne.

I'm sure Mr. Cherry and Miss Benson would like to meet some of the officers. I wonder if the hospitality of the ward-room..."

"A pleasure, sir." Aitkyne was tall and handsome and his uniform beautifully tailored as always. He hovered over Sarah as he escorted them below.

Smith was left to prowl the deck, eyes on the *Gerda*, ill at ease.

Arnold Phizackerly had awoken early, perforce. It was not long past noon when a hand shook his shoulder and he peered out through gummy lids at Perez and asked huskily, "Wassamarrer?"

Perez was a clerk in the port office but also on a retainer from Phizackerly. He whispered, "The British warship, *Thunder*, she is headed for the river. The signalling station has just telephoned." He added apologetically, "You said whenever she came I was to tell you. 'Whenever', you said. 'Day or night'."

"Ah, God!" Phizackerly covered his eyes for a moment but he was not a man to shirk his duty. He crawled slowly, painfully out from under the single sheet to stand in long-sleeved singlet and long cotton drawers that hung loose around his bony rump. They were none too clean and he smelt powerfully of stale sweat.

Perez whispered, awed, "Much woman, hey?"

Phizackerly followed his stare, his own eyes lingering with satisfaction on the huge mound of Juanita under the sheet. She was more than double his weight and stood a head taller. Theirs was a stormy relationship but in bed or out of it they worked well together. He said, 'Too much for you, matey." And cackled. He poked Perez's ribs with a bony finger and leered gummily, his teeth still in the cup on the dresser. "But you're a good lad. Come around tonight an' I'll get Juanita to fix you up with somebody special."

Perez left, whispering his gratitude. Phizackerly made his

way, painfully hobbling with early morning stiffness, down to the bar, stopping only to urinate on the way. Olsen the Swede was in the bar, lethargically clearing up from the night before. He got coffee for Phizackerly and slipped a stiff tot of rum into it. Phizackerly gulped it and felt better. Olsen shaved him. They did not talk. Partly because Olsen's English was fractured and Phizackerly's was thick Scouse although it was more than forty years since he had left Liverpool, but the real reason was that it was too early.

Phizackerly splashed water on his face, dried it and trailed back to his room. The rest of the house was silent; none of the girls would stir until the cool of the early evening. He was feeling more limber, moving with a jerky sprightliness. He opened the wardrobe and selected a suit from the darkest corner. He paused a moment. Next to the suit hung his old uniform, his pilot's uniform. He touched it with ritualistic pride, and proud not only because it was his own design. Down in the bar there was a big photograph of him in the uniform, a much younger Phizackerly, posed, contriving somehow to look stern, pompous and cunning all at the same time. It was a perpetual reminder of the original source of his wealth. Everyone knew that in the old days he had been a pilot, *the* pilot. He told them.

He gave a final stroke to the uniform then dressed in the suit: striped trousers, grey morning-coat, patent leather boots and spats. He did not bother with socks; it was a warm day. A jewelled pin went in the tie, cologne on his face and oil on his hair. He combed the scanty locks down on either side from a centre parting with twin little quiffs at the front. He picked up the topper, surveyed himself in the mirror and decided he looked what he was: a man of substance in this town. He no longer carried the cane since a merchant captain said he looked like a monkey up a bloody stick.

He left the room, closing the door gently behind him after one last fond glance at the mountainous Juanita, lying on her back now and snoring resonantly. Halfway down the stairs he turned and retraced his steps to the dresser beside the bed, fished his teeth from the cup there and bit over them, snapped them tentatively a couple of times. Now he was ready.

He strolled down to the waterfront. *Thunder* lay out in the basin and a small crowd on the quay stared and pointed at her. Only a small crowd because she had been here many times, they had seen her before. As had Phizackerly but he regarded her with pride as he always did. His narrow chest swelled and he strutted a little. He was British, by God. Then his gaze became pensive, calculating. They were not new calculations but a re-totting of old ones. He knew the size of *Thunder*'s complement almost to a man and the value of a man in terms of spending power. The unknown factors were whether any of them would be allowed ashore and if they were, where they would be allowed to spend their leave and their money. The latter factor was the reason for his being on the quay.

His contact in the telegraph office had told him of the Captain's death. A new Captain could mean a new start. At any rate, Phizackerly would give it a good try.

He came to where Vargas's boat bobbed at the foot of a ladder. It was a motor-launch, not very clean but serviceable. Vargas owned the boat and plied for hire. His bread and butter trade consisted of taking patrons of Phizackerly's and similar establishments back to their ships. At this time of day however, business was non-existent unless you went out and actively sought it. Vargas preferred to sleep under the awning he had rigged aft over the well.

Phizackerly climbed down the ladder and nudged Vargas awake with his toe. Vargas rubbed at his face and said politely, "It is good to see you, Fizzy."

"You're a lazy bastard." Phizackerly sat in the stern. "Let's 'ave a run around the pool."

"Why?"

"Why? Because I want to."

"But it is business, yes? You don't go around the pool for nothing so it is business and I wonder what may be in it for me, so I ask why?"

"For you? You'll get paid."

"Ah! I get paid."

"You always get paid."

"Ha!"

"And anyway," Phizackerly settled back comfortably, "if it hadn't been for me you wouldn't be in the position you're in today with your own boat and able to kip through the day. Living like a lord you are and you owe it all to me and don't you forget it."

"I will never forget it because each day for fifteen years you remind me."

Phizackerly did not answer that. A shadow crossed his face at the reminder of the passage of time. Fifteen years since he had —

Vargas said uneasily, "Hey! It was a *joke.*"

Phizackerly remembered that it had been hard work, out for long hours at all hours and in all weathers. Now he could go to bed drunk like a gentleman, wake for Juanita in the dawn and turn over again afterwards. He was a practical man. He flashed his teeth pink and white at Vargas. " 'Course. Get on with it."

And when Vargas started the engine and they puttered out into the basin Phizackerly said, " 'Ave a scout round the old *Thunder.*"

"We can't go close unless you keep under the awning. That Captain, he said he'd sink us if you went alongside again."

Phizackerly said seriously, "I have some sad news. He's dead."

"Dead? Ah. That is very sad." Vargas cheered up a little but then said, "There is still that First Lieutenant."

"He isn't Captain. The new Captain is *new.*"

"Ah-ah!"

"Ah-ah yourself. Get on."

So they cruised slowly around *Thunder* where she lay at anchor and Phizackerly took care to stay in the shelter of the awning. He saw Lieutenant Miles had the watch and Garrick was on the bridge. He knew them both; too well. He said nostalgically, "Still, I sometimes miss them days when you was running me out to the ships." Because that was how Vargas bought the launch, by working Phizackerly's pilot cutter for him. "Sometimes I even wish they were back, them days."

Vargas thought he was lying or mad. He knew Phizackerly very well and thought the odds were all on that he was lying. He crossed himself and said, "Sometimes, so do I."

Phizackerly saw Cherry's boat leave the quay and head for *Thunder*. He pointed and Vargas swung the launch around *Thunder*'s stern and tucked her in alongside Cherry's boat at the foot of the accommodation ladder. As the side-boy carried up the suitcase Phizackerly nipped across the Consul's boat and up the ladder with a facility born of years of practice.

Smith stood by the entry port, abstracted, uneasy.

Phizackerly appeared, grey topper in hand as he stepped on to *Thunder*'s deck. With the other hand he whisked a garishly printed handbill from a sheaf in the tail pocket of his coat and slapped it in the hand of the startled boy manning the side. He whispered hoarsely, "Special rates for young fellers." And winked lewdly. The boy gaped.

Phizackerly tucked the topper under his arm and ducked his head in a little bow. "G'morning, Captain." He swept the ship in one swift, fore and aft approving glance. "Ah! What a pleasure to tread the deck of a King's ship again. Fine ship you have, sir. Fine ship. Does you credit, sir."

Smith said cautiously, "Thank you, Mister – ?"

"Phizackerly, sir." He stepped forward and held out a skinny hand. Smith took it and found it a hard, dry claw. "Arnold Phizackerly. A prominent member of the British business community here. Entrepreneur an' impresario."

45

"What?"

Garrick came stalking and rasped in cold explanation, "Brothel keeper, sir."

"Oh?" Smith was off-balance a second, then amused. As he stared at the cheekily absurd little man and thought, 'Brassnecked little devil,' he had a strong temptation to laugh. It seemed a long time since he had laughed.

He showed no outward sign of amusement but Phizackerly sensed a lack of animosity and seized the opportunity. A number of men had found work in the vicinity and were listening. He said, "It takes all kinds, as you might say, sir. And the door of my house, Fizzy's Palace of Entertainment, is always open." It seemed that in an abstracted moment the handbills slipped from his fingers and scattered on the breeze, to be rescued by the men. "I reckon I provide a little bit of old England, a little bit of home, for these lads and that means a lot."

Garrick said, "Any lad I catch coming out of your whorehouse will certainly find it means a lot. It's out of bounds and has been for over a year."

Phizackerly pretended not to hear; he was there to try to have the ban lifted. "I know what it means because I had the honour to serve the old Queen, Gawd Bless Her. Wearing the Widder's clo'es as you might say."

Garrick said, "He deserted from a line Regiment."

Phizackerly did not bat an eyelid. "So when I had to leave the sea-faring profession my first thought was to use my little bit o' savings to make a little bit of England out here."

Smith asked, "You were a seaman?"

Garrick plugged remorselessly, "He was a river pilot."

Phizackerly finally acknowledged him. "That's right, Mr. Garrick, pilot." And to Smith, this time with genuine pride, "I was the first pilot here back in 'ninety-two when they opened the copper mines. I found the channel and brought the first ship in with me own hands and after that it was me an' the pilots as worked for me, apprentices like, and nothing

46

moved in or out of this port without us. Not until they bought the dredger and had the short channel dredged out, that's the one they use today. And they talk about the mist of a morning at the mouth of this river! Why, in my time – "

He had to pause for breath and Garrick admitted grudgingly, "That's true. Only he and his pilots could thread that channel and he made a fortune before the mining company decided it would be cheaper to buy the dredger."

Phizackerly had finally made a point but he threw it away. Smiling paternally at the young Commander he said, "Why bless you, sir, I've had more fine ships through my hands than you've had fine women." He heard the catch of Miles's breath, saw the expression of bad-tempered dislike on Garrick's face replaced by no expression at all, and he saw Smith's lips tighten and the pale blue eyes grow hard. He knew he had gone badly wrong. He said cheerfully, but watchful, apprehensive, "Just a joke, sir. To make me point, as it were."

Smith smiled at him and Phizackerly did not like it. "You've made your point, Mr. Phizackerly, and now I'll make mine. The next time you set foot on this ship I will throw you into the cells or over the side. That is a promise."

He was still smiling and he had spoken quietly but Phizackerly found comfort in neither. He lifted the topper before his narrow chest like a shield and mumbled, "Time I was getting away." He retreated behind the cover of the top-hat, clapped it on his head as his feet found the ladder and dropped from sight.

In the launch he mopped his face with a handkerchief. Vargas opened the throttle and asked, "Good business?"

"That's an honest man."

"Ah! That is too bad."

Smith turned from the side and found Knight waiting with the decoded telegram. Knight seemed excited. Smith read the telegram and said only, "Very good," in dismissal.

He read the telegram again until laughter broke into his thoughts and he saw Cherry and Sarah Benson attended by a little group of grinning officers who shredded away as Smith looked up at them. He said flatly, "Signal from Admiralty to be passed to all H.M. ships. The German cruisers *Wolf* and *Kondor* are now known to be at sea and to have been at large for some weeks. Their location and destination are unknown."

Cherry burst out, startled, "Good Lord!"

Smith stared past him. They would have slipped through the North Sea blockade in vile winter weather, not an easy feat but by no means impossible for two fast ships. *Wolf* and *Kondor*. He needed to be given no details nor to consult the silhouette book. He had patrolled the North Sea beat for long enough, watching for these two ships and the rest of the High Seas Fleet. Like a policeman. And like a policeman with known criminals he could recite all of their descriptions and histories, their idiosyncrasies and dangerous strengths, though many of them he had not seen.

He had seen these two.

On a wild black night they had obliterated his ship and his men and thrust him to the point of death. They haunted his dreams.

Cherry was saying, "Commerce raiders. They've had some success before so they're trying that game again."

Raiders. Aimed at Allied shipping. They could wreak terrible destruction before they were hunted down and that would be more than difficult. They could be on their way to Africa or preparing to slash across the Atlantic trade routes, Britain's jugular vein, or – His mind took a leap in the dark. Sarah Benson said the Germans were watching *Thunder*. The Pacific was the last place but . . . His thoughts raced and then were still. He felt cold.

Cherry murmured vaguely, "Maybe the African coast but more likely the Atlantic . . ."

Smith said with certainty, "No."

Cherry stared at him, as did Sarah Benson and it was she who asked, "You think they're coming here?"

Cherry shook his head but stopped when Smith said, "Yes."

And went on: "They're watching this ship, following her movements. There are two ships, the *Gerda* and the *Maria*, flying neutral flags but in fact German and loaded with Welsh steam coal. Yes?" And as Cherry hesitated, then nodded, Smith said, "They're tenders. *Wolf* and *Kondor* are coal-burning ships."

Cherry was silent a moment, then he said doubtfully, "It's possible, I suppose."

Smith was to see that look of disbelief on many faces but he did not see it on Sarah Benson's. She asked, "You know these ships?" And when he nodded: "What are they like?"

"Of a size with this one but only half her age. They're slightly faster and decidedly better armed."

"Then you can't fight them." She said it with cold common sense.

Cherry went pink. "Really! You can't tell the Captain his duty –"

"Duty my foot! It isn't his duty to commit mass-suicide with the six-hundred-odd men aboard here. Either one of those ships could run rings around this old tub and blow her out of the water! He's just *said* so!"

Smith's smile was bleak. Sarah Benson had summed up the situation with brutal clarity.

There was an uncomfortable silence until Cherry asked, "What will you do?"

Smith would not add to his worries. He said slowly, "I will sail now, heading north again but only for the sake of appearances. I have a rendezvous with a collier but I can't keep it now. Will you see she is sent here to wait for my orders?"

"Of course. And you will patrol these waters?"

Smith side-stepped the question. "That seems the obvious course."

Thunder sailed.

Every man aboard her knew that she had come to this port

49

at the urgent request of Cherry and they had seen them talking. They knew something was afoot. But Smith conned his ship and was silent.

As *Thunder* slid past the signalling station at Punta Negro and lifted to the sea, Garrick ventured, "The wardroom would be pleased if Miss Benson and yourself would join us for dinner this evening, sir."

Smith's lips twitched. He was sure the invitation was aimed at Sarah Benson and courtesy demanded it be extended to himself. But maybe he was being unfair. "I'd be delighted and I'm sure Miss Benson will be. Will the gunroom be present?"

"Yes, sir. We rather thought that, as this will be your first visit as Captain, it would be suitable."

So he had been unfair. "It will suit very well. I have one or two things to say."

He turned to leave the bridge but glanced at the log and read the entry 'weighed and proceeded'. He laid his finger against the figure of coal remaining and did the sum in his head: sufficient for seven days at an economical ten knots.

Garrick said, "We'll complete with coal from the *Mary Ellen*, sir?" The *Mary Ellen* was their collier.

Smith said absently, "I hope so."

Garrick blinked. Coaling was a chore as vital as it was filthy, a labour of hours in choking dust that took place almost weekly, vital because the ship moved by burning coal. A Captain coaled his ship or she lay a helpless hulk. Now Smith said he "hoped" they would coal. *Hoped?*

Then Smith added, "I've arranged for her to come down here." He left the bridge.

Garrick watched him go, relieved, but only partly so. He knew that with the rest of the crew he had been wary of Smith from the moment he stepped aboard and was uncomfortably aware that Smith knew it and had kept himself remote. They knew him only by reputation and rumour.

Garrick could never guess at the thoughts behind that impassive face but he suspected they were a deal quicker than his own.

Smith shifted restlessly around his cabin and rubbed at his face that had become a stiff, expressionless mask. He had to make a decision. No, that was not right. He had already made the decision but it appalled him and he was seeking an alternative. He had a cold knowledge inside himself that the cruisers were racing for these waters, and why.

The Atlantic trade routes might be an attractive hunting ground for a pair of cruisers but the Navy had a cruiser squadron off the States and another in the West Indies and reaction from both would be swift. But on the Pacific seaboard the defence of Britain's trade, and there was more than a hundred thousand tons of British shipping on this coast, rested on one ship: *Thunder*. The cruisers could sweep British trade from this coast and their marauding would draw ships from the Atlantic, maybe as many as fifty ships that were already desperately needed to blockade the High Seas Fleet and fight the growing submarine menace. And fifty ships would be none too many to find and destroy the cruisers. Hunting them in the vast Pacific wastes would be a heartbreaking business, a thousand times worse than seeking a needle in a haystack.

But that would be later. *Thunder* would come first. They would know about *Thunder*; she was under observation. She offered them a victory that would resound around the world. They could annihilate him or bottle him up in some port so that *Thunder* was interned, humiliated.

He would not have to search for these cruisers.

They would hunt him down like the wolf-pack they were.

There was a tap at the door and Horsfall entered. "Sir. Wondered if you'd like a — "

Smith snarled at him, "Get out!"

Horsfall got out. As he passed the marine sentry he spoke from the side of his mouth. "Watch it! Skipper's lookin' murder!"

It was a pleasant evening. For the second time since they had sailed from Esquimalt the gunroom were present en masse and Wakely brought his gramophone. The Captain's death, if not forgotten, was behind them. Sarah Benson was here and now. She wore a simple dress that was shattering in its effect on the wardroom. Smith thought with surprise that he supposed she was a very pretty girl, but that medallion that swung and drew the eyes to the top of the low dress — She flirted outrageously with the midshipmen, subtly with the tongue-tied Garrick, and halfway through dinner the First Lieutenant was joking with her.

Benks, the steward, leapt nimbly, arms loaded with plates. He was a God-fearing little man and a frequent but brief convert to temperance. Daddy Horsfall, pressed into service for the occasion, creaked around in stiff best boots and a pained expression with bottle and napkin. He spent a lot of time close to Sarah who persisted in talking to him and including him in the general conversation with solemn devilment. Garrick wasn't sure about that but he saw his Captain smiling broadly.

Smith had been in good humour all evening, smiling, joking. Aitkyne thought it was a textbook demonstration in total relaxation when duties were ended. Several others had thoughts of a similar nature.

Smith's mouth was dry but he drank only one glass of water. The food almost choked him.

They drank the loyal toast, Sarah Benson caught Smith's eye and stifled a feigned yawn. "Well, me for me haybag." There were exaggerated groans but sincere disappointment, because the last light had barely gone, dusk still rolling down across the sea. But she went. Smith had seen her before dinner and been polite but explicit on that and she had, as stiffly, agreed.

Benks and Horsfall withdrew to the pantry.

"Now then, gentlemen." It was said quietly but it cut through the buzz of conversation and the voices were stilled. Daddy Horsfall found, without any surprise, that the bottle he held was half-full. He and Benks saw it away while they listened to Smith beyond the pantry hatch, Daddy at first only thinking that soon he could nip away and get those damn boots off.

He listened and left, walked forward to the mess-decks and the first crowded mess he came to was that of Nobby Clark, Leading Seaman and Captain of a six-inch gun. Nobby stared at Daddy's white jacket and said, "Stone me! Here's a feller just joined us from the P.S.N.* Siddown you old bugger afore you fall down." He indicated the wardroom aft with a jerk of his head. "Is she still in there? What's going on back there?"

Daddy did not sit down. He sniffed. "I dunno what's goin' on, but I know what's coming off."

"Eh?"

Daddy told them, and as he did so *Thunder* heeled as she turned so they had to grab for a handhold as they stared at him, and still she turned.

* Pacific Steam Navigation Company.

4

THERE WAS A brooding hush about the night, black, close. *Thunder* lay once more off Punta Negro, the hill and its signalling station marked by a pin-point of light while Guaya was a glow against the sky far inland. Bullock, the Coxswain, muttered ominously that it was a weather breeder and Aitkyne gave cautious endorsement from the glass. The Coxswain shifted his quid from one cheek to the other. "Dunno about the barometer, sir. I'm going off Daddy Horsfall's feet."

Thunder swayed gently in a long, slow swell, without a light save the occasional dim blink from a shaded lamp. Smith walked aft and found his party forming up in that black dark as the pinnace and whaler were hoisted out, men swarming to tail onto the falls because he had forbidden the use of a clamouring winch to shatter that still darkness; they could sense the loom of the land, see the shore marked by a line of phosphorescence.

They all wore navy boiler-suits and blackened canvas shoes, their heads were wrapped in balaclava helmets and their faces smeared with soot until only the eyes showed. There was always plenty of soot to be got on *Thunder*. They were lost in anonymity, sinister in the dark. And they were, of course self-conscious, a little sheepish. It all seemed unreal.

To Garrick it was a bad dream.

Every man was armed with a revolver; a rifle made no sense in this operation. One chamber of each was unloaded and the hammer lay over that with the safety catch on. There would be no careless, accidental shot.

Someone guffawed, the laugh cut short as Smith stood before him. "What's the joke?" The question came softly.

The man grinned uneasily. "Just seemed a bit funny, sir."

The man was Rattray. Smith knew him as a hard case with a reputation as a brawler. He sniffed and caught the whiff of rum. A man like this could imperil them all. Smith rasped, "Hand over your pistol." And as he took it : "You're a bloody fool! Master at arms!"

"Sir!"

"This man's been hoarding his tots. Take him to the boiler-room. He can spend the night there and work the grog out with a shovel."

Rattray was hustled away. Smith glanced around and saw young Gibb in one of the parties manning the falls of the boats and thrust the pistol at him. "Get some soot on your face and fall in."

Smith went on with his inspection and wound up with Gibb as he returned and fell in, breathless from running and the excitement that gripped them all. Smith checked every pistol again himself and his attention to details impressed them as it was meant to do, to bring their concentration to bear. He spoke to them. The man in the wardroom had gone and his voice was harsh and urgent, sending a shiver through them. "I want no noise at all! No shooting except in direct defence of your lives!"

They stared at him, serious now. When a man licked his lips it was like a pink wound in his face.

They went down into the boats.

Somers was in the whaler with a dozen seamen. Lieutenant

Kennedy, a Reserve officer re-called from the mercantile marine and a man with knowledge of explosives, was in the pinnace with Manton and Wakely, ten seamen and ten marines under Sergeant Burton. The tow was passed from pinnace to whaler. Smith, standing by Manton who had the helm, stared up and saw Garrick on the deck above him, Aitkyne on the wing of the bridge, both of them peering down at him. He could not make out faces but he did not need to, the stances and attitudes of his officer were familiar now. He did not have to see Garrick's face to know he was a very worried man. Smith's cold assessment of the situation and his flat statement of his intentions had taken the wardroom's breath away. Most of them thought his assessment *might* be right, only – *cruisers*. It seemed so unreal. The war had been so far away. And what Smith intended! Garrick was shocked. Later, privately, he had pointed out the dangers and the probable, in his eyes certain, penalties. Smith was unmoved. Quite simply, Smith believed he was right while Garrick and the others were far from sure. It was too big a gamble for them. For him it was a risk he had to take.

He was taking as few officers and men as possible. If something went badly wrong, and it easily could, *Thunder* must still be able to function. He lifted one hand, saw Garrick's acknowledgment and said quietly, "Carry on, Mr. Manton."

The screw of the pinnace turned, bit and she eased away, towing the whaler. The ship fell away behind them, changing to a humping shapeless mass, to nothing. He had not seen Sarah Benson where she shivered in the shadows below the bridge.

He stood by the compass but it was not needed. Manton steered for the signalling station at Punta Negro, its lights pricking the dark. Beyond it the lights of Guaya, though hidden by the bend in the river and five miles of forest and swamp, cast a pale glow against the sky. Smith leaned with his arms on the coaming, relaxed, as if this was just one more item in the day's work. When they were a mile from the mouth of the river he said laconically, "Steer a point or two to starboard." Manton, like all of them, had been well briefed and was expecting the order. The bow of the pinnace moved away from the light and laid on the right bank of the estuary, so when they entered it they were tucked right in under that bank, invisible to the men in the signalling station if they watched, though there was no reason why they should.

They passed Stillwater Cove, keeping to the shallows and the greatest darkness by the shore, avoiding the deepwater channel. The pinnace made an easy three knots despite the drag of the tow because the tide was flowing now and urging them on. They rode smoothly through the night with only the slow, dull churn of the picket-boat's engine, the muffled scrape and clink of Jenner's shovel in the tiny engineroom and the clump of the closing furnace door. Here there was no one to see or hear them. Smith ordered an increase in speed and as the shovel clanged like a bell below: "Quinn."

The signalman started. "Sir?"

Smith's tone was mild but had an edge to it. "Tell Jenner that if he does that again his shovel goes over the side."

"Aye, aye, sir."

"And him with it."

He maintained the attitude of calm throughout the long haul up the estuary. He found himself continually stifling yawns, but far from being drowsy he was strung to a tight pitch. This was an awful gamble. Success could ruin him while failure would be an ignominious disaster. He thrust the thoughts aside. His decision had been taken and he believed it right. And now he was committed.

They rounded the bend and entered the pool with an odd mixture of relief and heightened tension. The waiting was over but now the action would begin. The men shifted and wiped sweaty hands for the hundredth but the last time. The pool was open before them, picked out by scattered lights along the shore and more lights marked the ships that lay there. U.S.S. *Kansas*, the battleship, was a floating mountain far across the pool. The collier *Gerda* was a squat shadow, barely lit but seen against the lighted backdrop of the shore. And something else showed against that backdrop. Smith called softly, "Stop engines." They closed the collier, slowing as the way came off the pinnace, stopped. They drifted in silence but for the burble of water under the bow.

Smith stared, and saw it again, was sure now. A boat was rowing around *Gerda*. It was halfway along the port side and creeping towards the stern, hardly moving at all, the deliberate pacing of a sentry. He watched until the boat worked around the stern of the collier and disappeared from view. It was odd behaviour for a neutral vessel in a neutral port.

Kennedy said, "A guard-boat. That does it."

"That does it." Kennedy had spoken his thoughts aloud: the operation was off. Kennedy could not dissemble. He was a sea-officer not a diplomat and he had patently disbelieved in the cruisers heading for these waters. He was not alone. Smith knew that most of the officers sided with him, including Garrick, and regarded this operation as an act of madness. He had not called for volunteers. He knew the men he wanted and named them. Kennedy was here reluctantly but because he was needed. He disliked his orders but he was obeying them.

Smith turned to look at Kennedy and met his gaze that was both expectant and relieved. Smith saw the twitch of surprise when he said, "Not by a long shot, Mr. Kennedy. Bring up the whaler."

Wakely answered, "Already coming, sir."

The whaler sprouted oars like a man waking from sleep, arms stretching. The oars came in again as it ran alongside the pinnace. Smith gave Kennedy his orders then stepped over to sit in the stern by Somers. He paused, then called, "Sergeant Burton! Come with me." Burton's square bulk rose from the block of marines and he picked his way lightly between them to swing over into the whaler. Smith ordered, "Give way."

The whaler headed across the pool, giving *Gerda* a wide berth, keeping out in the sheltering dark, passing her. So for another half-minute then the whaler turned and pointed back downstream, heading for the collier. Now Smith could see there was a light on her deck, aft of the bridge on the starboard side, and he could make out a dangling ladder on that side. The light was on the superstructure amidships but he could not see a man there. But there would be a lookout, somewhere. He could see the guard-boat creeping again up the port side of the collier towards the stern. He gauged the relative distances and speeds as the whaler slid down on the ship and saw that they would meet the guard-boat under *Gerda's* stern and was content.

He spoke in a hoarse whisper but his voice carried down the length of the whaler: "No shooting except in self-defence, and at this moment no shooting at all. Mr. Somers, you will need four men." Somers picked them. They were closing the stern of *Gerda* now. The guard-boat had seen them, Smith could tell that from the accelerated beat of its oars and the swing of the bow towards them, before the voice lifted, the words incomprehensible but the tone enquiring, suspicious.

Smith replied nasally, *"Kansas!"* The man nearest him, bent over the oar, face only inches from Smith, gasped, "Blimey."

Smith continued his drawling, "Have you fellers seen anything of a swimmer? The son-of-a-bitch went over the side because his furlough was stopped and when I get my hands on him – "

The whaler came from the direction of *Kansas*. There were two men in the guard-boat and they waited, listening to Smith's impersonation, a poor impersonation but good enough to get him alongside. At the last moment one of the men yelped as the whaler swept down on him and Smith snapped, "Oars! Somers!"

The oars came in, the whaler thumped against the boat and Somers and his four men leapt over the side like frogs to smother the men in the boat.

"Shove off! Give way!" Smith left Somers to drift away down the port side while he took the whaler skimming down the starboard side of the *Gerda* to the dangling ladder. The oars came in again and he snatched at the ladder and started climbing. He heard a voice on the deck above him but right aft, a voice that called, puzzled. He was aware of Burton at his heels and that he had started climbing without taking his pistol from its holster. His head lifted above the rail and he swung one leg over then the other, took a pace forward and saw the man hurrying from the stern towards him. The man halted a couple of yards away, just in the pool of light that flooded over Smith. He gaped and the hand at his side lifted. It held a pistol.

Smith snapped testily, "Put that away. I am a British officer." For an instant the man hesitated, the pistol still pointed at the deck and Smith took a long stride and grabbed it with one hand, the man's throat with the other. Panic twisted the man's face and he jerked back. Thick-set and strong, he hauled Smith with him and his free hand came up to claw at Smith's face. At the instant that Smith realised he was out-matched in weight and strength, Burton appeared. In one smooth movement he plucked the man away from Smith and threw him face-down on the deck, Burton's hand at his throat, Burton's knee in his back.

Men spilled around Smith, hurrying soft-footed forward and aft. He crossed the deck, fumbling the torch from his pocket, blinked it twice and got one flash in return from the pinnace. He turned and stared into the muzzle of a pistol, had the briefest gut-sinking impression of an officer's jacket pulled on over pyjamas, a bearded face and eyes that glared death at him. Then a figure plunged from the gloom and crashed into the officer, flame blinded Smith and the discharge of the pistol deafened him.

He rubbed at his eyes and when the wheeling circles were gone he saw Somers crouched on the officer's chest, pinning him to the deck. Somers held the pistol. Smith's ears still rang and he swore. The cat was out of the bag. He ran forward and saw a door open below the bridge, a man framed in that door and behind him the lighted interior of a cabin, the paraphernalia of the wireless office. He saw Able Seaman Beckett leap for that door and have it slammed in his face. He added his weight to that of Beckett but the door was bolted solid and the port clamped shut. He swore again and snarled at Beckett, "Guard it. He comes out with his hands up or you shoot him."

He reached out to grab another seaman as he raced past. "Get on top of this wireless office and rip all the aerials adrift!"

"Aye, aye, sir!"

Smith ran on and met Sergeant Burton. "All secure forrard, sir. And we've got all the officers, I think."

"Keep searching. One of the officers nearly got *me*. Mr. Somers is sitting on him. What happened to yours?"

"Made fast, sir. And a mouthful o' rope for him to chew on."

"Add Somers's man to your collection."

Then the pinnace thumped alongside and moments later Wakely led his party aboard, swarming across the deck. The ship was theirs. Kennedy came over the side with his two assistants carrying the wares of his trade and they disappeared below.

Smith was not happy. That damned shot! He could not see or hear any sign of an alarm being raised, except – was there activity on *Kansas*? He could not be sure.

He made a rapid tour of the upper deck and returned to find the captive crew lined up below the bridge, officers and men, most of them still dazed from sleep, peering owlishly, shivering in the night air. Burton brought the bearded officer to join the others. He held his midriff, badly winded, and wheezed out: "I protest – "

Smith cut him short, savagely, "Shut up or I'll shoot you!"

Wakely, coming up then, flinched at Smith's words then said, "There isn't a safe in the Captain's cabin, sir. Just a desk with three locked drawers." It had been Wakely's job to take the safe. "I broke them open and emptied them into a sack."

"Very good."

Rudkin, the picket-boat's engineer, panted up from *Gerda's* engineroom. "She had steam up, sir. Could ha' sailed in half-an-hour if she'd wanted."

"Thank you. Carry on."

Rudkin swung over the rail and down to the pinnace.

Smith turned to the silent master. "This ship sinks in ten minutes but you will be clear of her by then. Lower your boats."

"This is a neutral vessel – "

"Or swim." Smith offered the choice.

The master swallowed and bellowed an order at his crew. In German. They ran to lower the boats.

Smith glanced at his watch. They were on time, in spite of the enforced change of plan caused by the guard-boat. Just. He saw a rent in the left-hand side of his boiler-suit and used his torch to inspect it. The hole was surrounded by a powder-burn. As he switched off the torch he faced Somers. "Where did you spring from?"

The soot on Somers's face was now striped by sweat-drawn channels. "Checking on the look-outs, sir."

Posting the look-outs had been one of his duties. Smith said, "I mean before. When you came up from the deck like the demon king."

"We'd run their boat right in under the stern. Some chap in the stern shouted but he couldn't see us and went away. I shinned up a line that was hanging and came forrard and there I was."

"Yes. And here I nearly wasn't."

"Sir. *Kansas* seems to be manning a boat."

Smith stared across at *Kansas*. There was activity on her deck, tiny figures moving under the lights. But the rest of the pool was quiet, undisturbed.

Kennedy reappeared, breathing heavily, like all of them his soot-mask was lined and smeared now. "Five minutes, sir."

"Right." Smith turned on Somers. "Those two prisoners in the boat – return them to their friends."

"I've done that, sir."

"Then call in the look-outs." Smith raised his voice : "Over the side, all of you. Five minutes."

The ship's crew were already in their boats and pulling away. The seamen and marines padded across the deck and went down. Burton swung one leg over the rail. Smith cast one final glance around the deserted deck, at the falls hanging loose from the davits so the ship looked untidy, abandoned. As she was. He hated to do this to any ship.

It was time to go.

He called to Beckett where he guarded the wireless office : "Give him the word, then it's up to him!"

Beckett hammered on the door of the wireless office. "Abandon ship! Ship kaput!"

There was no answer, no reaction. Beckett hesitated and Smith shouted, "Come *on*! We can't hang about all night!"

Beckett left his post and started towards him. He had taken only three strides when the door swung open behind him and a man loomed in the doorway pointing a blue-gleaming, threatening finger that suddenly flamed and the shot cracked out.

Beckett cried out and fell forward, his face, slack-jowled in shock, turned up to Smith. The man put one foot outside the door, holding it open with his left hand, aiming the pistol with the other. Smith ran at him in black rage at the sudden attack, at himself for not, somehow, preventing it. He ran in, tugging his pistol from his belt. The man fired again, so close the flame seared the eyes but his aim was wild, panicked by Smith's mad rush, and Smith was already throwing himself to the deck. He fell close enough almost to touch the man whose pistol waved above his head. Smith squeezed the trigger again and again and the hammer clicked on the empty chamber then fired three times. The other pistol that waved above him fired only once, the slug howling off the deck then the pistol fell, clattering. The man reeled back into the cabin. Smith crawled to the door and saw him sprawled, used his torch and saw the arms thrown wide, the eyes staring.

He turned and saw Burton bending over Beckett who was feeling gingerly with his right hand at his left side. Smith used his torch again and saw little blood. The minutes were ticking away. "We'll look at it in the boat."

Beckett went down on Burton's back with his wrists lashed together around Burton's neck so he could not fall if he fainted, but he clung on grimly. When the hands reached up eagerly from the pinnace to take him he grinned down at them, shakily.

Manton reported, "All present, sir." And Somers from the whaler: "All here, sir."

Kennedy growled, "Less'n two minutes."

"Full speed ahead," Smith ordered.

The pinnace eased away from the side of the collier, towing the whaler again but Somers had the oars out and was working furiously. Smith saw outlined against the lights of the shore that *Gerda*'s boats were well clear then the pinnace swung around the bow of the ship and thrust out into the pool, heading for the deep-water channel. Wakely's voice came from the bow as the pool opened out before them: "Boat fine on the port bow!"

Smith saw the lights and then made out the boat, a steam pinnace bigger than *Thunder*'s, and that it was altering course to intercept them. It was moving at speed, throwing up a big, white bow-wave. The intervening distance shrank rapidly until the hail came: "What boat is that?"

Kansas's pinnace. Smith answered: *"Thunder!"*

The American pinnace swung neatly on her heel to come around and foam alongside a dozen feet away. A boyish figure stood at her wheel, white face turned towards Smith, as were all the other faces in her. *"What* boat is that?" As if he doubted the evidence of his eyes.

Smith repeated cheerfully, *"Thunder!"*

For long seconds the two pinnaces ran side by side as the Americans peered fascinated at the bizarre parties in the opposite pinnace and whaler. Then the explosions came, muffled, dull thumps, seeming more physical vibrations than sounds. Smith saw the collier heave and then settle. Kennedy had blown the bottom out of her. Smoke and steam suddenly roared from her funnel and she began to list. Smith said, "Very effective, Mr. Kennedy."

Kennedy did not answer and sat stone-faced.

A voice on *Kansas*'s pinnace cried, *"Jee-sus!"* And another: "What the *hell*?" She spun away and headed for *Gerda*. She was the last vessel they saw.

In the channel they met the flowing tide and the crew of the whaler spat on their hands and bent to their oars in earnest. With their efforts and the pinnace punching along at her best speed they passed the signalling station at Punta Negro before the dawn. Running without lights as they were it was unlikely that they would have been seen from the station but before they reached Stillwater Cove the mist swirled and curled thick and dirty yellow over the channel. They pushed through it, the look-out in the bow fanning at it mechanically as if he could cut a path for them. Now they used the compass.

The mist held them cocooned in a muffled, closed world for a half-hour, then the yellow turned pink shot with golden light as if they moved inside the silence of some church and the sun came at them through stained glass. Then they ran out of the mist and were clear of the estuary, on the open sea in the dawn's light, and *Thunder* patrolled, cruising slowly across their course, a mile ahead. There was a ragged cheer and the men looked at each other, exhausted but exhilarated, grinning uncertainly at first but then broadly. In the light of day with their streaked faces and their hair matted and spiked where they thrust away the balaclavas now, they looked very odd. Even funny.

Someone said to Beckett, "There's the old cow standing in for us." *Thunder* had seen them.

Beckett had lain in a daze or a doze, he was not sure which. Now he stirred and sat up to stare at the ship. He looked back at Smith. "You should ha' seen the old man run at that feller. Run right *at* him! And the bastard firing away like mad. But he never faltered, and you should ha' seen the look on his face." He would not forget it. "What daft bugger said he was windy?"

Thunder rounded to and the pinnace ran alongside. Smith stared back at the estuary and saw the mist already shredded to almost nothing, the sun sucking it up greedily, the wind rolling it away. He could see the signalling station and no doubt they were watching *Thunder* and wondering. They would know by now of the sinking of the *Gerda.* He could see no sign of pursuit in the estuary but it was too early for the authorities to have assessed the situation, much less to react. But they would.

He turned and said to Manton, "By God, Mid, I'm famished." He was honestly surprised at the discovery. As he climbed aboard he knew he was very hungry and very tired and that before he ate or slept he had work to do. Garrick looked relieved to see him, but not overjoyed. Smith grinned wearily at him, and at Aitkyne behind him. "A course for Malaguay, pilot, and revolutions for fifteen knots." And: "Pass the word to Miss Benson. I would be grateful if she could spare me a few minutes."

He found cheerful words of congratulation for the crews of pinnace and whaler as the boats were swung in. He received Albrecht's report that the bullet that hit Beckett had entered his back on the extreme left side, run along the ribs and out. He would be sore and his ribs bruised for some days and Albrecht was keeping him in the sick-bay for twenty-four hours. Then the messenger returned and said Miss Benson was ready to see him and Smith walked aft and below.

Garrick watched him go then shot a haggard glance at Aitkyne, who said, "He's got his nerve. That's one rumour nailed for a lie. By God, he's got his nerve." He shook his head over it. Smith had sunk a neutral ship in a neutral port. The enormity of the offence left them silent. It was unthinkable, except to Smith. He had done it.

It tempered the exuberance of the crew as they welcomed back the boarding-party but still there was a lot of back-slapping and Gibb came in for his share. He had been the last to board the *Gerda* and he had seen neither shooting nor fighting. Still, he had been one of them and he blushed under the smeared soot.

Rattray took no part in this. A night spent in back-breaking labour under the cursing driving of a Stoker Petty Officer had left him exhausted and filthy. He had boasted of what he would do when he boarded *Gerda* and then Smith had humiliated him and taken that green squirt Gibb in his place. He had heard Smith tell Gibb that he had done well, as he told all of them.

Rattray would get even with both of them. He was not sure yet how he would get at high and mighty bloody Smith but he would start with Gibb.

Sarah had not needed to be wakened; she woke long before dawn. The previous night she had watched the boats leave. Now as Smith entered and she saw the strained, blood-shot eyes in the dirty face, the hair sweat-stuck flat to his head, she asked only the one question and that was almost a statement: "You sank the *Gerda*?"

"Yes."

She sat up in the Captain's bed, wrapped in a silk dressing-gown lent by Aitkyne. It was too large and loose but her case had held no night-clothes.

He had expected her question and she expected his. "What can you tell me of Malaguay?" Another collier lay there.

They were polite to each other, business-like. There was a working truce to tide them over till their ways should part and that would be soon. Sarah shrugged and the robe slipped to reveal a glimpse of white shoulder and a lift of breast. She adjusted the robe absently. "Natural harbour between two headlands with a muddy river at the head of it and wharves on either bank of the river. But that's not what you want from me; you've charts and sailing directions.

"Let's see ... A German gunboat was interned there late in 1914. She's been tied up in the river since then. Disarmed of course, but otherwise untouched. Her crew live aboard and the Chileans have a guard on her. That's only a gesture; there's nowhere she could go.

"Strong German influence, a large German colony. Usual few British with the usual British club. Some Americans.

"Cherry sent me down there not long ago because a man called Medina, a Chilean, had applied for a licence to carry mails by air."

Smith stared. "What?"

"Exactly. Everybody's eyebrows went up and particularly because he didn't have an aircraft. Besides, Cherry had him on the books as a German sympathiser. Soon after a new American arrived as an assistant to the local representative of a firm selling farm tools. In a couple of days everybody knew he had been a pilot with the United States Naval Air Service and handed in his commission because the money wasn't good enough. He also hinted that his fondness for a gamble might have had something to do with it and he said he wasn't pro-British nor pro-German just pro-Jim Bradley. Inside of a week he had a reputation as a gambler, winning and losing big sums but mostly winning, and everybody knew he could fly any God-damn aeroplane you cared to name, anytime, anywhere – if the money was right.

'I'm certain he's working for his government. I think he suspects I'm working for mine." She stopped abruptly. "That's all about him that matters.

"Ten days ago Cherry ordered me north but the day before I left an aircraft arrived for Medina from the States and a pilot and two mechanics came with it, all of them 'civilians' invalided out of the German service with things like stomach trouble or rheumatism. They looked very fit to me."

Smith put in : "You didn't mention this aircraft yesterday."

"Well, you can't carry much coal in the thing!"

Smith did not elaborate, but it was another factor added to the colliers. He thought about what she had told him and she watched him and thought that he was a solitary character and a million miles from her, remote. She wondered about those stories now and the letter from her sister. He was a lonely man . . .

Smith asked, "This Jim Bradley – you've met him?"

"I've met him in the way of business. That was part of my business, meeting people like him, strangers."

"What is he like?"

Sarah shrugged again but this time when the robe slipped she was self-conscious in her quick adjustment of it. "Tall. Six feet two. Broad shoulders. Brown hair, brown eyes, small scar on right cheekbone, 'go-to-hell-and-I'll-come-with-you' expression. He's a good man."

She met his gaze straight-forwardly but he remembered that would be part of her stock-in-trade. He felt she was holding something back. "Anything else?" The girl's cool look was stiff-faced now. "Anything else?"

"He has several other scars on his upper body, the result of a flying accident, and one on his lower abdomen. He's tried to get me to bed but I didn't go. I learned this from somebody who did. *Anything else?*"

Smith was embarrassed. The girl had been holding back but only to save herself and him from embarrassment.

She said, "Why, Commander, I think you're blushing under all that dirt."

He felt a fool and knew that she knew it. He mumbled some apology. There would be a British ship at Malaguay and then he would be free of her. Soon. He held on to that thought as he stood up, rubbed at his face and smiled stiffly, blearily at her. "I'm grateful for your help." And he was, his awkwardness could not hide that.

"You're welcome, Commander." The door closed behind him and she stared at it, fingering the medallion that hung on her breast. She said softly, "You'll need all the help you can get."

Smith tried to put her out of his mind and concentrate on the information she had given him. Bradley—a good man. Then as he climbed to the upper deck he met Garrick, who said, "Young Wakely had a sack of stuff he brought aboard from the *Gerda*, sir. He's in the Captain's – your deck cabin with it, sir."

Smith ignored the slip but it was a sign of the newness of his command; he was a stranger here still. "Right. You'd better come along and give a hand with it." And as they went: "I will mention them in my report. Manton, Wakely, Somers, Kennedy, Burton. They all did well." He did not mention Somers particularly but the boy impressed him. He said, "And I'll mention your loyalty *and* the objections you raised."

"Sir?"

Smith paused outside the cabin and his smile was lopsided.

70

"Just in case. It will keep your nose clean if it turns out I have been a bloody fool."

Half-an-hour later the law of probabilities insisted he had been just that. The sack held the *Gerda*'s log, her master's diary, copies of manifests, letters from owners and agents and his wife, personal papers. Smith, Garrick and Wakely sifted through it painstakingly and Albrecht was sent for because there was a great deal of German in the papers. The master of the *Gerda* had been born in Argentina but as Albrecht explained, "No doubt he spoke German at home and with his friends." He shrugged. "There's nothing at all in that. We often spoke German at home." And there was nothing at all to cast doubt on *Gerda*'s neutrality.

Nobody wanted to look at Smith. He dismissed them. Later Aitkyne asked Garrick, "Well? Anything?"

Garrick shook his head worriedly. "Nothing at all. As far as evidence goes that collier was as neutral as a Swiss hospital ship."

Aitkyne said, "The general opinion is that he's mad as a hatter."

"Nonsense!" Garrick snapped it, but he peered uneasily at the navigator.

Aitkyne smiled wryly. "Don't jump down my throat, old lad. I didn't say it was my opinion. But it could be his salvation."

"What?"

"If he's lucky they'll decide he's mad – and they won't shoot him."

5

THEY MADE MALAGUAY in the late afternoon, *Thunder* trudging in over a slow, leaden swell under a grey and lowering sky. There was a strong, gusting wind that snapped the crests from the waves in spitting spume. The weather was worsening.

Thunder came to anchor in the bay but before she was stopped the boat carrying the Consul ran alongside and he jumped for the dangling ladder, clawed at it desperately and clambered up. He was obviously in a hurry. Smith spoke to the bridge messenger. "My compliments to Miss Benson and I would be grateful if she would spare me a few minutes of her time." And then he added, turning the seeming request into a command, "Immediately." He might also have added that the lady was right forward in the bow but there was no need. The messenger was as aware of it as everyone else on the bridge and no doubt as appreciative. The wind moulded the dress to her body and whipped at the skirt around her ankles. Looking for her American?

Thunder rode to her anchor. Garrick said, "Can't see any *Maria*, sir."

Smith had already made his inspection of the vessels at

anchor. "No. She must be up-river." Ships lined the wharves in the river that ran into the bay, a small forest of masts but it was impossible to pick out a particular ship at that angle and that distance. He could see two British ships at anchor, one a commonplace tramp but the other bigger, smarter. They called for another decision.

Garrick said, "That's *Ariadne*, sir. Commodore Ballard. This is her regular run, right up the coast to Vancouver. Usually around forty or fifty passengers and cargo."

"And the other one." Smith lifted his glasses and read the tramp's name. "The *Elizabeth Bell*?"

"Don't know, sir. She's a stranger to me."

"My compliments to both of them as well. I want someone to explain the situation to them and that I request neither will move without my protection." He paused. That smacked of arrogance. He added, "I will go myself if I can, but if not then Aitkyne shall go. Tell him to be tactful."

But Aitkyne was behind them, looking pensive as well he might because the explanation would be difficult and they wouldn't want to believe him when they heard what Smith wanted; that might mean delay and time was money to both skippers. And Aitkyne did not believe it himself. He said unhappily, "Aye, aye, sir."

Smith said, "Be tactful." But he finished definitely: "But firm!"

He left the bridge and Aitkyne muttered, "They've had the news from Guaya, that's sure. See the Consul come aboard? Like a scalded cat. This is where the sparks start flying."

Smith met Sarah Benson and the Consul on the upper deck. Thackeray was a thin man, thin-lipped. He eyed Smith severely. "You've stirred up a hornet's nest, Captain, if reports are correct."

"I don't know what reports you've heard. The truth of the matter is that there was a German collier lying at Guaya, masquerading as a neutral. I sank her."

Thackeray jerked as if struck and glared at Smith. "You can prove she wasn't neutral?"

"I can't prove it, but she wasn't neutral. You know about the cruisers? *Wolf* and *Kondor*?"

Thackeray did because Cherry had telegraphed to him and Smith went on to explain why he had sunk *Gerda*. Thackeray listened impatiently, lips pursed. At the end he shook his narrow head. "They're outraged and I'm not surprised. It will get worse, I'm sure. The Germans are playing it up with all their might, of course. They're bandying around phrases like the wolf sneaking into the fold to murder the lamb."

"An unusual lamb – fitted with brand-new wireless!"

"So you say. Did you know they've had a gunboat, the *Leopard*, interned here since 1914? Now they're demanding her release or the internment of *this* ship."

"That's nonsense. They should be told as much."

Smith was hinting that this was the Consul's job but Thackeray looked down his nose. "Suppose the Chileans agree?"

"*I* wouldn't. You can make that clear. If they try to intern this ship illegally they'll have to do it by force." And he looked around at the crowded port and the town.

Thackeray muttered, "It's an indication of the trouble you've caused. Over the years I've built up good relations, *very* good relations with everyone in this port. Now my friends cut me and peasants shout at me in the streets!"

Smith caught Sarah Benson's eye on him. Her face was impassive but one eye closed, opened. So Thackeray's cosy little world had been upset and Smith was to blame. He'd get little more aid from the Consul than from the Chileans. It couldn't be helped. He said, "The collier in this port. I want *her* interned. Where is she lying?"

"She isn't." Thackeray sniffed. "She sailed about nine hours ago, a half-hour after the telegrams began to arrive with the news of your – er – *escapade*." He said the word with distaste

74

but he was relieved. Smith could wreak no damage here. "She headed to the west."

So there it was. Smith stood on his upper deck, aware that the picket-boat was in the water, smoke streaming from her stubby funnel, Somers at the helm and Aitkyne going down into her. He was not surprised that the *Maria* had fled because it was always a possibility, nor at the speed of her departure; she must have been lying with steam up ready to sail when called. Like *Gerda*. But it was a blow. It was one more piece of circumstantial evidence pointing to her guilt but that only added to his reasons for wanting her. He had considered the possibility of her running and her probable course and destination. There were several, scattered around half of the compass. North? South? West? She had steered west and that could mean she was bound for Juan Fernandez, a dot in the Pacific where raiders could coal in peace. Or was that merely a ruse to gain sea-room so as to swing north well clear of *Thunder* as she had run down to Malaguay. Or a ruse before she turned south.

The cruisers would not rendezvous to the north . . .

Garrick said, "The Port Captain wants to come aboard, sir."

The words sank in slowly and then Smith said, "Yes. Due honours." And he sent a messenger running to his cabin.

Maria was carrying coal to the cruisers but Smith stood on his quarterdeck and met the Port Captain, saluting at the head of the accommodation ladder.

The Port Captain was big and full of bluster. He protested. A neutral vessel sunk in a neutral port; insolent violation of neutrality; representations in the strongest terms were being made to the ambassador, to London . . .

South or west? *Maria* had nine hours start and she would be making eight, possibly nine knots. If *Thunder* sailed now and made fifteen knots she should overhaul *Maria* in nine or ten hours. *If* Smith was right about her course. If he was wrong he would have lost her.

The Port Captain paused for breath as the messenger returned, still running, and panting, and handed Smith the envelope from his desk. Smith handed it to the Port Captain with the words: "This is a copy of my report of the incident."

"*Incident!*" The Port Captain exploded the word.

"Incident." Smith went on doggedly, "It details the reasons for my action, the evidence I had, that the vessel in question was not a neutral but a tender of war manned by a German crew."

"A tender – " That set the Port Captain back on his heels.

"It is all in my report."

The Port Captain turned the envelope over in his hands. "I will present this – document to the proper authorities. But meanwhile you are unwelcome in this port, you will receive nothing and no one from this ship will be allowed to land."

It was Smith's turn to protest. "Are you aware that this ship has neither coaled nor provisioned in a Chilean port for the last three months and that under international law – "

"In normal circumstances, Captain. These are not normal. Be sure you understand me. You receive nothing, no one lands, and you sail immediately."

Smith shrugged. "Very well. Please believe me when I say I am sincerely sorry that our former excellent relations have deteriorated to this point and I hope they will soon return to happy normality." If they wanted diplomatic waffle they could have it. "I have the greatest respect for yourself and your country. I have a little engine trouble, nothing serious, and my engineers are at work on it now." That was true. Davies wanted to put out some of his fires and clean them of clinker. Smith might let him do it now. "I will be ready to sail in a few hours. Meanwhile I undertake that not one of my crew will be landed for any reason."

After that came the stiff formalities of departure and all the time the alternatives competed in Smith's head. South? West? And *Maria* already over seventy miles away. Within the stark choice between south or west there were sub-

76

divisions: the Pacific was a large ocean. But the first basic choice was still south or west. Though *Thunder* was a slow warship she still had twice the speed of a collier, but he could not go in two directions at once. He had to commit himself to one. And Sarah Benson had bitten her lip – because she would not be seeing a young man she had 'met in the way of business'? Thackeray was hovering uneasily, a troubled man. The picket-boat was plugging through the chop, the sky was low and heavy, the wind gusting with the first rain flying in it.

There would be three, maybe four hours of daylight. If he sailed now and guessed correctly, enormous assumption, it would be night when he came up with *Maria*. If he was wrong? He dared not be wrong. He had to shorten the odds somehow. *Had* to.

The Port Captain descended and Smith's hand snapped down from his cap. "Miss Benson! Would you take me to your American friend, discreetly?"

For a moment she gaped at him, taken off-balance. "Well, I—"

He was aware of the risk she would be taking; Cherry had spelled it out. She would be aware of it, too.

She said, "Yes." She did not ask 'Why' but the question was in her mind.

Smith swung on Thackeray. "Will you put us ashore?" And: "I am formally requesting your assistance as His Majesty's representative."

Thackeray hesitated. Smith knew the cause of that hesitation was only partly the promise given to the Port Captain but he said acidly, "My word given was that no member of my crew would go ashore. I said nothing of myself or Miss Benson."

Thackeray admitted grudgingly, "It will be possible. I believe it has been done before." Then he added, "But I advise *you* formally of my disapproval and I accept no responsibility at all."

"Understood. A moment, please."

Smith hurried aft to his cabin but returned quickly, uniform jacket and cap discarded and buttoning an old tweed jacket, cramming a soft hat on his head. "Mr. Garrick, you're in command in my absence, of course."

"Aye, aye, sir." Garrick thought that he was being left to his own devices in a port technically neutral but decidedly hostile to the ship. Something of this showed in his face.

Smith said dryly, "Don't sail without me, Mr. Garrick. And arrange with *Ariadne* for Miss Benson to transfer to her as a passenger."

Thackeray had gone down into his launch with Sarah Benson and Smith followed. Sarah crouched in the tiny cabin as it thrashed across the harbour while Thackeray remained standing in the well. Smith said, "You heard what the Port Captain had to say; I'll get no coal in Chile and I must coal soon. The collier *Mary Ellen* is making for Guaya. Will you send for her to come here?"

Thackeray nodded woodenly and Smith ducked into the cover of the cabin as the launch drew into the river.

Thunder had coal for six days of economical steaming but for the last ten hours she had steamed at fifteen knots and at that speed she ate coal.

Smith heard Thackeray speak briefly to the man at the wheel in rapid Spanish, and the helmsman nodded, smiled as Thackeray made a promise, a bribe. Smith thrust his other problems behind him. The launch slowed as it entered the river, puttering gently past the ships moored there. Thackeray, without a glance at the cabin, said clearly, "We'll soon be passing a line of boats tied up below the wharf. There is a ladder. This boat will be tied up a hundred yards further up-river from that point and will wait there for you."

"When I give the word . . . *Now!*"

Smith plunged head-down out of the cabin and saw the line of boats sliding past only a foot or two away on the brown, murky flow. He vaulted without straightening over

78

the side of the launch into the nearest boat and scrambled across the thwarts towards the wharf. Right under it he paused just long enough to see Sarah Benson scrambling after him, skirts held up with one hand, and the launch sliding away. He was close to the ladder and in a moment was climbing. His head rose above the edge of the wharf and he saw it was empty except for a little knot of men working at a stacked pile of bales about thirty or forty yards away. Their backs were to him. Dust swirled on the wind and rain spat briefly into it. He felt Sarah Benson on the ladder behind him, climbed up onto the wharf and held down a hand for her. They walked across the wharf, down a gap between two warehouses and emerged in a cobbled street of chandlers and little bars. Sarah tucked her arm inside Smith's and they walked up the street to the broad thoroughfare that ran across the head of it. There was a hotel and two cabs, each drawn by a head-hanging scarecrow of a horse, waiting for hire outside it. The pressure of Sarah's arm urged Smith over to the cabs and into the first. Sarah spoke briefly to the driver then joined Smith inside. A whip cracked and the cab jolted away.

They drove for barely fifty yards and then stopped. Sarah said, "I can get Bradley out to you, getting you in to him would be risky." They were outside a shop, its window crammed with farm tools and beyond them Smith could see the counter with a man behind it facing a customer and to one side a stairway. Sarah said, "He has a room upstairs."

Smith saw her pass through the shop and climb the stair. He leaned closer to the window of the cab so he could see the windows above the shop and waited, watched. After a minute he saw a curtain pulled aside. He could not see the face beyond it but he lifted his hand and took off his hat, stared up at the window.

The curtain fell back. He waited.

The *Maria* was getting away from him with every passing second. He might well lose her altogether.

If he was wrong, if the cruisers were five thousand miles away in another ocean, or lying at anchor again in the Jade with the rest of the High Seas Fleet, then it would have been as well if he had lost both *Gerda* and *Maria*.

Bradley had been up and about for almost an hour. He had been involved in a long game with some miners and landowners from upcountry that had lasted all night. At the end of it he had counted his winnings, eaten a huge breakfast and then slept. Now he had brewed himself coffee on the pot-bellied stove, heated water and shaved and washed. He was still naked to the waist, drying his face and smoothing the full moustache, when Sarah entered.

He gaped at her then surprise gave way to pleasure. "You're just in time. Come on in." He tossed aside the towel and held out his arms to her.

She fended him off. "Not now or any other time. Get dressed. I want you to meet somebody."

"Who?"

"Commander Smith."

"*Who?*"

"The Captain of H.M.S. *Thunder*."

"The Captain – *Thunder?*" Bradley snapped his long fingers, remembering. "Hold on. While I was eating breakfast there was a lot of hoo-haw going on among the local boys about a British ship and a British captain. They were raising hell over him but I gather he raised it first. They reckoned he raided into Guaya and blew a neutral ship to bits."

"Rubbish!" Then Sarah admitted grudgingly, "He sank a collier that *claimed* to be neutral."

Bradley whistled softly. "That'll do. Boy! The Navy can only shoot you once and that'll do! Where is this lunatic?"

"He's not a – He's outside. In a cab."

Bradley crossed to the window. "I'd better take a look at this character while he's still around for viewing! If they catch him ashore they'll lynch him!" He twitched back the curtain, stared down and saw the face at the window of the cab that returned his stare. It was a thin face, young but drawn. He said, "That's him? Young feller, sort of –" He stopped, not knowing how to put it into words. "He's not what I expected."

Sarah's lips twitched. "What did you expect? Somebody with a beard and a cutlass between his teeth? There's only one man in the cab. Smith."

Bradley stared down and the eyes below held his. He said, "On second thoughts, maybe ..." He let the curtain fall and shrugged his broad shoulders so the muscles slid under the brown skin. Sarah watched him. He asked, "What does he want with me?"

"I don't know. But he needs all the help he can get."

"I'll go along with you on that." Bradley reached for his shirt and pulled it on. "Well. Let's go see the little Admiral. Can't do any harm." He would remember the words with bitterness before long.

Smith saw Sarah returning with a tall man who, hat in hand, opened the shop door for her and handed her into the cab after speaking to the driver. The cab moved off.

Bradley sat beside Sarah, facing Smith. He eyed Smith with obvious interest and grinned broadly when he saw that interest returned. "From what I hear you're in trouble up to your neck, Admiral, and sticking that neck out at this very moment."

Smith saw he was bronzed with strong white teeth. Not handsome, but it was a good face with a reckless cut to it. Smith suspected this man would live up to first impressions, and hoped so. He said, "A man called Medina has a seaplane, or the Germans have one, I think it comes to the same thing. I also think you may know something about it."

Bradley replied blandly, "No more than anybody else

81

around here with a tongue in his head." Then he added, "Provided they knew what they were talking about and listening to, Admiral."

"And what did *you* see and hear?"

Bradley shrugged. "It's a Curtiss twin-seater seaplane. Observer sits up front and the pilot behind him. Maximum speed around ninety knots."

"The pilot told you this?"

"Richter? The hell he did! I've *seen* it and that's enough. Richter told me he was a real flyer with combat experience, not a feller who found the money better or easier on the ground." It was said easily and the half-grin was still there, but fixed.

Smith asked, "Where is it?"

"Just outside of town in a little inlet, really a wide creek. They've fixed up a hangar there."

"Guarded?"

Bradley chuckled. "Who could steal a seaplane around here?"

Smith chuckled in his turn. Then he said. "You."

Bradley straightened in his seat. "Me! Why should I –"

"To take me up. You can fly it?"

"How should I know?" Bradley glanced, amused, at Sarah, a glance easily interpreted: Mad or drunk! I'll humour him.

Smith said, "I haven't much time, Mr. Bradley. I think you can fly it, I think you *know* you can fly it. I think you are still in the service of the United States Government. I think that if you really wanted Richter's job at any time then he would have a nasty fall or get caught up in some brawl so that the position would become vacant."

Bradley laughed then looked serious. "You're not thinking at all, Admiral. Plenty of people are saying you're off your nut and I'm starting to agree with them."

Sarah said quietly, harshly, "Jim!"

Bradley gripped her hand. "It happens, girl. Loneliness of command and all that."

Smith said, "Take me up. You're here to find out why that seaplane is here. Take me up and I'll tell you."

"How do you know?"

"I know."

Bradley stared at him.

Sarah said, "You could do it, Jim. You said no one was there."

He snapped at her, "That makes no difference. As soon as she takes off everybody in town will see her, and before that they'll *hear* her. And you know one reason why nobody will be out there now? Because nobody in his right mind would take off in this weather." And he thought that wasn't half of it and Smith did not know the rest.

Smith said, "You mean Richter wouldn't."

Bradley replied grudgingly, "He would if he had to. Give the devil his due."

"So it could be done."

Sarah put in impatiently, "You're not scared of a little bad weather!"

Smith swore under his breath. That was a dirty blow and if Bradley reacted and ditched them –

Bradley did not. He stared down at his hands that were clasped between his knees, fingers tight. "It's not just a 'little bad weather'. Maybe that's what it is for the Admiral in his ship but *that* isn't made out of plywood and canvas." He paused, staring at Smith.

Smith asked again, "Take me up."

Bradley muttered, "I'll say one thing for you, Admiral: you never give up." He was being driven into a corner and he was proud that he was so cool about it but he wondered how long he could keep that up. He backed further into the corner: "You were going to tell me why."

Smith nodded. "Two German armoured cruisers have slipped the blockade in the North Sea and are heading for this coast. The seaplane is to scout for them."

Bradley sat still. He said softly, "Jesus." And then: "But

why ship it out here? Why couldn't these cruisers carry their own seaplanes?"

"There are numerous hazards in flying off and recovering seaplanes at sea. Whereas with a land-based aircraft?" He put it as a question and left it to Bradley to answer for himself. He finished with another: "And has Medina set up other bases as part of this proposed mail contract, like dumps of fuel and mooring facilities?"

Bradley nodded slowly. "That he has. Plenty."

Smith went on, "There was a collier at Guaya that called herself neutral but was a tender for the cruisers."

Bradley put in wryly: "I heard about her."

"Another collier, the *Maria*, sailed from this port a little over nine hours ago. She's gone to a rendezvous with the cruisers. She may have sailed south or west and I need to know which before I start to chase her. I need to know. Badly." He did not say that he had offered Bradley a bargain and Bradley had taken his share. Bradley had not accepted the bargain, he was not even bound by his word. There was only an unspoken understanding between them.

A ghost of the grin returned to Bradley. "That Richter. Oh, boy!" He leaned out of the window of the cab, and Smith realised that all the time he had been noting with a part of his mind that the cab had walked steadily around the same four streets, around and around the block. But now as Bradley yelled up at the driver the whip cracked and the cab rocked as the horse broke into a trot. Bradley hung there for a moment, head and shoulders out of the window, feeling the wind on his face and not having to smile. He thought he had taken a step forward. Toward the edge of the plank.

Five minutes later the cab halted and they climbed down. Bradley paid the driver and told him to wait. They stood on a dirt road lined with trees but Bradley led them on a path into the trees and they followed its windings. In less than a minute they came to the little inlet. A large shed stood at the water's edge. The sea broke gently in this inlet and washed in little ripples around their boots as they walked around to the front of the shed. The big doors were locked with two massive padlocks but Bradley fished a bunch of keys from his pocket, selected two and opened each lock and tossed it aside. He said solemnly, "Fitted myself up with the keys a coupla weeks back. Good idea to check up on your competitors' stock once in a while."

Smith replied equally seriously, "It does no harm. I believe the farm tool trade is very competitive."

Bradley guffawed.

They pushed back the doors that concertinaed on themselves.

Bradley said, "And there she is. Single-engined biplane made of fabric an' wood. Curtiss engine of one hundred and fifty horses, maximum speed ninety knots – but I told you that." He rattled on but as he talked he swung up on a staging beside the engine, looking it over then checking the fuel. He dropped down and pushed the staging aside, hesitated a moment then said, "As I thought. She's all ready to go." One more step.

He glanced around, moved to one wall where two long, leather flying coats hung from nails with leather flying helmets and goggles. He tossed one set at Smith who stood peering up at the flimsy aircraft where it stood on its bogey. They both dressed, took off their boots and pulled on the waders that lay by the wall, dropped the boots in the cockpits of the seaplane. Bradley said, "It'll be cold up there." And he shivered despite the coat and the closeness of the air in the shed. Smith noticed but said nothing.

The seaplane stood on a wide-wheeled bogey. As they shoved the bogey forward out of the shed and across the narrow strip of sand, a line attached to the float-struts snaked out behind them. Its other end was anchored in the shed. The bogey disappeared under the ripples that washed the beach. They pushed it another foot and the seaplane floated, lifted clear of the bogey and rose and fell gently to the wash of the waves under the floats and, under the wind's urging tugged impatiently at the mooring line.

Bradley beckoned Sarah Benson and showed her the loop in the line where it was made fast to the float-strut. "When I lift my hand you pull that loop, the line comes free and she goes. Right?"

She nodded, eyes watching his face and worried now.

He turned away from that look and waded out to climb on to a float. Smith waded out after him. Bradley felt the wind thrusting at the seaplane and thrumming through the fabric. Little waves chased across the inlet. Beyond its mouth he could see the bay and the ships anchored there, a tramp and a liner and far out the ugly shape of a warship. The cloud ceiling was low and dark and clouds ran in on the wind. There was rain in the wind that touched cold on his face. He wondered if Smith really had any idea – ?

Smith asked, "I have to swing the propeller?"

"That's right."

"I can do that."

"Yeah?" Bradley reached up and clamped his hands on the side of the cockpit, staring at the fuselage inches before his face. Smith saw sweat standing on his face but Smith himself was sweating in the leather coat. Bradley said thickly, "I think in fairness I should tell you I flew one of these things into the sea a while back and I couldn't face flying after that. So they sent me down on this job, where all I had to do was talk about it and know about it." He licked his lips and went on: "I got as far as this because I thought I should fight it, give it another try; and because you're in one hell of a mess. And because Sarah asked me." He paused, then said, "I can't do it."

Smith could barely hear the words. He hesitated, weighing this new factor against his instinctive judgment of the man, weighing the possible gains against the possible loss if they went on, and in that mental exercise not overlooking the fact that loss might be his life. Then he decided that basically the situation was unchanged. He said, "I told you I have to know where that collier is. I think you can fly it."

Bradley sighed. "Look. Have you ever flown in one of these things?"

"Once. A chap in the Naval Air Service took me up for a spin. Strictly against the rules, of course, but Tubby didn't worry much about that sort of thing."

Bradley said, "Uh-uh. So you had a joy-ride with friend Tubby. Great. He sounds like a great guy. But the way the weather is today – "

Smith said, "He was. I saw him killed a couple of days later, trying to take off in bad weather. Total loss."

Bradley turned his head slowly to look at Smith. "Weather like this?"

"Yes."

"You're hell-bent on this." Bradley whispered it. "But you know the odds and you think it's worth the gamble?"

Smith nodded. "You're a gambler."

Bradley said bitterly, "It takes one to know one, Admiral." And: " 'Can't do any harm.' Ha!" He splashed back to the shore where Sarah Benson waited, lifting the long tail of his coat as he went and digging into a trousers pocket. He brought out a wash-leather bag and dropped it, chinking heavily, into her hand. She held it, feeling the weight of the silver inside. He said, "The Bradley fortune. Hold on to it for me. And get the hell out of here as soon as we've gone."

He stared at her seriously a moment then turned and splashed back to the seaplane and climbed into the cockpit, kicking his waders off into the water. He pulled on his boots and took the paper Smith handed him and looked at the course Smith had pencilled on it. He heard a voice outside himself calling instructions to Smith on the swinging of the propeller and was aware that his hands and feet and eyes were going through the cockpit check, the old routine, the movements of a puppet that he watched perk to the strings.

He noted that the wind would be right on the nose so he could take off straight over the breakers and into the wind and the breakers looked huge out there away from the shore. This would be bad enough but coming back would be a bloody sight worse. If they came back.

The cloud ceiling was a thousand feet at most and there would be better than two hours of daylight left, maybe three. The rain was flighting heavier on the wind and looking out across the bay he could see the squalls running in, the rain painted dirty grey. He could see the ships and the squat, old, gun-bristling bulk of *Thunder* and the smoke that wisped from her funnels confirmed the direction of the wind for him.

He closed his eyes and saw the sea blurring below then rushing up at him and felt the shock and then the agony as the flames burst around him and the sea took fire – and he opened his eyes as the engine fired, caught and raced. Smith scrambled around and up into the observer's cockpit forward and Bradley hated him. If Smith had not come this would not have happened. He could have been telling himself still that sure, he could do it if he wanted to and if the chance was there.

He could have been alive.

Smith was mad.

Oh, Sarah!

He ran the engine up for several minutes, sitting there, staring out to sea across five thousand miles. The snarl of the engine drowned the sound of the wind and the surf. It would be clearly heard, unmistakable, in Malaguay and Richter would already be running. The seaplane tugged on the anchoring line, fretting to be away.

Smith dragged on his boots and turned to stare at Bradley. The pilot had pulled his goggles down over his eyes and the light reflected from them so Smith could see no expression in the eyes nor was there any on the face below the goggles. Smith turned away.

Bradley knew he could wait no longer. He lifted his hand and felt the jerk of release as Sarah Benson set the seaplane free. They raced out across the breakers and he held the stick back so the floats would not dig into the breakers and cartwheel them, and with these big waves that would be easy. It was a question of getting the speed and judging it right and if you were wrong it was – *bang*! But the speed built up, he eased forward and the tail lifted and now the floats were smacking across the tops of the breakers with great thuds and the spray was bursting, tossed on the slipstream. He pulled back and they lifted off. The ships fell away beneath the lifting nose that pointed at the sky and all the sky was his.

Something burst inside him and the seaplane rocked and yawed under his hands until he brought it under control, the master once more. He reached forward and nudged Smith who had been peering over the side, seeing *Ariadne* slip beneath them, a pale speckle of white faces against the yellow timber of her decks. Then he caught the movement at the corner of his eye and turned to see Bradley laughing like a maniac. Smith laughed with him.

Bradley wheeled the seaplane in a gently-climbing, banking turn then levelled off and straightened out on course just below the cloud base, at a height of a little under one thousand feet. The course was west.

It was cold. Smith was glad of the leather coat and wished fervently that he had worn sea-boots with thick stockings. He moved his feet continually to try to keep them warm. These were sensations forced upon his attention by his protesting body. He acknowledged the protest but then ignored it, had no time for it. He had flown once before and so knew what to expect but was still fascinated by the panorama opening swiftly below him like the unrolling of a huge chart. The sea was a white cross-hatching on green, the coast-line ragged brown and a deeper green and fading behind them as their course took them out to sea. The cloud base kept them comparatively low but still visibility was a good fifteen to twenty miles in any direction. At sea level in this weather he would be lucky to have half of that visibility. And they were making four or five times *Thunder*'s best speed.

He was still afraid. He remembered the crash of the Naval Air Service seaplane only too well and not only because it had cost him a friend and he knew he had few friends. But Bradley had survived a crash like that and yet was flying again. He marvelled at the man's courage.

Bradley flew straight and level on the course for a half-hour then banked gently to the left on the first leg of a series of zig-zags, each leg ten miles long, working up the line of the course. They searched like that for more than an hour and in all that time they saw only two ships. Bradley took the seaplane down in a shallow dive to investigate each of them, sweeping low overhead and circling close, just skimming the surface of the sea so they could read the name on bow and stern. Neither was the *Maria*. But when Bradley lifted the seaplane from the sea to slip bellowing over the bow of one of them he set a seaman running in blind panic. Bradley roared with laughter.

He finally reached forward and held out a note-book to Smith. Bradley had printed neatly: We're making about seventy knots over the ground. *Maria* could not have passed this point. Light is going. Must turn back.

He took it back from Smith and watched the thin face, pale where it was not blue with cold, for a shadow of disappointment. He saw none. Smith nodded and put up his thumb.

Smith had found out what he wanted to know but he was not happy. He had gambled with Bradley's life because he had to, because of *Wolf* and *Kondor*, and the game was not over yet. They had to get back and Bradley was flying for their lives while Smith, the cause of it all, was a useless passenger.

Bradley put the seaplane into the turn. The period of release and soaring elation had passed. The gut-tearing terror had not returned but neither was he uncaring. He was alert to danger and there were plenty of signs. The day was dying; the sun, wherever it was behind the masking cloud, dropping down into the sea. They had an hour of daylight at best and the cloud ceiling was lowering.

They were down to four hundred feet and cloud wisped around them when the coast loomed, darkening now, within two miles of them. Bradley turned and flew along it. It would not do to miss Malaguay because that was the only place on this coast where they might put down and it was now no better than 'might'.

Visibility fell to barely a mile with the coast-line a black silhouette against the dirty grey of cloud. Rain was continuous now, thrumming on the fabric, sluicing over them in the open cockpits. Flying was a nightmare but Bradley was unruffled, totally absorbed, except for a nagging regret that he had not found the collier; he had failed Smith. And he owed Smith so much. He held the seaplane on its course, riding the weather, eyes straining against the gathering gloom, straining even more when his watch told him the headland of the bay should be coming up. It was dusk now and they were down to two hundred feet, the coast was right under them as creamy phosphorescence of breaking seas on a rocky shore and visibility was only hundreds of yards and closing in.

He sensed the loom of the headland before he saw it and was already pulling back on the control column as the black mass rushed at them out of the rain-filled dark. The engine roared under power as he set it climbing, the seaplane seeming to stand on its tail but still the mass towered above the spinning circle of the propeller, a pinnacle. He knew they could not crest it and threw the seaplane into a banking turn that dragged them away and around the pinnacle, so close that Smith could see the thrusting rocks and the wiry scrub that grew among them and a goat that rose from them and hurled itself, terrified, down the hill. The seaplane scaled past the pinnacle standing on one wing-tip, the pinnacle slipping away beneath the floats and more rocks below reaching for that dragging wing-tip. Then they had cleared the headland, were flying level and Bradley took them down through the cloud in a shallow dive.

They burst out of it; a thinning of the murk then it was ripped into flying ribbons and they thrust through them as if they were a curtain. Visibility was instant but only comparatively good. It was still good enough to show them the water very close under them and even as Bradley eased back the stick and levelled off he had to bank again to avoid *Thunder's* bulk that was suddenly ahead of them in a strung necklace of lights blinking at them out of the dusk. They skimmed past down her starboard side and Smith saw Garrick clearly, standing on the wing of the bridge and looking *down* at them. They also passed through the smoke that trailed from *Thunder's* funnels on the wind and Bradley saw the direction of that wind and swore.

It had swung through a quarter-circle and now it blew at an angle across the breakers. The shore came up as he climbed to gain height for the turn and he saw a little group of figures outside the box of the hangar and he thought: Welcoming committee. Richter would be there, and the mechanics. If they were unarmed he would be lucky to get off the beach alive, while if they were armed –

He made the turn, swept out around the curve of the bay and came in again from the sea. Smith turned his head for a second and Bradley glared grimly and mouthed against the bellow of the engine: "Hang on!" He saw Smith's nod of comprehension, then he was taking her down, intent on landing out in the bay, carefully clear of the wrecking shore and the waiting Richter.

He took her down gently until he could see clear water below and ahead. This was not a hatching of lines on a crinkled surface far below but the surface of the bay, close under them, waves snapping like teeth. He held her off for a second, steadying her against the wildly quartering wind, picking his place and time. Then he eased her down so the floats kissed gently and the spray flew. They were almost down, the floats flicking through the snapping teeth and Smith started to exhale, ready to shout congratulations, because although he was no flyer he could recognise a near-impossible feat superlatively accomplished. Then the wind gusted and blew them over, one wing slammed into water suddenly as substantial as concrete and the seaplane twisted and dived forward on its nose.

There was a ripping of fabric and the twanging of parting wire stays. Smith had crashed his head against the cockpit coaming. Through the whirling, blood-tinged kaleidoscope he was aware that the seaplane was tipping further nose-down into the vertical and only the seat belt saved him. Saved him? The seaplane was sinking, jerking from side to side as the sea shook it but settling all the time. The belt would take him down with it. His vision cleared as realisation came and he clawed at the belt. He could see the waves breaking and sucking on the fragile hull and that Bradley was out, standing with one foot on what remained of the upper wing-strut above water. One hand lifted Smith off the cockpit coaming and the other tugged at the belt with practised fingers. The belt slipped away and Smith fell out of the cockpit as the seaplane rolled, sea-thrust, over on to its back. He fell on Bradley and they went down into the watery darkness together, the seaplane slamming down over them like a trap-door.

The fuselage forced Smith under but he kicked and turned, Bradley beside him but Bradley was not kicking, he lay sluggish and drifted. Smith grabbed him, kicked again as his lungs clamoured for air, clawed at the fuselage and dragged the pair of them to the surface. He managed to get his head out, paddling with his feet, fingertips of one hand clamped on the fuselage and the other around Bradley so the pilot's face was lifted back, just clear of the water. The sea slapped over them and Smith coughed and spat it out, coughed and spat again. He could hear Bradley coughing but he still lay inert, a rapidly increasing weight as his clothes took on water, as were Smith's. The weight was dragging him down. He clawed his way, inching desperately, further up the fuselage but it did no good. The seaplane was sinking. The sea washed the blood from Bradley's face but it oozed again from a cut on the head. Smith thought it would be all up to Garrick. God help him. The dark was closing in.

He saw the light but felt rather than heard the beat of propellers as the picket-boat's prow thrust up high above him then swung away as she turned. Her side came down towards him and he saw Buckley, Robinson, Exton and Lambert all kneeling there. As Exton and Lambert reached down to grasp the hand he lifted from the fuselage, Buckley plunged in beside him and lifted away Bradley's weight. They hauled Smith out of the bay and he fell over the side to sprawl in the well like a stranded fish. Seconds later they brought Bradley in to join him, Buckley crawling in after, spitting and swearing. Somers spun the wheel and the picket-boat swung away, straightened out. Smith got his legs under him and stood up, holding on to the cabin's coaming and peered back through the gathering darkness to where the seaplane lay. He was in time to see the tail slide down as the water rushed up inside the hull and the weight of the engine dragged the wreck to the bottom. It left a little vortex and a crowd of bubbles that held brief life and died. The sea closed over the place; it was as if the seaplane had never been.

He turned away. They had rushed Bradley into the cabin and he could see Buckley in there, still dripping wet but helping to wrap blankets around the limp body. Smith called, "How is he?" He was furious that his teeth chattered.

Buckley replied cheerfully, oblivious to his own wetting, "He's alive all right, sir, but he's still out. Looks like he took a clout on the head."

Somebody tried to drape a blanket around Smith. It was Lambert. Smith shrugged it away impatiently, "Use it in the cabin." He moved to stand between Somers and Quinn, who was clicking the hand signal-lamp. The clicking stopped and he saw the answering blink from *Thunder*.

Somers said, "I told them to expect survivors, sir."

"Very good." Smith's clothes were clammy against his skin, seeming to freeze in the wind. He was an impatient fool. He should have taken the blanket. He was cold to the bone. He said, "You all did very well. You were very quick."

Somers kept his eyes on *Thunder* as she came up. "We saw the aeroplane take off, sir, and where it came from. Then when Miss Benson came off a while ago and said you were up in it, well, we hung about more or less ready to bring you off."

"On whose orders?"

"It just seemed like a good idea, sir, and Mr. Garrick said I could do it."

"I'm glad you followed me."

Somers said absently, preoccupied with the business of bringing the pinnace alongside, "Follow you anywhere, sir." And was instantly embarrassed by his own sincerity.

Somers swung the pinnace alongside the ladder, Lambert and Quinn hooking on. Smith snapped, "Get that man aboard as quick as you can." And ran up the ladder.

Albrecht was waiting for him with a little group of hands with stretchers and blankets. "If you'll come this way, sir."

Smith pushed past him. "See to the man coming aboard."

"Your head, sir."

Smith ignored him. Garrick was there beside a number of others. He stepped close to Smith and muttered, "*Ariadne* and *Elizabeth Bell*, both masters here to see you, sir."

Smith said, "Prepare to get under way."

"Aye, aye, sir."

Garrick left and an instant later the pipes shrilled to his bawled order. Smith turned to the group that waited on him on his quarterdeck. Sarah Benson was there and she looked drawn, eyes fastened on the head of the ladder. He turned his back on them briefly while he saw Bradley brought aboard and hurried forward to the sick-bay but not before Smith said, "Word at your earliest, please."

Albrecht answered, "Aye, aye, sir." He did not lift his eyes from his patient.

Smith turned back to the group. "Miss Benson. Gentlemen. I don't want to appear perfunctory but you'll realise my time is limited."

Hands were shaken. Smith's was wet and the water dripped from him to form a widening pool around his feet. His face was very pale and his hair was plastered to his skull. A thread of water and blood ran thinly down over his temple.

Ballard of *Ariadne* was hefty and handsome, his uniform well-cut. He looked the picture of what he was, the commodore of a line. Graham of *Elizabeth Bell* was short and solid with a little round paunch that shoved out his waistcoat with its looped watch-chain. He carried a bowler hat in his hand to go with the blue serge suit and his hair was a halo of fluffy white round an island of pink scalp.

Ballard said, "One of your officers brought us word that we couldn't, or shouldn't sail. Some story about German cruisers being loose in these waters!" He grinned.

Smith nodded. "My information is that two cruisers are out and I expect them on this coast at any time."

Ballard's grin faded. "That's what he said. They've been sighted?"

"No, they have not."

Ballard looked relieved but puzzled. "Then what makes you think they are bound for these waters?"

Smoke billowed and rolled around them as *Thunder* raised steam. Smith eyed that smoke, pleased to see it. "I haven't time for a lengthy explanation, but among other factors I received information that two colliers were on this coast, loaded steam coal and manned by Germans. There is no doubt

in my mind that the cruisers have this coast as their objective."
His voice was hard with certainty.

Ballard glanced at Graham. Neither seemed happy. Graham
said, "Understand, Commander, we don't want to be un-
reasonable nor rash but in the merchant service time is money.
If I waste time idling here my owners will take a loss and
they'll want to know why. All you're saying is that you *think*
those cruisers are headed this way."

Smith nodded sympathetically. "I appreciate your diffi-
culty." But he went on firmly, "I'm certain about the cruisers.
Now look here, gentlemen. I expect to return to this port
within thirty-six hours. If I do not then you may decide at
the end of that time whether or not to sail in the light of the
situation then. If you sail before without my escort then you
do so against my advice."

Ballard glanced at Graham then turned to Smith. "Well,
that seems reasonable. It will give us time –"

But Albrecht appeared and Smith asked quickly, "Yes,
Doctor?" He was conscious of Sarah Benson, intent.

Albrecht said, "Slight concussion and shock but nothing
serious, sir."

"I'm glad to hear it. Can he be moved?"

"He can."

"Get him up here." And to Ballard: "Can you take Miss
Benson and that injured young man as passengers? Neither
would be welcome ashore. I'd be grateful."

The request was also a broad hint that it was time to leave.
A party was already hovering, waiting to stow the accommodation ladder and both skippers knew what they were
waiting for.

Ballard said, "As I've told your First Lieutenant, I'm already
overcrowded. I will disembark a number of passengers at
Guaya, but until then – I can put the man in the sick-bay, of
course. Graham?"

Graham said immediately, "I've a cabin for the young lady
and she's right welcome, but we're no liner, miss."

Sarah grinned at him. "Lor' love you, I'm no fine lady, either." She winked at him impudently but Smith saw Graham smiling.

Smith sighed with relief. "Excellent."

Sarah looked at him ironically but Graham was addressing Smith. "Only one more thing, Commander. There are a lot of rumours flying about ashore and those fellers spin a yarn a bit and we can hardly credit . . . they say a neutral ship was boarded in Guaya last night by a British naval party, and blown up."

"That is not a rumour. She was German though claiming to be neutral but I've explained that. I sank her." He waited as they stared at him then: "Anything else?"

Graham sucked in his breath. "No." He thought, 'That'll do to be going on with.'

Smith shepherded them to the head of the ladder and as he handed Sarah on to the ladder he said awkwardly, "Thank you, I'm grateful – we're all grateful for all you've done."

"No more than my duty, Commander." But she added, "Good luck." And he saw her fingers touch that barbaric medallion. So they parted.

Before Bradley on his stretcher went down into *Ariadne*'s boat he managed a fragile smile at Smith. "Seems I bust one more airplane so nobody can straighten it out again. But I've been thinking: if I hadn't smashed it up you would ha' done because you wouldn't have left it for Richter to fly reconnaissance for those cruisers. Right?"

Smith nodded. "Right. But it was a gallant piece of flying. No one could have done more."

Bradley shook his head and winced. "They were right. You're mad." But his grin took the sting out of the words. He said seriously, "For you I'd try it again. I'm just damn sorry I didn't find that ship for you."

"I know where she isn't and that will be enough."

Bradley went down and the boats pulled away. Smith

found Garrick and Aitkyne on the bridge and retired with Aitkyne to the chart-room, leaving Garrick to take the ship to sea.

He stared at the chart and fiddled with a pencil, shivered with the cold of the wet clothes. He was unaware of Aitkyne watching him.

He 'knew where she was not'. That ruled out one of a long list of possibilities, that *Maria* had sailed west for Juan Fernandez. But there were still a thousand places spread over the hundreds of miles of coast to the south, seamed as it was with channels and inlets, where the collier could hide. *If* she could hide. What if she had a rendezvous to keep at all costs, with cruisers that had traversed the Atlantic and rounded the Horn, coaling secretly and precariously from colliers like the *Maria*? They would want to meet without delay. And there was a place the Germans knew and had proved in the far-off days of 1914 when Von Spee had cruised this coast. His fingers were tight on the pencil now.

It was logic allied with intuition and faith.

It was all based on his conviction that the cruisers would come.

He jabbed the pencil down at the chart. "A course for the Gulf of Peñas, pilot. Revolutions for fifteen knots."

Thunder headed south.

6

Thunder PLOUGHED OUT of Malaguay and into the night and the storm. She was rolling and Smith was grimly aware that rolling was made worse by the lightness of her bunkers. The seas were black mountains in the night, capped with the snow of driving spray. *Thunder* thrust her bow into those seas to lift then fall, bow going down and stern lifting and all the time she rolled.

He stood by Garrick on the bridge and Garrick glanced sidewise at him and said, "Coal, sir."

"I know. I asked Thackeray for help. The *Mary Ellen* will be waiting for us here."

Garrick chewed worriedly at his lip and scowled out at the humping seas. "Going to get worse before it gets better."

He referred to the storm but Smith thought of the cruisers, out there, somewhere, in the all-surounding darkness.

Smith said, "Yes." Garrick thought they were on a wild-goose chase, that there would be no cruisers to meet the *Maria*. Smith *knew* they were there. He said again, but tiredly, "Yes," and, "Call me at first light or immediately anything, *anything*, is sighted."

He went to his cabin below the bridge, stripped and

towelled himself dry, holding on to his bunk with one hand against *Thunder*'s pitching and dressed in dry clothes. A hot meal had been cooked while they lay at Malaguay, a stew of corned beef. Horsfall had kept some warm for him and brought it now, even managing to keep it warm through the journey forward. Smith sent Horsfall away and wolfed the meal. He laid himself down fully-dressed. He might get a few hours sleep before first light.

But he knew that sleep was impossible. *Thunder*'s rolling and pitching and the continuous hammering of the sea on her hull would see to that if his thoughts did not and they were black enough.

He was acting only on the evidence of one collier that had been suspect and another that seemed to fly at his approach. The seaplane could easily be a coincidence. He had no scrap of evidence that the cruisers were or would be in the Pacific. It was like assuming a murder without a body.

If he was right there would be a murder and *Thunder* would be the victim.

If he was wrong he faced professional ruin and worse. He would be the man who single-handed upset the pro-British feeling in South America at a time when Britain needed all her friends. There would be a clamour for his blood and no reason at all why that clamour should not be satisfied. If he was wrong.

And again, if he was right? The cruisers loomed huge in his mind and he twisted in the bunk and put a hand to his eyes. He had to sleep.

Bradley had done well. Do it again, would he? Guts. Bradley. Graham. Sarah Benson. He was rid of her now. He was grateful for her help, God knew! She had brought the word that the Germans were watching *Thunder*, spotted the oddity of the collier with wireless and but for her he would not have flown with Bradley. Because of her *Thunder* would not sail unprepared into an ambush.

If ambush there was.

Only Sarah Benson believed he was right.

He threw an arm across his eyes. But she was a prickly, short-tempered – Her face when she killed that man. He would not sleep. Somers: 'Follow you anywhere, sir.' The boy meant it. Thackeray, Graham. The water closing over him.

Sarah Benson . . .

He slept.

Dawn came in a full gale and as Smith clung on the bridge the seas broke over the bows to sweep aft like a green glass wall and smash against the conning-tower. Visibility was maybe three miles. There was no ship in sight.

He ate breakfast there, a sandwich of the inevitable, monotonous bully beef that tasted vile and was washed down by tea that was cold before he drained the cup. It was all gulped down, forced down, eaten one-handed as he held on with the other. The galley fires were out. There was no hot food nor would there be until this weather abated. The mess-decks were in chaos and awash. Visibility was no better and the storm was even worse than in that heaving dawn. *Thunder* was reduced to ten knots and making hard work of that. In the stokehold men were thrown about as they fought to feed the fires and were bruised and burned.

Garrick said, "*Maria*'ll be no better off, sir. She'll be lucky to be making more than five knots in this sea." His face was grey as the sky under the prickling black stubble and there were shadows around his eyes.

Smith grunted in black bad temper, "I suggest you turn in, Number One."

"Aye, aye, sir." But Garrick hung on, reluctant, until Smith's baleful glare caught him. He left the bridge.

Kennedy had the watch. He took one look at his Captain and ventured no comments at all. Smith swayed to *Thunder*'s heave and roll and peered wearily out at the wild sea. They would be making better speed than the collier but that did not mean they would catch her. In an ocean of millions of square miles Smith could see only a tiny circle and beyond that was lost to him in rain and leaden cloud. It was like seeking a needle in a haystack, and he could well be searching the wrong haystack.

He wailed it out.

At mid-morning the visibility was scarcely improved, variable as the squalls swept in over the mountainous seas.

For what seemed the hundredth time Kennedy hailed the look-out: "Masthead! Anything seen?"

The answer came down from the man miserably wet and cold on his swaying, swooping, dizzying perch: "Nuffink, sir!"

Smith opened his mouth but shut it again, biting back the irritable chiding that came to his tongue. He waited a moment then said in as normal a tone as the wind allowed, "He's a good man, Mr. Kennedy?"

"Picked, sir."

"Then I think we'd do well to leave him alone."

"Aye, aye, sir."

He was trying to maintain an air of calm certainty but he knew they saw through it. He had been on the bridge for four hours. Waiting. Wait and see. But would they see? They could pass the *Maria* within a few miles and not see her in this weather. They should see her if Smith was totally, completely right, but if her course varied from his by only a degree that divergence would take him past her. He cursed the absence of a consort. If he had another ship with him, any ship, an armed merchant cruiser say, it would widen his search and be another pair of eyes.

What if *Maria's* rendezvous was not the Gulf of Peñas, if she was already lying snugly hidden in some sheltered inlet? *Thunder* could sail on for ever like the Flying Dutchman, chasing a similar phantom.

No. At a point in time he would have to acknowledge that he had made a mistake and turn back. That time would be soon. They should have caught her by now but she would be running for all she was worth. He would have to set a time. He did a little sum in his head, involving the speed of *Thunder* and the probable maximum speed of *Maria*, and the relative times of sailing, and he arrived at an answer.

Noon.

If they had not sighted her by noon he must turn. He must return to Malaguay and give clearance to *Ariadne* and *Elizabeth Bell*. And make his report by cable.

Then wait for the cable in reply that would relieve him, break him.

Garrick, unable to sleep, came onto the bridge.

Smith felt bleakly, briefly, sorry for him, for the mess he would inherit. Then he remembered again what his own state would be and grinned wryly at himself. Sorry for Garrick. That was almost funny.

Garrick caught the grin and misconstrued it. "Sighted her, sir?"

Smith shook his head and saw the worry that dragged Garrick's mouth down at the corners and the glance he threw at Kennedy. Smith said, "There's time yet, Number One."

There was neither hope nor resignation on Garrick's face, just worry. He did not know whether they would come up with the collier nor how it could help if they did. She had happened to sail before they arrived at Malaguay and that was all. Smith was just jumping to conclusions.

Garrick had said it all before and now Smith could read it on his face, and on the other faces. In a casual glance Smith covertly examined expressions on the bridge and decided they were not fools and had done their sums as he had. They knew that any chance of a sighting had slid into improbability and was sliding fast towards impossibility.

At 11.30 the weather worsened in a belt of squalls, visibility fell to less than two miles and spray burst continually over the bridge.

At 11.50 the bridge was ominously silent and they were

all waiting as they had waited all through that long morning, but now they were waiting for the change of course. All of them were immobile as statues except that they rocked and swayed to *Thunder*'s rolling that now seemed as heavy and sullen as the atmosphere on the bridge. Smith was cold to the bone.

At 11.55 the squalls swept by and visibility marginally lifted to possibly five miles.

At 11.58 the masthead look-out howled: "Masthead! Ship bearing green two-oh!"

Smith fumbled at the glasses hanging on his chest, swept the arc of sea over the starboard bow and thought he saw something through the rain and blown spray, a shadow, a shape, but could not be sure.

"Masthead! I think she could be the *Marigher*!"

Smith could make out a ship now but what ship he could not tell. She was ploughing into the seas, gamely but slow and they hid all but her superstructure. The man at the masthead had a better view from his perch high above the deck. Smith lowered the glasses. "Steer two points to starboard."

Thunder edged around and started to close the ship ahead and to starboard. She slowly came up through the rain until she was within a mile and they could see her with the naked eye, but Garrick used his glasses. "It's her, sir. The *Maria*."

If he expected Smith to be delighted and relieved then he was disappointed. If anything Smith looked grimmer. "Very good. Make: 'Heave to'."

The signal was hoisted and on Smith's orders a searchlight repeated it in morse.

Garrick said, "Of course, we have right of board and search, sir, but launching a boat in this sea – "

"Yes." A boat would not live a minute. "We'll cross that bridge when we come to it."

Garrick blinked and Knight said, "She's flying 'I am a neutral', sir."

Maria maintained her course and speed.

Smith said deliberately, "Make: 'Heave to or I will sink you'."

Knight swallowed. "Aye, aye, sir."

The signal broke out, the flags laid flat as boards on the wind. The collier steamed on.

Smith said, "Close up the starboard twelve-pounder battery." And as the guns' crews scrambled to the guns and the 'Ready' reports came in: "Put a shot across her bows, Number One."

A twelve-pounder cracked and sea spurted ahead of *Maria*. She sailed on.

A messenger came staggering. "Wireless reports signalling, sir. Very close, they think it must be this ship an' it seems to be in code."

"Very good."

So *Maria* was signalling furiously to someone out of his sight, quite possibly out of range of her wireless anyway because this weather would play the devil with wireless. Or whoever it was could be within a few miles. The eternal guessing game. The two ships ploughed heavily on through the breaking seas, the driving rain, lost in a little world of their own that was bounded by Smith's vision. But there was a world outside this where diplomatic protests were flying concerning a naval officer who had flouted International Law and sunk a neutral vessel in a neutral port. Where two big, fast cruisers hunted. Somewhere.

Smith's thoughts crystallised, ending his hesitation. He had known what the end of this would be and that hesitation was only a faltering of nerve. He had been right in his reasoning from the start and he was right now. Or had been wrong, 'A wolf sneaking into the fold to murder a lamb'.

May as well be hung for a sheep.

"Close up the upper deck six-inch batteries." The main-deck guns were unusable in this sea. "And sink her."

106

"*Sink* her, sir?" Garricks' voice rose on the word, the heads on the bridge jerked around.

Aitkyne said, "Sir, if I might suggest, we could lay right alongside and hail her. I'll take a party of volunteers – "

Smith cut brutally across the protests. "They're playing for time! First hours, and now for minutes! Sink her and quickly!" His voice was harsh and flat, denying argument or delay.

The men waded and clawed their way across the deck through the seas that washed it and manned the six-inch casemates. They reported ready. Garrick exchanged an agonised glance with Aitkyne, Kennedy, Knight – and Smith saw those exchanges. Garrick tried once more: "Sir – "

But Smith would not wait. "Open fire!"

The two starboard six-inch guns bellowed bass to the tenor cracking of the twelve-pounders. At that range, the trajectory near flat, hitting was almost inevitable, a miss inexcusable. The six-inch bursts were clearly seen, one forward and one aft on the *Maria*, opening great holes in her on the water-line. She seemed to stop dead in her tracks and fall away before the sea. There were men forward and aft of the super-structure, struggling waist-deep in the seas that swept her, attempting to lower boats.

The messenger again: " 'Sparks' reports she's still sending, sir."

"Very good." One brave man sticking to his post in the egg-shell protection of a wireless-room in that exposed super-structure. One man calling down the pack on *Thunder*. "Concentrate fire on the superstructure!"

Another exchange of glances on the bridge, sick. His own face showed nothing but – it *had* to be done!

The salvo crashed out, a hammer to crack a nut, the guns recoiling with the tongues of flame licking long and orange over the sea, the smoke blossoming dirty yellow to shred and disperse on the wind. Smith did not see it, his eyes on the *Maria* so he saw the superstructure burst open under that concentration of fire, the funnel lean and fall. She was listing badly and *Thunder* was drawing ahead of her.

"Starboard ten!"

Thunder swung ponderously around to head across the bows of the sinking collier. There was a boat in the water, a dozen men in her and thrusting away from their ship. Then the third salvo hit her, the effect instantly seen and appalling at that range. She broke in half, bow and stern lifting as the coal in her belly dragged her down, and sank. A billow of smoke and steam and she was gone.

"Cease firing! Midships!"

"Midships, sir!"

Smith rubbed at his eyes and lifted his glasses again. "Stand by to pick up survivors."

Thunder straightened on a course that took her down towards the wreckage and reduced speed until she rolled to the seas, barely making headway. There was flotsam: the wreckage of the life-boat, a few splintered planks, a cap. *Maria* would have carried a crew of twenty or so but there was not one survivor.

The guns' crews had stood down and *Thunder*'s company braved the seas to line her rails, staring silently. There was no jubilation.

The crew of the forward 9.2 made a little group in the shelter below the bridge. Chalky White, the gun-trainer, muttered, "He's gone off his rocker."

Farmer Bates, Leading-Seaman and the gunlayer, snapped edgily, "Oh, shut it!"

"I mean it. Do you reckon he knows what he's doing?"

Farmer was silent a moment. Both Benks and Horsfall talked to him and he knew the feeling in the wardroom. "I hope so."

Gibb opened his mouth to speak but found Rattray's hot eyes on him and stayed quiet. Rattray was making his life a misery. In any rare, brief moment that they were alone Rattray would crowd him, face shoved close. "Bright boy. Smith's little pet. He thinks you're a boy wonder but I'll see what you're made of one o' these days." The words changed slightly but the message was always the same. If they met on a crowded mess-deck or companion then Gibb got Rattray's elbow in his ribs or Rattray's foot crushing his own. And Gibb did not know why. He was afraid to tell anyone and so reveal his fear of the man because he was very young. It was wearing him down.

Rattray's eyes slid away and up to the bridge. Smith. Shoving his neck in a noose. They would break the bastard and Rattray would laugh in his face and break Gibb.

Garrick did not look at Smith, nor did anyone else on the bridge. Then the messenger came running. "Wireless reports she's stopped sending, sir." Smith glared at him. Was this some macabre attempt at wit? The man flinched under that glare but carried on: "Reports another signal, sir. Distant and it's stopped now, but they think it was Telefunken."

Telefunken transmissions were distinctive. And they were German.

Smith took a breath. "Thank you." Now they were all looking at him but he had had enough. "Pilot, a course for Malaguay. Revolutions for fifteen knots."

He staggered to his cabin to stretch out on his bunk and pull a blanket around him. He was cold, cold, and his body ached with the constant strain of those hours on the bridge. There was a tap at the door and he groaned softly. What now? He called, "Come in!"

Albrecht entered, in one hand a glass that held three fingers of golden liquid. "I took the liberty of prescribing for you, sir." He held out the glass. "Brandy."

Smith jerked onto one elbow and rasped, "I don't need Dutch courage, Doctor!"

Albrecht did not acknowledge the over-reaction, nor did

he argue. "No, sir. You led a night attack only thirty-six hours ago, yesterday you smashed into the sea in an aeroplane and today you were more than six hours on the bridge and then – " He broke off, then finished, "It will warm you and help you to sleep."

"I have nothing on my conscience, either."

Albrecht did not answer but he did not look at Smith.

Smith sighed. "Doctor, I had to sink that ship. They were signalling and they got a reply. I *had* to."

Albrecht said, "The surgeon's knife." And: "You're still certain that these cruisers – "

He stopped. Smith's weary grin stopped him. "If I say that they are after us, that they are sailing ten thousand miles to hunt *us*, you'll think I'm mad." He reached out and took the brandy and sipped at it and sighed. Albrecht saw in that weary smile a deal to frighten him but no madness at all. Smith said, "Because this ship can offer them a smashing victory, and then they can annihilate British shipping along this coast and that will draw forces to hunt *them*, not just from the West Indies but from the Atlantic and Scapa Flow. It will take a lot of ships to track them down and ships of force to deal with them. At best they can lengthen the war and at worst they can, by weakening the Grand Fleet, win it. But first they sink this ship." Smith drained the glass and handed it back to a staring Albrecht. "Goodnight, Doctor. And if you can't sleep, try a drop of brandy. It's all the thing."

But left alone, Smith did not smile. The brandy had warmed him, burning down into his stomach. His body was exhausted but his mind was only too active. He closed his eyes and saw them coming up over the rim of the horizon, murderous.

'Distant.'

The signals had been distant. That might mean a hundred miles or more or even, flukily, a thousand; but surely not so far in these conditions. No.

A 'distant' signal that the men on *Thunder*'s wireless thought might be Telefunken. It was still not evidence of the presence of a German ship, let alone two warships. Garrick and the rest did not believe in their existence while Albrecht? He – was uncertain now.

Smith was certain.

On the bridge, Aitkyne said quietly to Garrick, "What chance that our wild man *may* be right? After that wireless report? Thousand to one against?"

Garrick grimaced and shook his head. He muttered, "And if he's wrong we've just been witnesses to murder. Or accessories to it. By God, after the things he's done he'd better be right!"

Aitkyne's brows lifted. "Better? Unfortunate choice of word, old cock. My will is with the family solicitor in Gloucester. If you haven't made yours then I suggest you get on with it, just in case the thousand-odd to one shot comes off and he *is* right. Hedging your bets, old cock."

Garrick swung on him sharply. He found Aitkyne smiling, but very serious.

7

THEY CALLED SMITH at dusk. Garrick's voice came urgent down the voice-pipe: "Captain, sir! Ship in distress off the starboard bow! I'm altering course!"

"Very good!" Smith could feel the heel of her as she turned tightly onto the new heading. Still stumbling from legs asleep, he yanked his oilskin from its hook and dragged it on as he climbed the ladder, the folds of it streaming out behind and clapping as the wind tried to tear it from him. The rain ran down his face and he was wide awake when he stepped onto the bridge gratings.

Garrick pointed. "There she is, sir."

Smith wrapped an arm around a stanchion to steady himself against *Thunder*'s pitching and rolling. Her engines still rammed her on at that punishing and coal-devouring fifteen knots because Smith was certain the cruisers were somewhere astern of him and *Ariadne* and *Elizabeth Bell* waited in Malaguay for *Thunder*'s protection. Such as it was.

He lifted his glasses, steadied them, focussed, swept and found. She was a black ship on a wild, dark ocean as the night came down on her, and close inshore. *Thunder* was racing down on her.

Garrick said, "We signalled her by searchlight and she

answered, She's only got a poor signalling lamp but we made it out. Her engines have broken down and she's sprung plates all along her bottom. She's sinking but she reckons she'll go ashore first. She lost one anchor and the other's dragging."

Aitkyne butted in, "Damn all chance she has either way. I know this coast. She'll break up in minutes when she goes ashore."

"What ship is she?" Smith asked, absently surprised that Garrick had not told him already. He stared at the image that danced in the glasses, thinking of the men aboard her, of their thoughts at this moment with that awful sea waiting to swallow them. Whatever the cost he would take them off. He lowered the glasses and rubbed his eyes. "I asked 'what ship?'"

Garrick's face streamed water but he licked his lips. "She's the *Mary Ellen*, sir."

Smith lowered the hand from his eyes and peered at Garrick, eyes strained, or wincing. "The *Mary Ellen*? Our collier? *That Mary Ellen*?"

"Yes, sir." And Garrick lowered his voice. "We – we're only a couple of hours or so out from Malaguay but we'll barely have coal to go on to Guaya, sir. At fifteen knots – "

"*I know!*" Smith snarled it at him. He peered at the *Mary Ellen* not wanting to believe it was her and ground out, "What the *hell* is she doing here? I told Thackeray I wanted her at Malaguay not – " Then he clamped his mouth shut. It would do no good to bewail the fact as it would do no good for him to plead excuses when they broke him for leaving *Thunder* powerless and helpless. The collier was here before him and sinking, that was the fact. And she carried a crew of frightened men who would be hoping now. He pounded softly on the rail with his fist. Aitkyne looked from him to Garrick and there was sympathy in their exchange of glances. Smith's fist was still, the knuckles white. Then he stared through Aitkyne and said huskily, "So you know this coast. Show me the chart."

They went into the chartroom and stayed there long

113

minutes. When they emerged Smith clung to the stanchion again and scowled stone-faced at the *Mary Ellen* as they closed her.

Then at last he came alive. "Slow ahead. Make to her: Stand by for a line. I will tow you." He swung on the gaping Garrick. "Make ready to tow her."

They could not believe it. Garrick looked at the shore and the sea then saw his thoughts mirrored in Aitkyne's stare: It was impossible!

It was dark now, the *Mary Ellen* a tossing black bulk. There were lights on her bridge and there were lights on *Thunder*'s deck now and men milling aft where they worked frenziedly to rouse out the big towing hawser. From the *Mary Ellen* a signal-lamp faltered through a reply.

Knight read: "She says: Ship is sinking. Will you take off crew?"

Smith had read the signal himself and his answer was ready. "Reply: Negative. Stand by for my line."

There was a shifting behind him on the bridge, a restive ripple that ran through the men there. He was aware of it, ignored it, eyes fast on the *Mary Ellen*. The lamp blinked again, still stumbling but faster now with a desperation about it. He watched and read it: Boats gone. Urgently request –

He did not wait for the rest of it. He could see for himself that her boats were smashed. She had taken a beating as she lay powerless under the storm. "Make: Negative. Stand by for line."

Again that shifting, that ripple.

Garrick knew their eyes were on him, that if anyone should speak to the Captain it should be he but he was learning about this Captain, had learned a deal today as the *Maria* exploded and sank. He hesitated.

Smith sensed that hesitation as he had been aware of the shifting. "Everything ready aft, Mr. Garrick?"

"Yes, sir."

The use of boats was out of the question in this sea. Ideally he should hold *Thunder* safely clear of the collier and drift a line down to her fastened to a cask. But *time* was against all of them. He said, "I want a man to throw a line from the stern. What about that big leading hand of yours – " he turned on Manton, "Buckley? Is he good?"

"V-very good, sir."

Smith turned back to Garrick. "We'll want fenders over the stern and this must be done handsomely. Better go aft yourself and see to it."

So Garrick took himself aft and his uneasy conscience with him.

Smith ordered, "Port four points."

"Four points of port wheel on, sir."

"Midships." *Thunder* steadied on the new course that would take her alongside of the collier. There was a light in the bows of the *Mary Ellen* now and figures moved on her fo'c'sle, crouched as the seas burst over them in spray. He could see the cable of the anchor she had tried to use to save herself. He snapped, "Starboard a point!" He would have liked the hawser made fast aboard the *Mary Ellen* to a length of her anchor cable. The towing hawser was wire, immensely strong but with little elasticity except that given by the curve in its length. The anchor cable was far heavier and would steepen that curve and give more spring, more elasticity to the tow to prevent it breaking. But there was no time for that operation. It was up to him not to break the tow. He edged *Thunder* closer as she drew abreast of the collier and crept past her. *Thunder* rolled and pitched and the *Mary Ellen* soared and fell and wallowed.

Smith was out on the starboard wing of the bridge now, eyes on the collier, gauging *Thunder's* crawling progress against the collier's dead rolling, narrowing on the strip of water that separated them. He was aware of the pale blur of faces on the bridge of the *Mary Ellen* and of one man who had to be her master, his mouth opening and closing and fists lifted and shaking at Smith.

Smith tore his eyes from the man and back to the task in

hand. He shouted against the wind, "Port four points!" And: "Midships!" And: "Ease on port engine!" *Thunder*'s bow swung around to point seawards and her stern swung to pass across the bow of the *Mary Ellen*. Close. *Close!*"

From behind him Aitkyne's voice came strangled, "Christ Almighty! She – "

But Smith knew she wouldn't strike. The figures on the collier's fo'c'sle scrambled away from the sudden towering steel cliff of *Thunder*'s stern hanging over them but that cliff eased away from them as the weighted line was hurled. It landed right across the men on the fo'c'sle and they tailed on to it and dragged it in. Both ships were driven towards the shore now, the *Mary Ellen* by the storm, *Thunder* because Smith held her close on the collier as if that thread-like line dragged her. The sea was setting *Thunder* down quicker than the collier because it exerted more pressure on *Thunder*'s vastly bigger hull and she wasn't dragging anchors. Smith had to keep just enough way on her to balance that pressure. "Slow ahead together! . . . Ease on port engine! . . . together! . . ."

A messenger cable of grass rope was bent to the line and drawn over to the collier because the line would not take the strain of hauling in the weight of the wire towing hawser. A donkey engine, the auxiliary engine to power her windlass, hammered faintly on the collier and hauled in the messenger cable and then the towing hawser that was bent to it. And all the time came the stream of orders to engines and helm as Smith juggled with them and the pressures of wind and sea on *Thunder*'s twelve-thousand-ton bulk and the three-thousand tons of the *Mary Ellen*. A mistake could throw *Thunder* astern on to the collier – or send her lunging away to yank the tow from the collier before it was secured and leave the whole painful business to be done again. Outside of the dancing, swinging lights on the cruiser's stern and the collier's fo'c'sle the night was a howling darkness.

But they could see the shore and it was close, the breaking surf marked by a line of phosphorescence.

A lamp blinked morse from the collier's fo'c'sle. The donkey-engine was silent. In confirmation of the signal Aitkyne called, "First Lieutenant reports 'Tow secured', sir."

"Very good!" Smith did not take his eyes off the tow. "Slow ahead together. Cox'n! Watch for the strain coming on!" Because the *Mary Ellen*'s weight would act like a huge sea-anchor dragged astern of *Thunder*. "Ease on port engine ...Slow ahead together."

The strain came on. He saw the hawser slowly straighten, the slack loop of it lifting from the sea. It tautened as *Thunder* eased away from the collier, and they all felt the shudder and an instant's check before *Thunder* paid off again. Smith's orders went on as he watched the tow for the first signs of the collier yawing and ordered again and again to correct it. Someone aboard the *Mary Ellen* was doing his best to steer and that was helping but while *Thunder* pulled her one way sea and gale tried to shove her the other.

It took over an hour to tow her out and around the headland into the little bay beyond. Smith grew hoarse. Someone brought him a mug of cocoa, hot so that it burned his fingers and scalded his tongue, grease floating on the top of it. He gulped it down when he could and then was hoarse again.

"Rig fenders and boarding nets. When we secure I want a party of men forward and another aft, both under a good Petty Officer who knows what he's about on this kind of business."

"Aye, aye, sir." And Aitkyne hesitated then burst out, "Congratulations, sir!" He still could not believe they had plucked the *Mary Ellen* off the shore. Smith saw no reason for congratulations. He had done what had to be done. Had to be done. He said tiredly, "For God's sake get her people off as soon as you can." And: "Hands to coal ship!"

In the, only comparatively, sheltered waters of the bay Smith laid *Thunder* alongside the *Mary Ellen* and anchored fore and aft. The ships were bound together forward and aft with securing warps, and ground on the fenders hung between

117

them. The searchlights crackled and blazed out, beams flooding on the collier's hatches and the working parties swarmed on to her deck.

Smith squinted against the glare. If the cruisers came up with them now – ! But they were not so close – if they were there at all. He thrust aside the recurring doubt and shouted, "Mr. Garrick! Use the boat derrick as well!"

Garrick lifted one hand in acknowledgment.

Normally the collier's derricks were rigged with the crusier's the winches of both of them working together to hoist the coal from the collier and swing it across and inboard. That would only work so long as the collier had steam for her winches. The big boat derrick that hoisted in the pinnace was the only one long enough to reach out over the collier's hold and hoist out coal on its own. The hands were still setting up the rigging between cruiser and collier of the other derricks when the boat derrick yanked out the first load.

'Hands to coal ship.' It was a fact of life for the ship's company that she coaled every week or ten days. It was heavy, filthy work and only the Captain was excused. But this time they would remember.

Because of the gale. Aboard the collier they threw off the hatch-covers and jumped down into the holds with their shovels. The coal was packed tight and the devil to break into as always but now they worked in a gale that rolled both ships together so that the coal shifted and slid in an oily, mountainous flow and they staggered and fell as they worked. They shovelled the coal into sacks and these were swung up out of the holds by the derricks, ten sacks to a strop, swayed over and lowered to *Thunder*'s deck.

Between the coaling scuttles in her deck and the bunkers far below were the mess-decks. So canvas chutes were rigged between scuttles and bunkers. The sacks were wheeled on barrows to the scuttles and the motion of the ship set the barrows grinding hard or trying to run away with the men. It was hard and it was dangerous. They emptied the sacks down the scuttles and the coal fell down the chutes into the bunkers. There was never a chute that did not leak but coal-dust found its way anywhere, anyway, so the mess-decks were filthy.

In the dust-filled gloom of the bunkers they worked with smarting eyes, soaked sponges tied across noses and mouths, trimming the coal. They staggered with the lift and plunge of the ship and the groaning and creaking of the two ships working together was a hellish noise in the steel drums of the bunkers, punctuated by the roar and crash as the coal came down. They always counted men into and out of the bunkers because men had been buried by coal.

In spite of the gale they worked in a frenzied haste, coaling faster than they had ever done because there was not a man who did not know what coal meant to the ship, and that time was against them. This coaling was different because the collier was sinking. Aboard *Thunder* they could see it. They would glance at the collier and when they looked again they saw she was a little lower in the water. The Petty Officers and men on the securing warps could feel it because as the collier sank the warps had to be eased. While they held her in to *Thunder*'s side they would not hold her up from the sea that claimed her. It was delicate nerve-racking work. Ease the warp too much and the collier would swing away to slam back against *Thunder*'s side, ease it too little and the strain would part it and the whip-crack of a parting warp could kill a man.

In the holds the coal shifted and slid and the sea pounded against the side but every now and again they would hear the surge of the water inside her. The hatch was a black rectangle against the lights and far above the men as they shovelled and sweated and cursed.

The crew of the collier were taken off as soon as she was made fast alongside. Garrick brought her Master to the wing of the bridge.

He was wild-eyed. "You should have taken us off. She could have gone down anytime. Man, you've only got to *look* at her! Every minute I thought she might go, every second!

You could have taken us off. I watched you handle this ship and, by Christ! You're a seaman! So you could ha' taken us off but you *wouldn't*. I *pleaded* with you to take us off and you passed us a *bloody tow*! *Why?*" His face was haggard.

Smith did not look at him or answer him. Instead he asked, "Why did you sail south when I asked that you wait for me at Malaguay?"

The Master peered at him, bewildered. "What's that got to do with it? But wait be buggered. The Consul said you needed the coal and I was to find you. You don't suppose I put to sea in this weather for sport, do you? I did it for you, you —" He stopped, not speechless but holding back the last words. Then he said, almost pleading again, "We all thought our number was up, then you came along but you wouldn't take us off. We're men like yourself. Sailormen. I don't see how you could —" He stopped again and shook his head.

Smith finally turned to him a face as haggard as his own and the eyes as wild. "I had to have coal. *I had to have coal!*"

The Master stepped back from those eyes but Smith turned away and back to watching his men. The Master whispered, "You're mad! A bloody *madman!*"

But then Garrick took his arm and led him away.

Smith stood alone. He watched the collier sinking and his men slaving in her at risk of their lives and the Master's charges hammered in his head . . . '*bloody madman . . .*' But his answer was the same. He had to have coal. Because of the cruisers. And because of *Ariadne* and the *Elizabeth Bell* and the other British shipping and hundreds of British seamen along this coast. Because of *Thunder*.

He knew that he was right but in his mind he saw the Master's face and took no comfort from being right.

He handed over the bridge to Garrick and went down to the *Mary Ellen*. Not because of her Master nor for any fake heroics but he had sent these men down into the collier and he could no longer stand high on the bridge looking down on them like some little god. He paced her deck with that restless stride and felt the sluggish, water-laden dying of her under him. He went down into the holds where despite the searchlights the men laboured in a reeling near-darkness of dust-filled oppression and the coal slithered and slid around a man's knees, or his waist so another would have to cease his frantic shovelling to haul him out bodily.

They saw him.

Somebody coughed and spat filthy phlegm and croaked, "What's he doin' here? Don't say our old cow's goin' down faster nor this one!" And they laughed madly, coughed and laughed again and the shovels ripped at the coal.

He said nothing but he grinned at them through a mask of coal-dust. On deck he told Aitkyne and the Petty Officers: "When it comes you must be quick. Get them out and back aboard." And to the two men, one forward, one aft who stood with axes where the big warps came down from *Thunder* and were secured aboard the collier: "When I give the word, cut her loose and jump! Understood?"

"Aye, aye, sir."

He paced the deck of the *Mary Ellen* as the loads soared up from the holds, until the collier's winches faltered and died and the hands struck the rigging that connected her derricks to *Thunder's*. Only the winch of the boat derrick hammered on aboard *Thunder*.

The *Mary Ellen* was settling.

He felt the sudden, sick lurch of her and his mouth was open when one of the party on the warp forward leaned over *Thunder's* rail to scream through the clatter of the winch: "*She's going!*"

Smith shouted, "Cut her loose! Get those men out and all accounted for!"

The axes flashed as they rose and fell. The hands came clambering out of the holds, yanked out by the Petty Officers and thrust towards the side. They jumped at the nettings and clawed their way up *Thunder's* side like flies caught in a web.

121

"Number two hold cleared, sir."

". . . hold cleared, sir!"

"Get aboard!" He shouted at them. "Get *aboard!*"

He stood by the after hold with *Thunder*'s boat derrick projecting above him like a gallows tree with its dangling wire. The *Mary Ellen* was going down. He snapped at Aitkyne, the only man left on the deck, "How many men in the hold?" The wire from the derrick hung slackly down into the hold.

"Two, sir. Kennedy and young Manton."

Now Smith could see them down there, securing the sacks on the strop. One of them yelled, mouth pink against the coal-dust, Aitkyne lifted his arm and the wire drew taut.

Smith shoved him towards the side. "Get aboard!" He saw him on the nettings as the warps parted to slam against *Thunder*'s side and be hauled inboard. He saw the two men with axes throw them away, jump at the nets and scramble up.

He was a solitary figure on the collier's deck under the glare of the lights as the sea seemed to hang above the deck of the *Mary Ellen* and then fell in on him. The load came swinging up out of the hold with Kennedy and Manton clinging to the sacks and as it soared past him he clawed and caught hold and Kennedy's fist clamped on his collar. He was snatched off the deck of the collier as the sea smashed around his waist.

They swung like a pendulum, fingers hooked like claws and knees gripping the sacks above a boiling sea. The *Mary Ellen* had gone. Then the derrick swayed them in and down on to *Thunder*'s deck.

They had torn a hundred and twenty tons of coal out of the *Mary Ellen*. At risk of their lives they had won at most another twenty-four hours of life for *Thunder*. Now she had coal for just two days' steaming.

8

Thunder RAISED THE scattered lights of Malaguay at midnight, seen dimly through recurrent rain that drove in on the gale that thrust at her, rocking her still further in a sea that rolled her badly enough, and blowing her smoke down and across that sea. She still heaved lumpily in the shelter of the roadstead as she came to anchor. The pinnace set out for the shore with the crew of the *Mary Ellen* and the search-light blinked to *Ariadne* and *Elizabeth Bell*: "Prepare to sail with me forthwith."

Ariadne acknowledged at once but the signal had to be repeated twice to the *Elizabeth Bell*, and Smith was on the point of firing a gun to get their attention, infuriated at this delay, when a lamp replied limpingly from her bridge.

There was a hail from the deck and a moment later Wakely reported: "Boat alongside, sir. Mr. Thackeray coming aboard."

As Smith left the bridge he caught Garrick's eye on him and said flatly, "I know, coal. You'd better come along and hear what he has to say." *Thunder* had steamed at fifteen knots for most of the previous twenty-six hours and had devoured coal that at ten knots, would have lasted four days.

Now she was left with coal for only forty-eight hours' steaming. She had to coal before those two days were out or lie a motionless hulk at the end of them.

Thackeray came aboard in a glistening wet yellow oilskin that reached to his ankles and they went to Smith's deck cabin. Thackeray shook the folds from a clean, white handkerchief, wiped a face that was even longer than usual and asked in a tone between hope and apprehension: "Did you find her?"

Smith nodded. "She refused to heave to and continued to claim she was a neutral. Have you heard any report that she was calling the shore stations?"

"None."

"She was sending hard enough to someone, and in code. And our wireless picked up a reply that was a Telefunken transmission. That scarcely sounds neutral to me." He paused as Thackeray stared at him, then: "I sank her!"

Thackeray's lips tightened till they became a thin, sulky line as Smith pushed on, his voice dangerously quiet.

"She was not the only collier to sink. I met the *Mary Ellen* south of here. Her engines were broken down and she was being driven on to a lee shore where she had no damned business to be and her Master said *you* sent her! She sank!"

A nerve twitched a corner of Thackeray's mouth. "It seemed best."

"Best! If her engines hadn't broken down I'd have missed her altogether!"

" – and in accordance with your request for assistance."

Smith stared at him. "My request? I asked you to fetch her here to wait for me."

"You asked me to bring her down from Guaya because you badly needed coal. You didn't say she was to wait."

"I didn't need to! Because you couldn't send her anywhere because you didn't even know where *I* was going."

"I knew you sailed south."

"That is a very general direction in a very large ocean."

124

"I am no seaman."

"Yet you instructed the Master of the *Mary Ellen* to sail south."

"I was repeating your instructions."

"I told you – "

"I remember very well what you told me, Captain. I only wish I had a witness to the conversation."

Smith sat silent. There was a little gleam of triumph in Thackeray's eyes and Smith had not missed the point of his words. Smith did not have a witness either, so it was his word against Thackeray's. He looked at Garrick, who was peering at Thackeray with distaste. It was obvious who Garrick believed. Smith was confident he knew what a Court of Enquiry would believe if they were asked by Thackeray to accept that a seaman had left instructions to send a collier to sea with the vague direction to head south. No seaman in his right mind would –

His thoughts stumbled, then limped on. Three ships sunk in forty-eight hours, two of them claiming to be neutrals and the Master of the third believing him to be a madman.

Thackeray had sent the *Mary Ellen* south knowing very well the odds were that *Thunder* would miss her. Because Smith had wrecked his cosy little world. Because he hated Smith.

He looked at Thackeray and could read all this in the man's remote face. But prove it? He rubbed his hands across his face. He felt tired and said tiredly, "There will be a Court of Enquiry." He was done with Thackeray.

Thackeray was not done with him. He said with satisfaction, "No doubt. The attitude of the Chileans has hardened even further. I understand the Master of the *Gerda* is screaming to high heaven that she was neutral and there is no *evidence* to the contrary. They're really angry." He did not say they were howling for Smith's head but that could be read between the lines. "They were very suspicious about the seaplane and why the pinnace went to her. I told them I knew nothing about it." He was washing his hands of that. "They're very hostile. My protest about the German breach of neutrality was accepted and that's all."

"What breach of neutrality?"

"The *Leopard*, the gunboat interned here. There was no sentry aboard her, only one on the quay and last night, after you sailed, it seems he abandoned his post. She got up steam and slipped away."

"*What?*"

"There's quite a strong German faction here. So when she was interned her crew were left to live aboard. She wasn't disabled but all her ammunition was taken off and put in bond in the Naval Arsenal. That was partly because she is, or was, tied up close to the town and they didn't want a lot of explosives lying around there indefinitely, but it also satisfied the neutrality laws, in that she could not fight."

"So she went to sea toothless." Smith scowled but it was a comforting thought in one way. "With what object?"

"Object?"

"She can't sail to Germany and in her present state she can't fight. What reason could she have for going to sea?" He supplied the answer himself. 'She's gone to meet the cruisers."

It was one more piece of evidence, circumstantial no doubt, but it fitted. Garrick looked thoughtful.

Smith said, "The cruisers can supply her with ammunition, and what's more she will be one more pair of eyes for them." Thackeray would not appreciate that. He had not stood on the bridge of *Thunder* that morning, cursing the lack of an extra pair of eyes.

He prompted Thackeray bitterly because Thackeray was piling it on. "Anything *else?*"

Thackeray hesitated, seemed reluctant, then said, "I had a cable. *Kunashiri* is in these waters. She's a long way north but she's steaming south. She's due at Guaya in thirty-six hours or less."

Smith stared at him, slowly taking it in. Japan was an ally and *Kunashiri* was one of the big, new Japanese battle-cruisers, fast enough to catch a German armoured cruiser, her twelve-inch guns big enough for her to stand off and destroy the victims when caught. Smith had wished for a consort and now he had one with a vengeance.

He found he was on his feet, and laughing. Then he remembered: the battle-cruiser was his salvation but first he had to reach her. He said brusquely, "I must ask you to excuse me now. *Ariadne* and *Elizabeth Bell* should be ready to sail soon and I want to leave for Guaya as soon as possible."

And he wanted to be quit of Thackeray with his narrow mouth and narrow cunning, his stupidity.

Thackeray did not move. He was looking down at his hands that were clasped as if in prayer and Smith could not see his eyes though he saw the twist of the lips as Thackeray spoke. "I received a second cable. This one said that *Wolf* and *Kondor* have been sighted in the Indian Ocean and the hunt has started there." He looked up at Smith and the eyes glittered. He had held it back to the end though it made the rest irrelevant.

Smith could not speak.

Garrick said, "Could easily be a mistake, sir. Some of these merchant chaps ..." His voice trailed away and Smith knew Garrick did not believe what he had said because Garrick had always doubted. Only Sarah Benson ... Garrick did not look at him. Smith thought, 'Never kick a man when he's down.'

Thackeray said, "They're searching."

Garrick said, "I think it's time you went ashore Mister Thackeray." Now his voice held distaste.

Thackeray pulled his oilskin about him. "I'm not going ashore. I've booked a passage in the *Elizabeth Bell* as far as Guaya. I think it's time I compared notes with Mr. Cherry, particularly as he may be called home over this – this unfortunate affair."

Smith asked quietly, "Have you told Graham and Ballard?"

Thackeray knew what he meant – the cruisers being sighted in the Indian Ocean. He smiled. "No. I thought I'd leave that to you."

Garrick shouldered out of the cabin after Thackeray and Smith was left alone. He sat there for some time. Once he thought that Sarah Benson had believed and he wondered how she felt. Thackeray would tell her and Graham as soon as he set foot aboard the *Elizabeth Bell*.

He climbed up to the bridge. Aitkyne turned his back to the wind that hurled the rain in driving sheets, wiped at his streaming face and shouted, "They're both of them on the move, sir! Must have had steam up!"

Smith nodded. They would certainly have had steam up. By now they would have abandoned hope of *Thunder*'s return within the time-limit he had set and been preparing to take him at his word and sail on their own initiative. They did not know of the cruiser's sighting, that cable had been for Thackeray and Smith only.

He was aware that Garrick had muttered to Aitkyne and now both were watching him. They looked – sorry.

He said flatly, "*Elizabeth Bell* to lead at five knots, then *Ariadne* and we'll bring up the rear." The tramp was the slowest vessel. These were the dispositions he had decided before he reached Malaguay. He would play the game out to the end. "Make to *Elizabeth Bell*: 'Act on instructions from *Ariadne*'. And to *Ariadne*: 'Pass all my orders to *Elizabeth Bell*'."

Thunder weighed and left her brief shelter and went to sea again but moving dead slow as she waited for the other two ships as they came beating out of the anchorage and plunging into the big seas outside. *Ariadne* led but as she came up to *Thunder* and the signal lamp flashed from the wing near Smith her speed fell away. Smith thought that Ballard would be annoyed at the slow speed. It was a comfortable speed for *Elizabeth Bell* in this weather but a funeral march for *Ariadne*. He saw in the lights on her deck the white faces of a few hardy souls who had braved the storm to demonstrate their loyalty. They stood in a huddled group on the deck below the superstructure and he saw them waving.

Elizabeth Bell followed close on *Ariadne* and narrowing the gap. Seas were bursting over her fo'c'sle. The signal lamp flickered again on *Thunder* and was acknowledged. No one waved on *Elizabeth Bell* but he saw Graham in the lighted wheelhouse lift his bowler, and abaft the bridge a figure clung to a stanchion, skirt whipping out like a flag. Sarah Benson. Smith wondered why she was on deck in this weather?

Thunder was increasing speed and Smith ordered, "Make to *Ariadne*: 'Darken ship'." And then he shifted restlessly as he came back to partial life and the thoughts stirred. He leaned over the rail, staring not at *Ariadne* but at the darkness astern, black, white-whipped sea and beyond the lights of Malaguay. No one on shore would see them now. "Mr. Wakely."

"Sir?"

"I think I see a boat astern of us."

Wakely was silent a moment, leaning beside Smith, then he said quickly, "Yes, sir. Looks like a big motor-launch — can't make out a funnel — but I can't make out much of her at all. She's carrying no lights."

Smith faced forward. "Watch her." *Ariadne* and *Elizabeth Bell* had obeyed the order and their ports were covered and only navigation lights showed. "Make to *Ariadne*: 'Turn in succession, four points to port'." He waited as the signal was made and acknowledged and waited again as *Ariadne* passed it on. The minutes stretched out and then Garrick said, "*Elizabeth Bell* is turning."

Smith nodded. Then *Ariadne* turned and finally *Thunder* and the three ships headed out to sea. Neither Ballard nor Graham would be pleased. This was not a course for Guaya.

But they would draw the conclusion that Smith was taking a course far out of the normal trade route to evade pursuit.

Smith asked, "Well, Mr. Wakely?"

"She's still there, sir. Wait a minute, though – "

They had been ten minutes on the changed course and whoever manned the launch would be having a rough passage in this sea.

Wakely called, "She's turning! She's dropping back!"

She was. Smith could just see the boat, broadside on and falling away astern. She came around further still, showed her stern and now he saw a faint, dim light in the well of her, possibly the compass. A moment later the darkness hid her.

He waited a further ten minutes and then ordered the return to their original course. He had one crumb of comfort for Ballard. "Make to *Elizabeth Bell*: 'Proceed at best speed'." Now he knew they were neither watched nor followed he would make the best speed he could. It would add another two or three knots. *Ariadne* was still far from stretching her legs but at least she would feel she was moving.

He left the bridge. Wakely stared at him as if he had second sight but he would not explain tonight. He would not explain that he had expected the Germans in Malaguay to watch his course and to suspect that once out of sight of the land he might change that course. So he expected the launch to be there. She would think she had caught him laying a false trail and that his course to Guaya lay well out to sea. But why had she trailed him if the cruisers were a world away?

He wanted to be alone.

He was on the bridge before dawn and Garrick came to stand beside him and together they drank hot coffee and watched the blackness over the tossing sea turn to grey. The navigation lights of *Ariadne* and *Elizabeth Bell* paled in that greyness as the ships took solid shape. Then it was full day and he could see his little convoy clearly, *Ariadne* heaving solidly,

Elizabeth Bell plugging into the seas. Visibility was fair, no better than that, but it was enough.

Garrick hailed the masthead and the reply came back: "Nothing, sir, only *Ariadne* an' *Elizabeth Bell*."

Smith heard it poker-faced. That was all that was left of his calm pose. He could not converse casually because he did not want to face his officers. He did not want to see the embarrassment and the pity behind it. They were at last on his side but now he had to stand alone. He avoided them. He would not go below and they passed within inches of where he stood or paced the bridge but it was as if they moved in different worlds. The whole ship seemed to tip-toe around him. He passed the long hours of the morning in thought and at the end could remember none of it. Only at the end his thoughts turned to coal and his need of it.

He had sunk two colliers filled with prime Welsh coal. And men. *My God, men!*

But he still could not believe that his whole reasoning had been wrong.

It was long past noon and they would reach Guaya shortly after sunset. A sun that was bright but robbed of heat by the wind tightened his eyes. It seemed to smile on *Thunder* and on himself but it brought him no warmth nor comfort.

The call came down from the masthead: "*Smoke bearing green one-six-oh!*"

9

THE GALE WAS blowing itself out. *Thunder* still rolled wildly with seas bursting over her rails and spray flailing across the bridge, and the wind still snapped that spray from the crests of the big, green seas, but the sky was clearing, seeming swept clean by that wind. There was little of the day left but what there was promised to be beautiful.

Visibility was good and on the bridge they could just see the ship now, a speck under the marking black banner of her smoke. The masthead look-out could see her better. "*She's a gunboat!*"

Garrick said, "She's making up on us, but slowly."

Knight ventured: "Maybe she isn't the German."

That was a possibility. She could be Chilean or any of a score of warships pursuing their lawful business in these waters. Smith did not believe it. He turned away and lowered his glasses. Everyone else who could reach a point of vantage was straining his eyes aft but he would not. He would know soon enough. *Elizabeth Bell* wallowed ahead of *Thunder* and rolled as badly. He wondered how Sarah Benson was managing aboard her and decided he did not give a damn. Whatever she got she'd asked for. *Elizabeth Bell* was barely making eight knots. If this sea fell flat calm she might make ten knots but as it was eight was her best. Astern of her and ahead of *Thunder* steamed *Ariadne*, riding the seas better than either of the others. She could make another four or five knots in this. *Elizabeth Bell* had a crew of twenty-two. *Ariadne*'s crew and passengers totalled a hundred and thirty.

Once more the hail from the masthead: "*She's that German! Leopard!*" The look-outs had all seen the gunboat more than once when she lay at Malaguay.

Smith said, "Mr. Knight. Make to *Ariadne*: 'Proceed independently at best speed'."

Knight was startled because Smith had not spoken a word that day. But Smith again caught the interchange of glances between Garrick and Aitkyne. There was only one gunboat, only just escaped from internment, unarmed. He could be sending *Ariadne* away in panic flight while the Germans laughed at the success of their bluff.

"*Ariadne* acknowledges, sir."

"Very good."

"And *Elizabeth Bell* signals: 'Am making best speed'."

He was only too well aware of it. "Acknowledge." Another man might have contrived a humorous reply but he did not feel humorous.

Ariadne's smoke thickened and she swung out to starboard and surged past the tramp and on towards the distant coast.

"*Masthead! Smoke bearing red one-seven-oh! Astern of the gunboat!*"

The hail was whipped away on the wind. Smith turned slowly to face aft. They waited, all of them on the bridge and he could see the rest of his officers grouped on the after bridge with glasses and telescopes.

"*Masthead! Looks like a four-funnel ship!*"

Garrick bawled up, tight-nerved, outraged, "What the *hell* d'ye mean? *Looks like?*"

"*She's near bows-on, sir, an' the smoke what she's making –*"

Garrick fumed.

Then the look-out bawled again, aggrievedly sure now, *"She's a four-funnel ship!"*

There was the end of doubt. A four-funnel ship meant a warship was closing on the gunboat. No doubt at all now. Smith thought that somehow they had got the word from Malaguay of the course he had taken out to sea and they had spread out in a wide, sweeping line with the gunboat taking the inshore station. The other cruiser would be ten miles farther out over the horizon and would take time to come up, so it would be one-to-one for that length of time. One-to-one. But she had a broadside of six big guns to *Thunder's* two and an edge in speed. Once he stopped to fight he would never escape.

"Masthead! Two *four-funnel ships!"*

His head jerked back to stare up at the look-out then his eyes came slowly down. The other cruiser must also have been closing on the gunboat, possibly the squadron concentrating for the night or to run into Guaya. Whatever the reason, *Thunder* faced impossible odds.

He found he was staring at Garrick and that the First Lieutenant was grinning like an overgrown schoolboy. Aitkyne smiled broadly. And Knight. All his officers seemed delighted, and then he realised it was for him, because he had been right. *Wolf* and *Kondor.* He caught a glimpse of young Wakely, flushed with excitement and laughing. The elder officers were hardly more serious. Garrick said, "God knows who they're chasing in the Indian Ocean." He guffawed. There were few hours of daylight left but Smith thought they could all be dead by sunset.

He turned from them and climbed slowly, steadily to the fore-top, the big glasses bumping on his chest. There was no hurry. The cruisers would not go away. He stood in the fore-top holding on against the wild sweep of the mast as it swung like an erratic metronome. He lifted the glasses, aware of Garrick behind him.

He saw them coming up under the smoke, a great deal of smoke, they were steaming for all they were worth. Bows on and superimposed as they were he could not distinguish their silhouettes, but he knew them. He lowered the glasses fractionally until the bucketing gunboat lurched into focus. Only nine hundred tons and with barely ten knots of speed, *Leopard* only carried a pair of four-inch guns. Except for them, with her flush deck she might be taken for a rich man's yacht. Yet she had sighted them, had pointed the finger. Without her he might have got away.

He let the glasses fall against his chest. Garrick held the silhouette book. He frowned at it. "I'll lay odds they *are Wolf* and *Kondor*."

"I know." Smith started down. He had seen more than enough. He was pursued by an enormously superior force but *Thunder* plodded on at a leaden eight knots while the pursuit roared down on her at more than twice that speed. The reason, of course, was the *Elizabeth Bell*, rusty and dirty and shabby. She hung around his neck like an albatross. In half-an-hour or less . . .

He could abandon the *Elizabeth Bell*.

Looked at coldly and logically it was the obvious course but he knew he could not do it. The sun was going down, it was already in his eyes as he turned aft again to stare at his fate rushing down on him, his nightmare come to appalling life. The sun was going down but it would not set soon enough to save them.

Very well, then. "Number One!"

"Sir?" The reply was jerked out of Garrick. The jubilation on the bridge had turned to a façade that could not hide the tension that was a palpable thing and Garrick was not immune.

Only Smith felt cold. "I will want steam for full speed, and I want every man fed. There's time for a quick bite, say twenty minutes."

Garrick ran from the bridge and Smith started to follow

him but paused by Aitkyne to say casually, "I'll be in my cabin, pilot. If there is any change in the situation no doubt you will let me know." He took the silhouette book from Aitkyne and made his way to his cabin in leisurely fashion.

Boat-deck and upper-deck were crowded by the watch below, the eyes of all of them astern. One or two of them saw him stroll by and nudged each other, grinned. He was a cool one! But once in his cabin, alone, he opened the silhouette book and stared at it. That was not necessary. Now he could have drawn the silhouette faithfully from memory.

They were faster and each of them carried eight 8.2-inch guns that were equal to *Thunder*'s 9.2-inch and she had only two of them. Sixteen to two. In a broadside fight they could fire twelve to two, even in a stern chase like this they would bring eight to bear against one. Between them they carried twelve 5.9-inch that out-ranged *Thunder*'s elderly six-inch guns.

Sarah Benson had said: 'You can't fight them.'

She was in the *Elizabeth Bell*.

There was a tap at the door and Horsfall entered with a tray. "That there Benks, he's made sangwiches for all the gennlemen, bully beef an' a bit o' pickle an' I thought you might fancy a bottle o' pale ale." He set the tray on the table and touched the glass lovingly, making sure it was safe. It was only half-full so that *Thunder*'s rolling would not slop the golden, white-collared contents.

Smith said, "You may as well have the rest of the bottle."

"Thank you, sir." Smith was prepared to bet the rest of the bottle had already gone. He was right. Horsfall said, "Looks as if we'll be busy later on. Anything particular you want while I'm here?"

Smith shook his head. "No, thank you." Except another ten knots, or that battle-cruiser.

"Well. Might see you later on, sir."

Might. Smith looked up at Daddy's long horse-face. Daddy was under no illusions. Smith tapped the book. "Know this class of ship?"

Horsfall breathed over Smith's shoulder, then said simply, "Too bloody true, sir."

"Good luck, Horsfall."

"And the same to you, sir."

Smith drank the beer thirstily but he could not face the sandwiches.

When 'Cooks to the galley' was sounded, Gibb queued up with the others and drew the meal for his mess: more bully beef and bread, scalding hot tea. Some wanted to eat, some did not. Some started voraciously then sickened. Nobody stayed on the mess-deck. They all crowded up aft, heavy sea or no heavy sea. The spray turned the hunks of bread to soggy lumps in their hands and diluted the tea while the wind cooled it, but they all got something inside them, if it was only tepid tea.

Gibb found Rattray alongside him champing hungrily and sucking at tea. Gibb ate nothing, drained his cup and was still thirsty. Gibb ventured, trying to be nonchalant, "Looks like we'll have a scrap, hey?"

Rattray did not answer for a while, then he showed his teeth. "And we'll see what you're bloody made of, you and Smith together."

Smith returned to the bridge and moved out to the wing, staring aft. The two big cruisers had overhauled the gunboat now. Ten miles away, maybe a little more. They were eating up the distance, racing down in line abreast so both could fire with all guns that would bear forward, which would be three each at least and four if he lay dead ahead of them. Dead ahead. Unfortunate choice of phrase. He grimaced and swung around, eyes seeking the coast. It looked no nearer and the sun seemed suspended, refusing to move down the sky. Neither sanctuary nor night to save them.

He ordered, "Sound 'General quarters'."

Thunder's crew boiled into life and ran to their action stations. The reports began to come in as the guns' crews closed up, magazines were manned and all the hundred and one posts necessary to *Thunder*'s functioning as a fighting ship were filled.

Garrick went to the fore-top. *Thunder*'s fire control like everything else about her was outdated. She did not have director firing, that is all guns being laid and trained from one central director high above the deck. She had a range-finder and a device to calculate deflection and that was all. The guns received range and deflection through navyphones and from then on it was up to the layers and trainers to lay and train the gun. Garrick in the fore-top watched for the fall of shot and issued orders to correct it if it was over or short.

Smith stayed on the bridge. In the conning-tower below the bridge they would have the protection of that eleven-inch-thick armour plate but Smith wanted to see as much as he could, *had* to see. But exposed as they were on the bridge, a hit on the ship might send scything splinters to wipe out Smith and everyone else up there, while a direct hit on the bridge – It was one more risk he had to take. If he could neither run nor fight with any hope then he would have to seek an alternative. He thought this was the place to seek it.

"Make to *Elizabeth Bell*: 'Copy my changes of course'."

The signal was hoisted and broke out then the minutes dragged by as Knight muttered under his breath but finally reported. "*Elizabeth Bell* acknowledges, sir."

The reports were finished and the ship was quiet, her decks deserted.

The sea was moderating, still heavy but nowhere near as bad as the night and improving every second. It was a lovely evening but Smith took no pleasure in it. *Thunder* could be running now but she was tied to the eight knots plug of *Elizabeth Bell*.

Smith stared at the two four-funnelled ships, eyes narrowed against the sun but still able to make them out under the thick black smoke. God! They were steaming! He wished

Thunder was making smoke like that. He heard Wakely say to Knight, "Wonder how long before we get a shot at 'em?"

Smith lowered the glasses, rubbed at his eyes, looked again and answered the question himself: "Probably not very long now." Light sparked from the bows of the cruisers, smoke puffed brown and was whipped thinly away. "Steer four points to starboard."

"Four points of starboard wheel on, sir."

Thunder's bow swung through the arc, pointing away from *Elizabeth Bell*.

"Midships."

"Midships, sir."

Thunder steadied on the new course. Smith glanced at the *Elizabeth Bell*, opened his mouth to snap the order at Knight to signal her, then clamped it shut. She was turning to parallel *Thunder*'s course and was now on the port bow. Smith saw light flicker on the cruisers again and smoke shred. The first salvo would be falling now, past the culminating point of its trajectory three thousand feet up and plunging down on the target. On *Thunder*.

The report came down from the rangefinder on the upper bridge: "Range one-three-four-double-oh." And as Smith thought: 'Maximum range', the first salvo howled down from the atmosphere and the sea erupted astern of *Thunder* in four tall columns and crashing bursts.

"Hard aport!"

"Hard aport, sir!"

"Midships!"

"Midships, sir!"

Now *Thunder* was on the opposite leg of the zig-zag. *Elizabeth Bell* should follow. She was not. Had that salvo shaken them out of their senses? Smith snarled, "Come on, damn you!"

Knight stared at him, startled. The second salvo was on its way, plunging now. Smith snapped, "Make to *Elizabeth Bell* —"

He did not get the chance to finish. The second salvo rushed over them and burst, water lifting, noise beating at them. And Knight shouted, "Christ! She's copped one!" The *Elizabeth Bell* had taken a direct hit amidships and another forward, each from a two-hundred-and-forty pound projectile plunging at a near vertical angle. She listed immediately and her bow went down; smoke billowed, sparks flying in it and flames leaping beneath it.

"Hard astarboard!" And: "Midships!" And *Thunder* raced down on the *Elizabeth Bell*, now laying like a log and going down by the head. Smith rattled off orders to a string of rapid acknowledgments. "Slow ahead both! Dead slow! I want to edge alongside ... ! Mr. Knight, I want lines over the side and strong men on them. Warn the Doctor to expect survivors."

"Aye, aye, sir!"

"Open fire!"

He heard that last passed to Garrick. Seconds later the after 9.2 recoiled, spat flame and smoke and the *crack!* racketed through them, the shudder ran through the ship.

Thunder closed the wreck of the *Elizabeth Bell*, slowing. He could see a party on her superstructure just forward of the gaping hole in her deck that poured forth smoke. They were trying to lower a boat and making a hash of it in the smoke as the ship tilted under them, her bows already under water and the sea reaching up greedily for the superstructure. He snatched the megaphone and ran out to the port wing of the bridge. Close now. "Starboard a point!"

"Starboard a point, sir!"

"Midships!" He lifted the megaphone as a salvo crashed down and plummeted into the sea beyond *Elizabeth Bell*, hurling more tons of water aboard her and starting a few more plates to hasten still further her already horribly swift end. She was awash as far aft as the superstructure and sinking before his eyes. *Thunder*'s bow slid by her stern, creeping along her starboard side. *Thunder* rolled in the beam sea but the little tramp lay steady with the stillness of a corpse. *Thunder*'s funnel smoke coiled down around them and she rubbed against the other ship and ground along her side to side. Knight and his men were swarming along the rails right forward and hurling the lines far ahead, fishing for the survivors on the tramp's heeling settling superstructure. Smith picked out the flutter of a skirt. The Benson girl. He bellowed through the megaphone, "Take the lines! We'll haul you aboard!"

He moved up to them, over them, as *Thunder*, dead slow, ground forward. Through the swirling blanketing smoke from *Thunder*'s four funnels and the huge hole in the deck of *Elizabeth Bell* he saw the skirt fly like a flag then flicked away on the wind and the girl seized a line.

The after 9.2 roared again. The stern of the *Elizabeth Bell* lifted and Smith saw Sarah Benson tying the line around a man who lay on the deck. He saw through the smoke another man leave the deck of *Thunder* at the end of a line and walk down her side, or rather ran, going down in great bounding leaps as the seamen above him paid out the line. It was Somers and Smith saw him lunge at the girl as the man she helped was whipped away from her on the line and as the stern of the tramp reared and she went down.

A salvo burst and Wakely said behind him, "Short!" And: "That one was short, sir!"

They had dawdled only minutes but that was too long, far too long.

The *Elizabeth Bell* went down as the 9.2 shook their ringing ears. She stood on her head with her rusty stern and idle screw perpendicular, slid down with a roar of escaping steam and dull thumping internal explosions. Leaning far out he could see only six, no seven, figures swinging on the lines as they were hauled in and one of them was Somers and the other Sarah Benson.

The salvo roared over and burst in the sea in high spouts of upflung water, off the port bow and over by less than a hundred yards.

One under, one over. It was time; high time. He bellowed through the megaphone, "Mr Knight! Get 'em *aboard*!" Knight and the men with him were doing their best but he could give them not a second more. "Full ahead both! Hard a'starboard!" He strode across the bridge as the helm went over.

Corporal Hill had fumed and chafed internally from the moment the after-turret closed up through the long waiting when the glimpses he had of the big cruisers showed them overhauling *Thunder* hand over fist. He only caught glimpses because spray burst continually across the deck, misting his layer's telescope and because *Thunder* was trailing her own smoke, wreathing and rolling around the after-turret, blinding him. But finally the speed fell away until *Thunder* rolled in the swell and the spray was less. The crew of the turret eyed each other, not understanding it, not liking it. Why were they lying like this, a sitting target? Then the concussion came throbbing through the hull to reach them in the turret as a tremble of steel under their hands.

Somebody asked, "What was that?"

And somebody replied, "They dropped one close."

Day, Lieutenant in command of the after-turret, snapped edgily, "Shut up!" But then the order to open fire broke the tension.

Hill's long fingers laid the gun, eye clapped to his telescope, swearing softly as the target came in view, was obliterated by smoke, swam blearily into the telescope again. Bowker, the trainer on the other side of the breech, glared into his own telescope and matched Hill's cursing.

They fired three times, when Hill and Bowker could see the target and lay and train the gun. Slam of discharge, hiss of recoil, the acrid stench of the coiling fumes, the clang of the breech and the whirr and rattle of the hoist bringing up projectiles and charges from handing room and magazine in the bowels of the ship.

In the fore-top Garrick strained his eyes to spot the fall of shot and succeeded, bitterly. "Short." And again: "Short." And for the third time: "Blast and bloody hell! Short! They've got the range of us." He had expected it because it was a mathematical certainty; *Thunder*'s guns were old but even when she was new her guns had not matched those of the German cruisers. It was still a bitter pill. Garrick had less trouble with the smoke than did Hill and Bowker but the light was bad, the setting sun glaring redly into his eyes.

In the fore-turret Farmer Bates, the layer, settled comfortably on his little seat and rested his chin on his arms, giving easily to the motion of the ship, whistling softly, absently. Chalky White grumbled, "That Hill won't hit bugger all. He's a useless layer."

Bates said placidly, "He isn't useless. He's not bad."

"If we was –"

"If we was firing we wouldn't hit nothing either." The ranges were repeated in the fore-turret. "On account of we couldn't reach the bastards any more'n he can. At this range we stand as much chance farting at 'em."

They felt the increased beat of *Thunder*'s engines and then the heel of the deck to starboard.

Chalky White said, " 'Ullo! Now mebbe –"

"Mebbe. But I doubt it."

That was when the shell burst right before the fore-turret.

As *Thunder* hauled away from the few scraps of flotsam that marked the last of the *Elizabeth Bell*, Smith saw at least one survivor hauled in over the side. Then the salvo screamed down, but this time, a split second before the waterspouts rose, *Thunder* was hit. The impact was a hammer-blow, shaking the ship, deafening. The flash seared the eyes and splinters whined and droned and caromed around the upperworks of the ship. Smith was thrown against the telegraph, bounced off, staggered, grabbed at his cap. There was smoke and he could see flames but he could also see the fore-turret and it seemed intact, but forward of the turret the deck was ripped open and bent back as if some giant had hacked at it inexpertly with a tin-opener. Miles and his damage control and fire-fighting party came running towards the hole, canvas hoses snaking behind them.

Wakely squeaked, "Engine-room reports no damage, sir!"

"Very good. What about the fore-turret?" And: "*Messenger!* Ask Mr. Miles for a report on the damage forward, and quick!"

Hit or no hit, *Thunder* was working up speed now that she was without the *Elizabeth Bell*. Smith swallowed sickly. Had he wished her sunk? That was nonsense. He knew it was and told himself so, impatiently, but he knew it was a doubt that would return to rack him. Now he thrust it away, turned to peer through the smoke astern and saw the cruisers grown larger, orange flashes prickling together, smoke puffing, shredding. "Hard aport!" ... "Midships!"

From the wing of the bridge he could see Knight and his party and the survivors from the *Elizabeth Bell*. Sarah Benson was there, down on her knees on the deck, bent over someone lying there. Knight knelt beside her.

Smith bellowed, "Mister Knight!"

Knight jumped to his feet. "Sir?"

"What the *hell* are you doing there?"

"One of the survivors, sir. A splinter got him. I think he's dead."

"You won't do anything for him laying on hands! The Doctor's below. Get them all down to him and yourself up here." Sarah Benson's white face turned up to him, outraged. Smith bellowed, "This ship is in *action*, for God's sake!"

To underline his words the after 9.2 out-bellowed him and another salvo howled down into the sea to starboard, close enough to hurl water in tons across *Thunder's* deck, knocking the damage control party from their feet but helping to put out the fire they fought.

Smith swung back to the centre of the bridge. "Hard astarboard!"

Thunder turned on another leg of the zig-zag. Starboard, port, starboard ... Vary the length of each leg, the angle of turn, now two points, now four. Study the ships astern, watch for their firing. Look forward for *Ariadne* and beyond her for the coast. They were all factors to be weighed and used.

The hit had sent them all flying in the fore-turret and left them stunned, groping feebly, disorientated and with ringing ears. Bates lost his placidity with the agonising smash on his funny-bone. He swore in black bad temper, climbed to his feet, dragged Chalky up by his collar and jammed him against the breech. He snarled at the rest of them: "Come on, you bloody idlers!" And to Lieutenant Fletcher who commanded in the turret: "Are you all right, sir?"

Fletcher's face was bruised and bleeding, his lips cut and already swelling. He mumbled, "Never mind me. Check the piece." He lurched forward to join Bates and a few seconds later he was able to report.

Gibb stood at his post, pale but trying to be still. Rattray grinned at him madly and looked right into his terrified soul and Gibb knew it.

Wakely said, "No damage to fore-turret, sir."

"Very good. Hard aport!" It was good news. And now *Thunder*, despite her erratic, evasive course was steaming for her life and closing slowly on *Ariadne*, running for the coast and safety.

But *Wolf* and *Kondor*, running straight, were overhauling *Thunder*. He could see they had left the gunboat astern. He watched the cruisers and their firing and ordered the changes of course.

Knight returned to the bridge and Smith was aware of

him without looking as a salvo fell to starboard and spray slashed across them. "Hard astarboard! Mr. Knight! What was young Somers doing over the side? He was ordered closed up at his station in action."

"He says he knew there was no question of his gun firing because it was out of range and he reckoned Leading-Seaman McCann could manage without him, anyway."

That was probably true. McCann was old enough to be Somers's father and well capable of carrying out Somers's duties as well as his own. He had been Leading-Seaman-Gunner, off and on as he drunkenly lost and painfully regained his character, for the past fifteen years.

Smith said grimly, "I'll see him later." And dress him down because it would be good for his soul, but it had been an act of deliberate bravery, a decision coolly taken and executed with speed and determination. He would mention Somers in his report.

If he made a report.

Aitkyne said, "I think that boy might do well." Cautiously defending him, not looking at Smith.

Smith grunted. Aitkyne might be right.

He saw the cruisers fire and ordered the change of course as the after 9.2 fired. He had noted the fall of its shot the last three times it had fired and was certain it was within range of the cruisers now but off for line. He could guess at the gunners' frustration – who were they? Hill – Corporal Hill and Private Bowker of the Marines. They had the same low, blinding sun that hurt Smith's eyes and on top of that *Thunder*'s smoke, belching out now she was running at full speed and rolling down over the after turret and astern, blacking out the target. Add to that the continual sharp changes of course that meant big switches on the gun, continual relaying and training and an unstable platform. Conditions for gunnery were appalling. Another salvo burst frighteningly close and he hung on and shot desperate glances fore and aft but he knew they had not been hit. He would not need the evidence of his eyes for that. When they were hit they would know about it, that had been made clear to all of them.

Aitkyne said, "They're shooting very well."

"Yes, they are." And they were alive to his tactics of evasion and trying to anticipate him.

He ordered no change of course. The Coxswain on the wheel waited for it, ready for it, shifted restlessly when it did not come.

Corporal Hill, muttering under his breath, expecting it, found instead that his target was in sight for all of ten seconds and the 9.2 got off a round.

The next salvo plunged into the sea a quarter-mile away and Aitkyne yelled, "Fooled 'em!" And seconds later: "Hit her!"

Smith had seen it, too. He lowered his glasses. "Hard aport!" And to Aitkyne and Wakely and the others, all of them agrin, "Not a hit." The water-spout had been right on the bow of the leading cruiser but there had been no flash or smoke of impact. A very near miss. "But good shooting." A little encouragement would be good for all of them.

The sun was almost down, slipping below the horizon. The coast was close now but not close enough. *Ariadne* was a deal closer and her lead being cut every second; *Thunder* was making all of her top speed of nineteen knots so Chief Davies had proved his claim albeit under duress. Smith estimated *Ariadne* would not enter neutral waters for at least fifteen minutes and more. Before that they would be up with her and the cruisers might well allot her a share of their fire. At the moment they were concentrating on *Thunder*, their prime target. He had another decision to make, and soon.

The sea was moderating and the ship was making better speed. Down in the belly of the ship where that speed was created was a scene from hell where the black gang in the stokehold, stripped near-naked and oily with sweat that formed a glue with the coal dust, laboured like souls in tor-

147

ment to feed the roaring insatiable red maw of the furnaces. The life of the ship and the lives of all in her rested in the hands and strength of those men on the rack of continual physical exertion. There was no glory, only back-breaking labour in a killing temperature and the knowledge that at any moment a shell might rip into *Thunder* and turn the illusion of hell into reality.

There were places in the ship where that awareness was even more acute: in the magazines. Benks the steward worked in the magazine below the forward 9.2, his job to load the charge into the gun-loading cage beside the projectile fat with death, to be whisked up the hoist to the turret above. It was not heavy work and anyway, so far he had done nothing; the fore-turret had not fired. But it was claustrophobic. He sweated coldly.

He had waited, strung taut inside for the inevitable hit. When it came right above him the shock tore at those taut nerves. He had heard stories, only too many. *Invincible* was a battle-cruiser, twice the size of *Thunder*, but at Jutland she had taken a shell amidships, in the magazine there, and she broke in half and sank like a stone. The middle was blasted out of her. Where the magazine was. Just obliterated. Nothing left of anything, anybody.

He lifted his face, turning it up to heaven and the sky but he saw only the thick steel above his head that sealed him in. He prayed.

Thunder twisted her old frame at thrashing full speed, swerving, heavily jinking, like some lumbering old nanny puffily playing tag with her charges. But effectively. Barely effectively. The cruisers astern had her range and were firing well, very well indeed. Time and again only the change of course hauled *Thunder* clear of a falling salvo, sometimes seeming to pull in her skirts as the towers of water rose right alongside or astern. At times she seemed to steam through a forest of tall trees, dark green in the trunk and blossoming dirty grey, through a fog of spray. So that Ballard in *Ariadne* cursed and held his breath, to whoosh! it out and curse again as she came through trailing her black plume of smoke.

She bore a charmed life; or maybe she had a wizard on the bridge. On the bridge they thought so as they braced against the heel and turn, tensed not only to ride that but for the orders that Smith gave curtly, absorbed. They lived from second to second and he gave them each second and they knew it. They were naked on the bridge.

He had to make his decision. The luck was running out as the range closed. Knight said, "They're firing their secondary armament, sir."

"Yes."

The fire had intensified. Now added to the four 8.2s that each cruiser fired were the two 5.9s that would bear forward in this stern chase. *Thunder* could reply only with the after 9.2, her elderly six-inch being still out of range. Just. But soon . . .

The coast was close but so was *Ariadne*, very close, with a hundred and thirty souls aboard her. Sunset was upon them, the darkness rushing in over the sea. Smith watched and gave his orders. They had to give *Ariadne* a little more time, or let her take her chance, which would be miserable because she was a huge and fragile target. And *Thunder's* chances? Throughout the ship they would be mentally hunched against the continual salvoes they braved and could do nothing about. Chafing. Wanting to hit back, make a fight of it. That would be a madness, an invitation to disaster. But now . . .

Smith snapped, "Hard astarboard!" and *Thunder's* bow swung and this time kept on swinging until, when he ordered, "Midships!" she ran at a right angle to her previous course and that of the pursuit. The turrets were already drumming as they trained round. And the sun was down. Smith took a breath. Now then. *"Broadsides!"*

Thunder still charged along at her maximum nineteen knots

149

but she was running straight. She still belched smoke from the labour of the gasping, sweating stokers but now it rolled away to port on the wind and at last the layers and trainers could see. The sun was down, no longer sending shafts of blinding light directly into their eyes, but leaving instead just a red afterglow against which the pursuing cruisers stood out stark, clear black silhouettes, beautiful targets for gunners and the rangefinder.

She left one more salvo plummeting into her wake as the guns rose and fell like a blind man's questing fingers but *Thunder* was no longer blind. The long barrels steadied and an instant later the salvo bells rang and the broadside crashed out in tongues of flame and jetting smoke. *Thunder* heeled to it, recovered as the guns had already recoiled. The ammunition numbers in turrets and casemates shoved forward with projectiles as the breeches clanged open, the fumes swirled and the gun-loading cages rattled empty down the hoists. Shells were rammed, charges inserted, breeches closed, trainers and layers spun madly at their wheels then slowly as the sights came on. The layers' fingers went to the triggers.

Thunder fired again, heeled again.

Wakely said, "They're turning, sir, turning broadside."

Smith nodded. The cruisers were matching his manoeuvre to return broadside for broadside. It was what he expected and Garrick in the fore-top would be expecting it. The cruisers could fire twelve 8.2s and six 5.9s to *Thunder*'s two 9.2s and two six-inch, because the main-deck guns could not be fired in this sea even if they had been manned. The cruisers had an overwhelming advantage in firepower, but they were no longer closing the range. That was what he wanted.

He let the glasses hang, resting his eyes, and thrust his hands into his pockets. Oddly, while the engines hammered and the broadsides thundered out, while somewhere above him only seconds away the cruisers' monstrous salvoes fell towards him, he could relax. For just this breathing space he had no orders to give. Now it was up to the gunnery jack,

Garrick, and the long chain of men that stretched down from him in the fore-top to the layers with their fingers on the triggers. He had given them a target they could see and a stable platform.

He had given *Ariadne* time.

Given? Nothing was free. Somebody would have to pay.

Thunder got off three broadsides and two salvoes fell in return, one short but close, briefly interfering with vision, one very short. They were laddering, of course, in *Wolf* and *Kondor,* one salvo below the rangefinder range, one at it, one over. The third would be over – or a hit. This clicked through his mind as that second salvo hurled water at the darkening sky and as *Thunder*'s broadside heeled her again and the flashes of the cruisers' salvoes rippled with awful beauty along the black silhouettes.

"Hard aport! Turn sixteen points!" *Thunder* heeled again but this time turning in her tracks to plunge back along her course as the turrets hammered around and the crews of the two six-inch guns on the port side, not engaged thus far, hitched at their trousers and licked their lips as they held on against the sudden cant of the deck.

The salvo came down on the port quarter, where *Thunder* would have been but for the violent change of course, but one rogue shell burst so close that the hammer blow was felt through the hull. Corporal Hill felt it in the after-turret and swore, but just the continual cursing he had kept up since the action started, either angry or happy, now frustrated at the change of course when they had the bastards dead to rights for once ...

Benks felt it in the magazine and quivered.

Thunder steadied on her new course.

In the fore-top Garrick was a professionally exalted man. He had his problems; there was still some smoke and the way in which the entire ship vibrated to the pounding of her engines and the thumping discharge of her broadsides made use of the big, mounted spotting equipment a waste of time.

The images shivered to that vibration. Instead he did his spotting shifting around the fore-top with a pair of binoculars.

The rangetaker muttered under his breath at the vibration. The rangefinder with its twin lenses gave him two images of the target and by twiddling the adjusting screw he could make the two coincide and at that point read the range. The vibration set the images dancing. "Bloody hell! He's like to run them engines right through t'bottom. Wish they could come here and have a fist at it. Hold *still* yer daft cow!"

But he was reading ranges.

Garrick was a happy man. He had a good target at last and his guns were shooting well. He also noted with professional appreciation that the enemy cruisers were firing well. He could not judge the 'overs' that fell somewhere behind him but the 'shorts' were well together with little spread. It was good shooting, frighteningly good. He was aware also that *Thunder* was a broadside target and that the zone of the guns firing at him might be anything up to two hundred yards ; that is, that a shell aimed incorrectly to fall short of *Thunder* by a hundred yards or more might still carry and hit her. Hit him.

In a momentary fleeting glance he saw Smith, hands in pockets, out on the wing of the bridge.

Broadside.

Smith lifted the glasses again to watch for its fall as the salvo dropped into the sea well astern.

Wakely said tentatively, "Their shooting's going off a bit, sir."

"No." Smith's eyes were clamped to the glasses. "He's having trouble seeing us." The glow behind the cruisers was dying but they were still clear against it while, to them, *Thunder* must be a ship lost in the darkness, only a black pall of smoke against the black background of the coast and the night sky. They were still shooting very well.

Wakely yelped, "A hit!"

"Yes!" Smith saw the flash on the leading cruiser that was not the flash of a gun, and a second later the thread of smoke that was not instantly shredded and blown away like the gunsmoke; this smoke trailed on.

But the salvo rippled again down the silhouette.

Thunder fired.

Knight called, "Signal from *Ariadne*, sir. 'Am in Chilean waters under escort.' Looks like a Chilean destroyer lying off there, sir, lit up like a Christmas tree!"

Smith swung on his heel, staring. He could barely make out the bulk of *Ariadne* but the other ship was easy to see. Possibly she made it more difficult to see *Ariadne* because she herself was a blaze of light. A Chilean destroyer.

Aitkyne said, "She's not taking any chances of somebody dropping one on her by mistake."

And Wakely reported, "Enemy's turning, sir."

Smith swung back. The black silhouettes were blurring now as the last of the light went but they had foreshortened, were again pointing at him, again in pursuit trying desperately to close the range. They, too, had seen the Chilean ship and knew what her presence signified. They fired.

As did *Thunder*.

Smith rubbed at his face. *Ariadne* was safe. He stared around him, at the wake creaming phosphorescent in the dusk, the dark ship. Black humping sea and black sky, tongues of orange flame, the ensign snapping a pale blur against the smoke that swirled down from the four funnels and rolled away downwind, mixing with the acrid grey-yellow of the gunsmoke. The last glow almost gone from the distant rim of the ocean, the cruisers almost lost.

One more broadside. These men of his had earned that.

He saw the cruisers' winking fire and then *Thunder*'s broadside heeled her for the last time. As the echoes crashed away in a concussion of air, Smith ordered, "Starboard ten! Cease firing!" The cruisers were no longer a target, hardly seen.

153

The only way they would see *Thunder* would be from the flashes of her guns. He would not give them that opportunity.

He watched for the fall of that last broadside.

The cruisers' landed first. The familiar spouts rose off the port quarter but the shells that counted were the ones that hit them. There was a blinding burst of livid flame, and shock that sent him grabbing for handhold. He caught at his balance, recovered it and gaped aft. There was smoke but not a great deal, abaft the bridge but wisping away on the wind so he could see beyond the bite taken out of the port quarter, but no flames. The unmistakable long figure of Miles ran aft with huge strides, his filthy damage control party at his heels.

Smith thought he should have turned sooner and not hung on for that last broadside. He lifted the glasses, looking for it.

Aitkyne shouted, "Hit her, by God!"

Smith saw the winking yellow flash on the cruiser to port, right forward, the ship seen in that one camera-blink of light, then almost lost in the darkness as the night swept down over the sea. But flames flickered, tiny with distance, again. She had a fire.

Aitkyne crowed, "Gave 'em a bloody nose to remember us by! Ha!"

A seaman, soot-smeared and running with sweat, panted up the bridge ladder. "Mr. Miles, sir, says two hits, fire's out, wireless office wrecked but no casualties." A grin: "Sparks was away for a run-off when it 'it. An' no serious damage aft."

Smith took a deep breath and let it out. Thank God for that. He felt the tension running out of him, the excitement draining away and taking the nervous strength with it. They had been lucky. God! How lucky! He wondered if the rest of them really knew how lucky . . .

They came abreast of the Chilean destroyer lying in her pool of light and he saw her name: *Tocopilla*. There were plenty

154

of men on her deck. One yell came across the gap, the words incomprehensible, then another voice, authoritative, cut it short. The first voice had been jeering.

Aitkyne asked, "What was that?"

Smith knew very well. *Thunder* was unpopular here and now she was being chased into hiding. He ignored the question. "Revolutions for five knots."

Thunder's speed fell away. She was opening the channel now. *Ariadne* lay ahead of them, dawdling, Beyond her, to port were the lights of the signalling station. *Thunder* ran down on *Ariadne* whose rails were crowded with crew and passengers and as *Thunder* slid past, smoke-blackened, torn, filthy, they cheered her.

Thunder's decks were alive with men now, swarming like bees, wide-eyed and short of breath but they returned the cheers wildly and kept on cheering when *Ariadne* was left astern.

Their faces were turned up to the bridge.

Smith realised they were cheering him.

Garrick was down from the fore-top, grinning at Smith, who thought Garrick would have slapped his back if he dared. Aitkyne and Wakely and Knight, all of them on the bridge wore the same drunken grin. Smith thought that they had settled the colliers, brought *Ariadne* safe to port, rescued at least some of the people from the luckless *Elizabeth Bell* and fought a long action against a faster and vastly superior force. They had survived to fight again, were legally entitled to shelter in this port for twenty-four hours and *Kunashiri* joined them on the morrow. They had a lot to be pleased about.

He felt sick and his hands were starting to shake as they always did at this time. He jammed them in his pockets. He wanted his voice to be casual but it came out harsh and abrupt. "I'm going below, Number One. Set the men to work on the damage." At the head of the ladder he paused to say, "And well done."

155

He saw Garrick's expression had changed and that a messenger was with him. Garrick said, "Report of a casualty, sir."

"Yes."

"Not reported before because it wasn't really at the point where we were hit, the second one I mean, aft."

Garrick was rambling. Smith, desperate to be away, to find a few moments of solitude, of peace, snapped irritably, "Get to the point, man!"

"One of the loaders in the port after six-inch collapsed from fumes and they brought him out to take him down to the sick-bay. That was when we were hit. There were three of them, the man himself and two carrying him. This section of plate must have richocheted and passed them by inches and flew in the open door of the casemate." Smith stared at Garrick as he fumbled for words. "A chance in a million, sir. Young Somers . . ." Then he put it brutally simply, finding no other words for it. "It cut him in half."

"Signal from the shore station, sir." Smith became slowly aware of Knight, speaking his piece, repeating it for the third time to an unheeding Smith. He realised he still stood, half-turned at the head of the ladder. Knight's face was drawn like Garrick's and he read the message to Smith: *"Kunashiri* in collision two hundred miles north. Entered dock for repairs, estimated two days."

Smith said mechanically, "Very good. Acknowledge."

He turned and descended the ladder.

Somers.

That last hit aft. If he had turned away before . . .

Two days for *Kunashiri*'s repairs and then she would still be near a day's steaming away. She might as well be on the moon for any help she could be to *Thunder*. In twenty-four hours she would have to face the cruisers again, and alone.

They had cheered, those men of his because if they had not won at least they had not been beaten, they had survived.

Survived to be smashed to pieces.

It was as if he had climbed a mountain only to find he stood on the edge of an abyss.

There was a marine sentry at the door of his cabin who said, "Begging your pardon, sir – " And even lifted a hand. Smith snarled, "Get out of my way." He thrust past and burst into the cabin.

Sarah Benson was in there, though for a moment he did not recognise her. A heap of clothing lay on his table and a blanket on the deck. She was rubbing at her hair with a towel. She wore that barbaric medallion on the thin gold chain, it dangled, sparking light, in the valley between the taut-drawn breasts and that was all she wore.

IO

SARAH BENSON'S ARMS snapped down, spreading the towel before her, clutching it to her. Her hair hung stringy and tangled and the first sound she made as she moved was a squeak but then she shouted outrage and arrogance at Smith. "*What are you doing here!*"

Smith gaped at her, choked but finally grated out, "This is my cabin." Then all the pent-up strains and tensions took brief and furious charge. "*Get dressed, woman, and get off my ship!*"

He flung out of the cabin and charged away, oblivious of the wooden-faced sentry and unaware of the whistling blow-out of that sentry's breath: "Strewth!"

Smith strode the upper deck until he walked the rage away and they kept out of his way. He had blown off steam. He was sick at Somers's death and bitter over the *Kunashiri* but these were facts to be faced. He had a duty.

He went to the sick-bay and Albrecht greeted him with, "Oh, sir. The girl we picked up from *Elizabeth Bell*. Purkiss dug up some clothes for her, stuff that she left behind; she went over the side at Malaguay at short notice." Purkiss was the sick-berth rating. Albrecht went on: "I put her in your cabin to get dressed. Hope you don't mind, but there was nowhere else, a lot of the cabins are in a mess and I could hardly ask . . ."

Smith grunted.

Albrecht was relieved. He had heard of Smith's baleful pacing and the reasons for it. He would not have been surprised to have his head chewed off. He said, "She's in good shape, sir."

Smith snapped a sharp look at him. What was behind that remark? But it was impossible that Albrecht should know — yet. But he would, because Smith could not, or would not, order that sentry to hold his tongue so it would be all over the ship in no time. Then the humour of it struck him and Albrecht saw his bleak-faced Captain suddenly break into a grin.

"Have I said something funny, sir?"

"Wait and see, Doctor, wait and see." Smith got down to business. "What have you got?"

"One crushed finger and two cases of mild concussion. That's the crew. The crushed finger has returned to light duty and the concussion cases will be all right after a night's sleep. There are five survivors if you include the girl. One deck officer and three deck-hands. Shock, all of them. Except that girl. She's tough."

A picture of her standing in the cabin rose in his mind. Tough? He came back to the matter in hand. He saw the cases of concussion and the survivors and spoke to them briefly. To his crew: "Well done." To the survivors: condolences, awkward sympathy and a promise to get them ashore and into hospital as soon as possible. The officer was a tubby little man of fifty-odd, balding, with big hands that clasped and unclasped. "Poor old George. Our skipper, you know. Due for his pension, only stayed on because of the war. Bloody shame." His plump cheeks sagged miserably. The hands would not stay still.

Smith said, "I am very sorry."

"Not your fault, sir. Nobody could ha' done more than you did. It was just bad luck."

Thackeray, that twisted, bitter man was not among the survivors.

He paused for a final word with Albrecht. 'Thanks, Doctor. It's a funny sort of war for you."

"Funny?"

Smith corrected hastily. "I should say, strange. Being shot at by your former countrymen."

"Ah!" Albrecht nodded and smiled thinly. "I suppose there is a certain ironic humour about it. And it is conceivable there might be a distant relative of mine out there now." He paused, then added bitterly, "They'll be gloating, I suppose."

Smith shook his head. "Not them. Exhilarated, yes, like our chaps are, but for slightly different reasons. Their commander will be annoyed that he did not sink us. But not gloating. They are brave, determined men. They know that they can never get home, that at the end of the day they will be hunted down and destroyed. That makes them even more dangerous. There can be no turning back for them."

"And us?"

"Nothing has changed, Doctor."

Albrecht stared after his retreating back. Nothing changed? They were no longer discussing hypothetical situations: *if* the cruisers existed, *if* they appeared.

Thunder was caught in Guaya like a rat in a trap.

Smith returned to the deck. *Thunder* cruised steadily up the deep-water channel past the little scatters of lights that marked villages. The ship was not darkened now. Garrick had lights rigged forward and aft and men milled in urgent, disciplined confusion. He encountered Wakely. "I want the fires lit in the pinnace, Mr. Wakely, ready to put her in the water as soon as we anchor."

"Already seen to that, sir. Manton thought you might want the puncher."

"Good."

Both forward and aft the damage was at first sight horrendous, as it always was, as it might be expected from the blows of eight-inch projectiles of two-hundred-and-forty pounds apiece. Forward a hole gaped in the deck and below it the mess-deck was a devastated area, filthy with soot from the fire, dripping with water. Aft a huge bite had been taken out of deck and side. There was a great deal of work to be done, most of it ultimately dockyard work, but there was nothing that could not be patched by *Thunder*'s crew well enough to render her a fully effective unit, appearances notwithstanding. He found the work well in hand, which he had a right to expect, but when he ran into Garrick he made a point of saying, clearly and loudly, with a score of men in earshot: "Very good, Number One. The ship's company have behaved in very satisfactory fashion." It sounded pompous to Smith as he said it but it could not be called back and Garrick seemed pleased, as did the men who listened.

He passed Somers's gun, saw the door of the casemate hooked open and inside a section of the deck that had recently been washed down and sprinkled with sand.

Garrick said, "Chaps are in good spirits, sir."

Smith nodded. He was keenly aware of it, had been watching them, catching at the tone of a voice, the quick reaction to orders, the general air of them. They were working hard and cheerfully. Joking. There was occasional laughter, some of it a little high-pitched, still excited, but laughter.

Then they rounded the turn in the channel and opened the port and the pool. Smith took his ship into port and to her anchorage, performing the evolution neatly with his usual insistence that a job be well done, but with only a part of his mind. He was preoccupied with the thought that his ship was not welcome here. A reminder was there in the way the masts of the *Gerda* poked out of the water at an angle where she had settled on her side on the bottom. They would be attacked, not with crude force but certainly in diplomatic terms.

He was not inclined to wait for that attack. So that as *Thunder* anchored, the telegraph rang 'stop engines', and the derrick yanked the pinnace up and over the side, he said, "I'm going ashore."

"Yes, sir," replied Garrick, then asked, "Do you think they'll follow us in?"

Midshipman Vincent was on the bridge. Smith saw his startled glance and grinned. "Hadn't thought of that? They have as much right to come in as we have." He thought: And may well be more welcome. Then he said definitely, "But they won't." He did not explain.

Garrick followed him down to the entry port. "You're going alone, sir? Do you want Knight as interpreter?"

"No." Smith did not explain that, either, but the Port Captain would make his feelings clear enough without an interpreter and it would be unpleasant so he would go alone.

It was night, now. Darkness clothed and hid the hills but the town twinkled with a thousand yellow cats-eyes of lit windows. Half-a-dozen ships lay in the pool but *Kansas* loomed over them all. They were strung with lights, their decks crowded. The picket-boat, at Smith's order headed for the quay above which lay the house of the Port Captain. The quay was lit by one big lamp and he could see a crowd there, too. He stood quiet, still, alongside Wakely who had the helm.

The cruisers waited for him outside and there would be no help from the battle-cruiser, no help from anyone. His choice was to fight them or be interned. Suicide or surrender.

He had coal for only twenty-four hours' steaming.

They ran in on the quay. Two boats already lay there, tied-up clear of the steps. One belonged to the Chilean Admiral, the other to *Kansas*. *Thunder*'s pinnace slipped between them and Smith climbed the steps. At their head he found the crowd and in the forefront stood a little party.

There were several women, all in evening dress, hair piled, bejewelled, gaudy as parrakeets against the men. They were also in evening dress or full-dress uniform, black or navy-blue. The Chilean Admiral and the American, Donoghue. And Donoghue's Flag-Captain and two young men who were obviously the respective Chilean and American Flag-Lieutenants. All of them glittered with decorations.

He saluted and smiled at them all. "Good evening. I seem to have interrupted a party. I'm sorry." Like every other man in *Thunder*, soot streaked his face and his eyes were red-rimmed and stared. He presented a startling contrast to the group he faced.

Encalada, the Port Captain, fluent in English, almost choked at that opening remark. The Chilean Admiral had not understood a word but he scowled at Smith nevertheless. For a moment Encalada was bereft of speech and the American Flag-Lieutenant slipped into the gap. "If I may be permitted, sir, I have some knowledge of Spanish."

His Spanish was excellent and he made the introductions. One of the party was Herr Doktor Muller, the German Consul, tall and stiff, bald and hook-nosed. The Flag-Lieutenant rolled off the titles in English and Spanish spectacularly: "Contra Almirante Gualcalda, the Navy of Chile, Rear-Admiral Donoghue, United States Navy, Captain Encalada ..."

Smith thought he had done his homework.

The Flag-Lieutenant came to the end of the titles and the ranks, the long, aristocratic-sounding names. Then he stumbled, "And Commander – " Only then he realised he did not know the name.

Smith supplied it for him, tersely. "Smith."

And Donoghue remarked on that contrast, too, and grinned to himself. He said, "You didn't exactly interrupt. We were having dinner when we heard the firing, but in the tradition of Drake we finished the meal. Then we came down to see what we could." His eyes moved from Smith to *Thunder* lying in a circle of light out in the pool, aswarm with men. Through the hole torn in her side he could see the men labouring, tiny figures inside the smashed and mangled interior. His eyes moved back to Smith.

One more contrast. Donoghue was tall and broad-shouldered, deep-chested, strongly handsome. An aristocrat. He could trace his family back three hundred years to a house in New England and before that to a castle in Ireland. It was a family that had always held rank, in the last hundred years it had enjoyed rank and privilege and wealth. It was now considerable wealth.

Smith had nothing but his pay. No family.

Donoghue saw a slight, young man, too thin, the face drawn. He cut a frail and lonely figure as he faced them all. And yet – there was something about the man, a restlessness, an energy that could be sensed even now when he stood unmoving.

They had a great deal in common and they eyed each other warily.

Donoghue said, "I see you brought your consort safe to port."

"*Ariadne*? Yes. But we lost a merchantman, the *Elizabeth Bell*. She was hit and sank in minutes. I'm glad I was able to take off some of her crew before she sank, but the others were lost."

Donoghue thought about it. So did his Flag-Captain, Corrigan, lean and vinegar-faced, vinegar-tongued, puritan. Smith had been able to take some off before she sank? Both of them thought there was a deal left unsaid.

But that saw the end of the courtesies. Encalada asked, "What is your business here, Captain?" His face was set. He was angry, or rather still angry. Forty-eight hours before he had been outraged.

This was the attack Smith had come to meet. He met it coolly. "I escorted *Ariadne* to this port. As you know and

164

can see, I have been in action and I need to make repairs and coal – "

Encalada brushed that aside with a wave of his hand. "Your presence here is effrontery!"

"My presence here is of necessity, I assure you."

"You have flagrantly violated the neutrality of this port!"

"This port had harboured a belligerent for – "

"That has *not* been proved."

The Herr Doktor put in quickly, "I reiterate, neither my government nor myself accept responsibility for the collier, whose ever she was."

Smith rapped at him, "Responsibility or no, the *Gerda* was a belligerent and that was proved by the action of her sister ship, the *Maria*. She ran when I approached Malaguay." Muller smiled thinly, and shrugged. Smith said, "I caught her and sank her." This time the Doktor's eyes flickered, his head twitched on his neck. Small signs but enough for Smith, who went on, "And before she sank I intercepted signals between her and a German warship and two German cruisers lie outside this port now. That is a *fact*, Herr Doktor." He swung on Encalada. "As was also the matter of the *Leopard*, a German gunboat supposed to be interned at Malaguay but allowed to slip away to fight again and *she* is outside now! What kind of neutrality is *that*?"

"Do not lecture *me*!" Encalada shouted it. He swallowed, took hold of himself and said more quietly, "She was not allowed to slip away. She escaped because of gross negligence and indiscipline on the part of one junior officer and he will be dealt with. And that gunboat's violation of neutrality does not excuse yours, which preceded theirs and I believe made theirs possible. Cruisers there are but I refuse to accept their presence as proof that *Gerda* was a belligerent." He took a breath. "I tell you this, Captain. Under International Law you may claim shelter in this port for twenty-four hours to make your repairs. That you may have, but nothing else. You will not be permitted to land nor to receive supplies of any kind, coal, water – *nothing!*"

Smith said equably, "Very well." He would not beg. No, that was a lie. He would have begged for his ship and his crew if it would have done any good. But they did not need water or supplies. He had coal for only twenty-four hours' steaming but that was sufficient because he would not be allowed to steam for twenty-four hours or anything like it. The cruisers waiting out in the darkness of the Pacific would see to that.

Encalada took his watch from his pocket and clicked open the case. "The time is twenty-one-ten hours. At this time tomorrow you will get under way and quit this port."

"That is understood. I ask for nothing, except – "

"No exceptions!"

Smith carried on as if he had not heard. "There is a boy – a man – I must bury. He was killed in today's action."

Encalada stared at him. Smith's face was grey under the lights, a tired face, a hard face, closed now, seeming to give nothing away, yet the Port Captain felt the stirring of an alien sympathy. But he kept his voice hard as he replied. "I see. That will be permitted but only a small party, the minimum necessary for due honours. Officers may wear swords, but other arms will not be permitted."

"That, too, is understood." Smith thought there might be an element of sympathy lurking in the eyes of Donoghue and Corrigan. It was obvious in their Flag-Lieutenant but his seniors were an impassive pair. The Port Captain's fire and fury had turned to ice. Muller looked pleased.

The idea floated, bizarre, into Smith's mind and he acted on it before cold propriety could make it look ridiculous as it was. He said straight-faced, apologetic but patently sincere, "I'm afraid I've spoiled a very pleasant evening for many of you. In normal times I would have extended the hospitality of my ship, at least to attempt to make some recompense, but these are not normal times. However. Despite the times my officers and myself will be taking tea tomorrow afternoon and we would be delighted to welcome all of you. At, say, four in the afternoon?" Then he added, "With, of course, one obvious exception." He grinned at Muller.

Those who understood him looked suspicious, as if this was some sort of practical joke, or like Encalada suspecting a trap, but not Donoghue and Corrigan. As Smith saluted and went down into the pinnace Donoghue thought it was almost an actor's exit. An unusual young man. Corrigan wasn't going to drink their goddam tea, but he wanted to look at that ship and her crew.

The pinnace sheered off and headed out towards *Thunder*, still functioning with a jaunty efficiency despite the dents in her stumpy funnel and her woodwork down one side showing charred-black through the blistered paint. Smith took off his cap and ran his fingers through his hair. Donoghue became aware that the women were a-twitter and gazing after the pinnace and he thought with surprise: Well, now.

Smith said, "They've given us twenty-four hours and at the end of that we sail. That's all they'll give us. No coal, no supplies, no assistance – nothing. It simplifies matters, anyway."

Garrick breathed heavily. "They know what's waiting for us outside and they'll send us out with barely enough coal – "

"It will be enough."

"Damn their bloody eyes!"

Smith blinked at this explosion from the stolid First Lieutenant, and said mildly, "You can't blame them, you know. On the facts as they see them, as they know them, they're more than justified."

Vincent called, "Boat coming alongside, sir."

It was Cherry, and Smith took him to the little sleeping cabin under the bridge. There was a certain amount of peace there. The deck cabin aft and the main cabin in the stern would be ringing like great bells to the hammering.

"I didn't see you at the party."

"No." Cherry shrugged. "The British are in bad odour at the moment. But I heard and saw your meeting with Encalada."

"Oh?"

Cherry nodded. "Twenty-four hours. And the rest of it. I'll intercede and protest, of course. As soon as I'm ashore I'll telegraph to Santiago, but frankly, I think their government will back him up."

"So do I."

Cherry said helplessly, "Well, is there *anything* I can do?"

Smith grinned sardonically, "You couldn't rent *Kansas* for a couple of days?"

Cherry refused to be cheered and muttered, "And that damn battle-cruiser. Of all the luck!"

"One or two ways you can help —"

"Yes?"

Somers. They discussed the matter in practical terms and Cherry said he would see to all the necessary arrangements. "Anything else?"

"Newspapers, as always. Any English papers you can get hold of, we'll be delighted to see."

"Can do."

"And last, but most important, the *Gerda*. The Chileans regard my action as indefensible, but if I can *prove* she was German they might change that to excusable."

Cherry nodded agreement. "No doubt of it. They'd still hum and haw and they'd want an apology but the sting would be gone. Their old-fashioned looks would all be for the Herr Doktor." He went on, "All her crew were in one hotel for one night only. Next day they were gone. I never had a chance to talk to any of them. I've sent word to Argentina but when, if, they find out anything there, it'll be too late. I reckon the skipper might be in the German consulate but the others tucked away somewhere up-country, maybe on somebody's farm so I went out and scratched around but had

168

no luck. I was on the way back tonight when I heard the guns."

Smith told Cherry the details of the boarding and sinking of the *Gerda* and the papers they had taken from her. "Somewhere aboard that ship there must be proof. Has a diver been down?"

Cherry shook his head, puzzled. "No. One of my men has been watching her. Nobody's been near her." He finished definitely, "But tomorrow I'll see somebody goes down. If the proof is there we'll have it."

Cherry left, on his way to see Sarah Benson.

She was aboard *Ariadne* in a cabin of a comfortable size with a comfortable bunk. It called to her but she walked the deck away from its temptation and waited for Cherry, knowing he would come.

Smith had left her open-mouthed and speechless but when she went to Albrecht her protest was blistering. She received an icy reply, an apology, but: "The man didn't know you were there for a start. He'd just fought a difficult and dangerous action, he's been driven into a corner and there's no help for him and he risked his ship to save yourself and a few more. On top of that he'd just learned that the boy who dragged you off the *Elizabeth Bell* had been killed. He may owe you an apology. You owe him a damned sight more than that, young lady."

She had swallowed it, digested it, then meekly asked for more and he had told her about the desperate shortage of coal and about *Kunashiri*.

Now while she waited for Cherry she thought hard and when he came aboard he gave her more to think about. He told her what he had told Smith, was silent a moment, then said quietly, "They've given him just twenty-four hours. That's all. But mark you, he didn't ask for that. He asked for nothing. I was in the crowd and I saw him. He couldn't see me, but, by God I saw him! Stood there on his own, coated in filth

169

and dead beat, eyes like – like windows in a dark room with a fire back in there, somewhere." He paused, then said self-consciously, "Well, that must have been a trick of the light but that's how it looked. Stood there with his head up . . . One man." He shook his head. "That's an extraordinary man. Extraordinary."

He asked her what had happened and she told him about the seaplane and Jim Bradley and Thackeray, but she was abstracted, merely reporting, her mind elsewhere.

There was a silence and he glanced at her. "Was it very bad?" He had to repeat the question before she heard it and then she looked at him blankly. He said, "On the ship – *Thunder*, I mean."

She shuddered. "It sounded like all hell let loose. It – " She stopped. "I can't describe it." But she could hear it and see it and she shuddered again.

They had set Gibb to work with the others in the clanging bedlam forward and every hammer blow was a nerve-wrenching echo of the hits on *Thunder*. There was no peace. And once he had found Rattray's eyes on him and knew that Rattray only waited his time. Gibb walked away from it.

He needed solitude and he could only think of one place in the ship where he would find it. He slunk around and into the fore-turret and in the airless steel gloom he found the solitude of a cell. Light came in faint bands through narrow slits set high and reflected dully from the massive breech of the gun. There was the smell of oil and steel and the residual tang of burnt cordite that still clung from the recent action. He sniffed it, as he had sniffed the baking smell when he opened his mother's front door but that was only an aching memory now. He felt hounded, bedevilled and the turret shut him in but there was nowhere else to go. He squatted on the deck under the breech of the gun, arms round his drawn-up knees, head down, eyes closed trying to blot it all out.

Rattray. It was quiet in the turret, there was that at least to be said for it and for the first time in hours his thoughts found some clarity. Or maybe it was only the crystallisation of one emotion from many. But he hated Rattray. He was no longer puzzled by, or wary of, or frightened by Rattray. Now it was one single, simple emotion: hate. And at that point light flicked briefly over him where he crouched in the gloom, a second's searching beam of the light from outside that lit him up and then was gone. The door had quietly opened, clanged shut. Gibb blinked and focussed on the figure that stood smacking right fist into the palm of the left hand.

Rattray.

He took two long strides to stand over Gibb and he said with savage anticipation, "Home from home. Just you and me and a bit of peace and quiet where we can sort things out without a lot of interference from nosey parkers, nor your God Almighty Captain Smith." The words meant nothing to Gibb.

Rattray reached down and grabbed Gibb by the front of his overalls, lifted him from his hiding place under the breech of the gun and swung him out. Gibb came slackly, stumbling, and Rattray thought there was something odd about his vacant stare, not showing fear, not showing anything. So he hesitated for a second with one hand gripping Gibb, the other pulled back, and in that second he saw Gibb's face contort beyond recognition. It was a fatal second.

Gibb exploded in his hands. Gibb himself could never recall the few seconds that followed. It was a moment of black-out for his mind that under torment and stress briefly ran away from its duties. The body functioned on its own. It functioned without the meagre advantage of the little boxing science the Navy had striven to teach him.

Rattray's own recollections were confused and curtailed. A flailing fist took him in the eye and another in the lower abdomen, a boot smashed against his right shin and knocked that prop from under him. Almost blinded, hurt and staggering he instinctively tried to hold on to something, anything.

171

He held on to Gibb, clawing blindly now with the right hand and getting that also twisted in Gibb's overalls. That was the second and final mistake. If he had fallen or hurriedly backed away he may have gained a breathing space both for himself and Gibb that might have brought hesitation to the latter or let his wildly flailing fists connect on nothing but air. But he held on, right on top of Gibb, within easy reach and vulnerable.

A fist hit him between the legs with excruciating agony, crippling. It was finished at that point but Gibb did not know it any more than he knew what he was doing. Another fist slammed into Rattray's windpipe, choking, and another boot kicked his right leg away for good. Or ill. He had released Gibb, trying to curl over to hold himself and was falling, for an instant free of those thrashing fists and feet. Then his back banged against the breech of the gun and he bounced from it into another hail of blows and kicks that landed at first on his body and then, as he fell, on his face and head. He was already unconscious and toppled back limply, loose as an empty coal sack, tossed one way then the other as Gibb's blows thrust him. He ended on his back, his head and shoulders propped awkwardly against the side of the turret.

Gibb had nothing to hit. The curtain lifted and he was first aware of pain in his hands. He lifted them and saw the knuckles skinned and oozing tiny beads of blood. He put them to his mouth, sucking, and then he saw Rattray. He stared, with the thick, sick, salt of his own blood in his mouth, retched and ran blindly from the turret.

He stumbled aft along the boat-deck away from the light and the milling crowd of labouring men forward. But another crowd worked aft and he swung away and brought up against the rails, staring at the lights of Guaya.

Rattray was dead and Gibb had killed him.

Voices shouted hoarsely in the clamour forward, sounding like a pack at his heels but the water moved oily black below him. He went over the rail and dived. He would have dived from the masthead if he had to.

There was a crowd on the waterfront staring at *Thunder* out in the pool so he had to swim a long way downriver before he could drag himself out of the water without being seen. He was an excellent swimmer. He skulked across the quay and into the shelter of an alley, found a dark corner and collapsed there. The water ran off him. He sat with his knees curled tight under his chin and shuddered spasmodically.

Now at least he had quiet but he knew he had to have shelter, to get away from prying eyes. He had never been in Fizzy's out-of-bounds Bar but he knew where it was. He made his way through the alleys until he found the rear of Fizzy's Bar and climbed the wall to drop down into the urinal. From there he went to the back of the house and tapped at the first window he came to. He was lucky, a girl was in the room but alone. She was patting powder on her face when he rapped at the window and she pulled back the curtain and stared at him, a hand to her mouth. Then came recognition that he was a seaman and she smiled.

She opened the window and he climbed in. She threw up her hands in horror at his condition and rattled a spate of Spanish at him. His legs gave way under him and he sank down on the bed. He held up a hand weakly to stem the flow and said, "Tomorrow. Yes? Tomorrow." And laid head on his hands, miming sleep. She nodded and held out her hand. He fumbled his money from his belt and she took it all. He said, "No tell. No one." And put finger to his lips.

She nodded again and repeated his gesture.

He stripped to the skin, folded his sodden clothes carefully and laid them on a chair. The girl reached out to him but he shook his head. He would not look at her. He got into the bed and pulled the covers over his head.

The girl peered at him, puzzled, then shrugged, hid the money, undressed and blew out the lamp. She climbed into bed, shoving him over and in minutes she was asleep. It was not until dawn that he sank into an uneasy doze.

I I

Aboard *Thunder* the work went on through the night and into the day, the crew working watch and watch. At Smith's orders he was called when the watch was changed and inspected the work and talked with the men.

Garrick reported unhappily, "Able Seaman Rattray and Ordinary Seaman Gibb are missing from this working party, sir. They could have gone over the side. Gibb is a very good swimmer."

Smith bit his lip. He did not want to believe it. "Together? They don't sound a likely pair."

"No, sir. That's a fact."

"Well, make a search but quietly. I don't want this blown up." There could be others who might find desertion preferable to facing the cruisers. God knew he could sympathise but he had a duty and so had his crew.

"Master-at-Arms is looking about, sir."

Hobbs, the Master-at-Arms on his rounds spotted the open door of the turret and shoved in his bullet head. "Anybody working in here?"

The ship's Corporal with him said, "Somebody over there."

They entered the turret and then they saw Rattray properly.

For one horrified moment they stared, then the Corporal, who had seen the bloody debris of bar-fights from Chatham to China, said in a hushed whisper, "Gawd Amighty!"

Somewhere along the way in that mad quarter-minute Rattray's head had caught the breech of the gun and the laceration streamed blood that covered his face. His nose also bled so that at first they did not know him but then they went quickly to him and the Corporal said, "It's Rattray."

Rattray had a reputation as a brawler but not as a victim. The Master-at-Arms summed it up. "Well, I'll be buggered."

They started to lift Rattray and he recovered bleary consciousness so they stood him on wobbly legs. Hobbs asked, "Seen anything of young Gibb?"

Rattray blinked, muttered, "No. Never seen him."

Hobbs looked thoughtful, but shrugged. They walked him, shambling and stupid, down to the sick-bay, where Purkiss peered at him and said, awed, "What happened to him?"

"Don't ask me. I just found him," Hobbs replied comfortably. "Can you fix him up?"

"Somebody's already done it."

"You know what I mean. Return him to duty."

"Let's have a look." His examination was thorough but rapid and unsympathetic. He cleaned, and anointed where necessary, bandaged the torn scalp. "There y'are. Good as new. Who done it?" He started to wash his hands.

Hobbs said, "Gawd knows." The Corporal thought that, leaving God aside, two of them could make out a bloody good list of probables. He kept his mouth shut. Hobbs nodded at Rattray. "You can ask him, but o'course he won't split in case that big feller, whoever he is, gets ahold of him again."

Rattray glared balefully from the one eye still open, climbed stiffly from the stool to his feet and limped out.

Purkiss said, "Strictly speaking I ought to make a report."

"'Course you should." Hobbs nodded. "Same as me. But times like these, when I'm busy, I sometimes forget."

The Corporal thought, 'You bleeding liar. Memory like an elephant.'

Purkiss also nodded. "I'm rushed off my feet just now." He glanced around at the sick-bay that presented a picture of utter calm.

"I can see." Hobbs started to leave. "Sorry to have troubled you when you're that busy."

"No trouble," Purkiss replied, "no trouble at all." He was whistling happily as they left.

The attempted deception was a waste of time because Rattray had already met Albrecht, who stared at him. "What happened to you?"

"Accident, sir. Fell down in the fore-turret."

Rattray's thinking was still sluggish and it took him a second or two to realise what he had said but Albrecht did not question the fatuous excuse; Rattray could have fallen a dozen times in the fore-turret and sustained fewer injuries.

Albrecht said only, "Very well." And it was some time later before Rattray thought there might be some ambiguity in that simple remark.

In the sick-bay Albrecht glanced at the log, innocent of mention of Rattray – and said nothing.

Smith was at his desk before dawn. There was a letter to be written to Graham's widow, another to Somers's parents. They took him a long time. Then he wrote his report, adding his commendations of Garrick for the gunnery, and Somers. He was uncomfortable in full dress now with his cap and sword on the desk because later he had a formal duty.

As he finished he thought cynically that it would bring none of them honour or glory. It was a bald recital of a ship that had run for cover, been hit only twice and suffered but a single casualty – a decidedly unspectacular affair to the reader. It did not mention that every man aboard and many ashore thought he had performed a miracle, for the simple reason that he did not know it. But he would not have said so anyway.

He thought the next report would be a very different matter but he would not be writing it. He wondered what those men of his would think of him then, if any of them survived. They would know he had failed them. They followed him and asked for nothing but they were entitled to a fighting chance and they would not get it.

He pulled his head from his hands as Garrick knocked and was straight-faced though cold-eyed when the First Lieutenant said, "Burial party ready, sir."

"Very well."

"And Leading Seaman Bates and Sergeant Burton ask to see you on a personal matter, sir."

"Now?"

"They say it's urgent, sir." They had been evasive and stubborn but both were old hands. Garrick had ceased probing.

Smith said, "Send them in." And when they stood before him: "I hope this is a serious matter."

Bates said, "It's about young Gibb, sir. There's more to it than meets the eye. I don't reckon him as a deserter in the face o' the enemy. 'Course, he had the wind up like all of us but I reckon there was more to it than that."

"What?"

"Dunno, sir. But I reckon I could get him to tell me. If we could sneak ashore and bring him back, 'cause we know where he'll be, I could get the truth out o' him, give him a chance to speak up for himself. *Please*, sir." Bates was pleading because Smith's head was already moving in a slow negative.

It was too wild a scheme. Smith sympathised; he wanted Gibb back, hated the thought of one of his men labelled as a deserter or a coward and like Bates he sensed that Gibb was neither.

177

Burton broke in. "There's only one place he *can* be, sir. Fizzy's Bar. That's the only place he'll know and the only one as might hide him. We'd land downstream clear o' the town and we could get to the place by the back way. We'll wear old clothes. Should be easy but if we was stopped we'd say we jumped ship to get a few drinks and how about sending us aboard."

Smith pushed up from his desk and shifted restlessly across the cabin to stand at the open scuttle staring out at his ship and the men as they worked. He stood there a long time until Burton said, chancing his arm, "It's been known for a feller to slip ashore unbeknownst, sir."

Smith's lips twitched. They all knew about his escapade at Malaguay. But when he turned his face was serious. "It will not be as easy as you think. Now listen to me."

When he took up his cap and sword and went on deck, he found the day again in mourning with scarcely a breath of wind and the sky overcast, grey. For once no smoke trailed from *Thunder*'s four funnels because Davies had put out all her fires and the stokers were cleaning them of clinker, one more periodic chore of a coal-burning ship. The flag-draped coffin rested aft by the accommodation ladder. The party was a small one. There were eight pall-bearers, seamen from Somers's battery, at their own request. There was Kennedy and a boy bugler, sixteen years old, even younger than Somers had been. He was already nervous, pale.

Smith detected a slackening in the work throughout the ship. The sombre little group aft was having its effect. This was a duty to be done for a fellow officer. It was as well that it should be done without delay. The bugler sounded the 'Still', work ceased and the ship's company froze into immobility.

The coffin had come off during the night; Cherry had arranged that. Aitkyne was officer of the watch at that time and had signed a receipt for it. The boat's crew had gaped at *Thunder* and the signs of damage, the great wounds and the men working on them and in them under the lights. And they had stared at Aitkyne 'as if they were measuring me, the mercenary bastards'. That had been macabrely amusing.

This was not.

They lowered the coffin into the pinnace and the burial party went ashore and disembarked on the quay under the eyes of a considerable crowd, who were curious but quiet. There was a glass-sided hearse pulled by a pair of black-plumed, black horses. There was a large escort of soldiers. The Chilean army was modelled on the German and the troops in their field-grey and spiked helmets seemed more guard than escort. And there was Cherry. As the seamen loaded the coffin into the hearse, Smith muttered to him, "I need more time."

Cherry shook his head. "They won't – "

"I think they might. My essential repairs will barely be completed at dusk. I want until six in the morning, but tell them I'll move up to Stillwater Cove as soon as repairs are complete and I'll leave the river by six."

"It will be broad day!"

"What difference does it make? They have a gunboat patrolling the mouth of the river and I can't pass her unseen, however dark the night."

"It will make a difference to *them*, surely?" And Cherry was talking about the cruisers. "They will be able to lie off and engage you at extreme range, twelve guns to your two."

"Then Muller won't oppose such a request. And the Chileans don't want a night engagement virtually on their doorstep."

Cherry murmured thoughtfully, "Ye-es. It might well be ..." He stopped, then finished apologetically: "Of course you know your own business best."

"I hope so."

The cortege was ready.

They marched behind the hearse out to the cemetery, that was the graveyard of the English church. Smith stood as the parson droned through the service, his mind absorbed in his plans. Then a phrase cut through that absorption: ". . . man that is born of a woman hath but a short time to live . . . he cometh up and is cut down like a flower . . ."

Cut down. But not like a flower. "Cut him in half," Garrick had said. Like a bloody tree-stump.

". . . ashes to ashes, dust to dust . . ."

It was neither ashes nor dust but a horrible bloody mess on the deck. They had hosed it and scrubbed it away.

He had closed his eyes. He forced himself to open them. Somers had gone into the hole.

The soldiers fired a salute. The bugler boy's lip was trembling and big tears rolled down his cheeks. Kennedy snarled under his breath, a savage whisper that reached the boy alone and snapped him upright. The first notes quavered but then he got hold of it and did it well.

They marched back to the pinnace with Smith at their head, stone-faced.

The girl stumbled from the bed, pulled a robe around her and padded barefoot from the room.

In the kitchen she yawned as she brewed a pot of coffee and put it on a tray with two cups. Olsen asked, "You got an all-night job?"

"English sailor – " The truth slipped from her, half-asleep, and her hand went to her mouth.

Olsen said, "No sailor last night." He kept the door. And anyway, he knew as everyone did the political climate in Guaya prohibited the British from landing.

She pleaded, "He came in by the window. Did I do wrong?"

Olsen stood up and shrugged. "You? No. But the sailor?" He grimaced and crossed to the door then paused to point a finger at her. "Take the coffee but tell him nothing." He went upstairs to Phizackerly.

The sun was high but it was far too early for Phizackerly. Again. He woke reluctantly, bemused, to Olsen's determined shaking of his shoulder. The previous night had been difficult. He had been torn between a desire to celebrate *Thunder*'s escape from the cruisers and an awful fear as to her predicament. He was in a position to enjoy both sensations because he was not personally involved. Whatever happened he was all right. But that nagged at him, too. He compromised by officially delegating all responsibility to Juanita and Olsen, who had it anyway, and drank himself into a melancholy stupor.

So he tried feebly, as a man wishing at least to be left to die in peace, to push Olsen's hand away. He tried to turn over and burrow into the warm lee of the snoring Juanita but Olsen stolidly resisted both attempts, clamped both hands on Phizackerly's bony shoulders and dragged him half-upright so he sat in the bed.

Phizackerly said in the voice of a ghost, "Oh, Gawd! My bloody 'ead!" His mouth was thick and his skull pounded. From the slanted rays of the sun that shot hot needles into his eyes he could tell it was early morning. He would kill Olsen for this.

Olsen said, "There is a sailor from the British ship downstairs. If the police find out they will come." He continued to hold Phizackerly, stopping him from swaying, falling, as the words sank in.

It was like dropping a stone down a deep well. For seconds Phizackerly sat dumb, blank-faced, eyes slits. Then he reached out fingers like talons to claw at Olsen's arm. "Sailor? From the cruiser?"

"He came last night. Over the wall at the back. He's downstairs now."

Phizackerly groaned. "Give us a hand." Olsen helped him

181

from the bed and he sat on its edge, pulling on his clothes, and whispered huskily, "A mender. Get us a mender."

Olsen went downstairs. When he returned Phizackerly was dressed and splashing water on his face. He could not find a towel so pulled up the ample tail of his shirt and used that. Then he took the glass of rum from Olsen and sank it, gasped, coughed and chased it down with the black coffee. "Right." He headed for the door, still moving stiffly but drawn on by the emergency that caused him to leave his teeth grinning in the cup.

The girl whispered, "Coffee." And Gibb took the proffered cup and drank. It was stuffily warm in the room but he still sat huddled as a man in the grip of cold. The girl was afraid that her fear would show in her face but he never looked at her, only stared at the wall.

Phizackerly and Olsen entered. Phizackerly glared at Gibb with hatred and jerked his thumb at the trembling girl. "Out." She fled.

There was no room for doubt. Gibb's clothes lay on a chair. But to be absolutely certain : "You're a deserter."

Gibb did not answer.

Phizackerly yelled at him, with an old man's shrillness, "You're off the cruiser!"

Gibb muttered, "Yes."

Phizackerly chewed it over and his toothless jaws moved in time with his thoughts. He had to get the bugger out of it. That was the first thought that formed, because if the law found him here there would be a hell of a row. They might even close the place. Then he thought it was more difficult than just throwing him out on the street. His capture then would be certain, he would be questioned and he would say he had spent the night at Fizzy's Bar.

His head ached.

Thunder lay out in the pool and the cruisers waited outside.

182

This was a personal matter between Englishmen.

He said to Olsen, "Fetch the rum." And when it came, "Give us a half-hour. Keep that girl's mouth shut an' everybody else out of here."

Phizackerly poured the rum, got Gibb to drink it and saw him shudder, nodded to himself as he refilled the glass. It was an investment. Gibb would not be the first man to be taken unwillingly or unwittingly and dumped on a ship that waited for him out in the pool. Phizackerly had done that before now to oblige a skipper and turn an extra penny. This was a different situation altogether, mind, but his back was against the wall. Sometimes you had to use force and Olsen carried a blackjack but Phizackerly judged that this time the rum would suffice, that and a good talking to.

He poured and he talked, about England, the Navy, duty, honour, comradeship and the rum gave him a marvellous sincerity. But his sharp little eyes watched Gibb keenly and saw despair give way to bewilderment and then stupor as the words flowed over him and the rum ran down to sink its teeth into his empty belly.

Olsen returned and together they got Gibb into his clothes. He moved slowly, dazedly, as he was told. Olsen brought a coat to hide Gibb's working dress and Phizackerly muttered, "Right. He's going back. I'll see to him. You hold the fort here. Tell nobody nothing till I come back, only I'm out on business."

Olsen said, "He is good boy after all."

Phizackerly stared at him. "He's a mug. You wouldn't get me on that old bucket for all the tea in China! Now clear off!"

He heard the distant popping of musketry, a salute and the lonely call of the bugle and knew what it meant. He glanced furtively at Gibb as he worked the coat on to him but the young seaman had not noticed. The rum had him. It was going to be hard work getting him back to his ship. Phizackerly swore under his breath.

He turned as the window was thrust open and he saw a burly, grizzled man in overalls swinging a leg across the sill. Another half-dozen crowded behind him. Phizackerly said, startled, " 'Ere! What's all this?"

Farmer Bates said placidly, "All right, Fizzy, me old son. It's the Navy claiming its own." The others climbed in after him except one who stood on watch.

Phizackerly blew out his cheeks. "Cripes! I'm glad to see you." And as Burton crossed to the door, opened it a crack and peered out, "Don't worry. Nobody'll bother us. You won't have no trouble."

Burton closed the door and grinned at him. "Good. We don't want no trouble."

Phizackerly knew a tough bunch when he saw them but he was a much relieved man. It was going to be all right.

When the pinnace reached *Thunder* Smith said, "Stay alongside, Mr. Manton. I'll want the picket-boat in ten minutes." He ran up the ladder, returned Garrick's salute, went to his cabin and shifted out of his dress suit and into his shabby old uniform. He snatched his binoculars and as he stepped into the pinnace he asked Manton, "You've got the boat lead?"

"Yes, sir."

"Very well. Take her to sea, Mr. Manton. I'm curious to see our friends outside."

"Aye, aye, sir."

The pinnace swung away and headed out of the pool and downriver. Once more they ran down the broad deep-water channel with its steep, forest-clad walls, down to where Stillwater Cove opened up to port and opposite, to starboard, a bare quarter-mile beyond the old channel, stood the signalling station on its little hill. Smith saw light wink there as a telescope or binoculars was trained on them. They would be reported by telephone. He shrugged and lifted the glasses to his eyes. The cruisers were in sight.

One lay close outside Chilean waters and the gunboat was alongside her. The limit of Chilean waters was clearly defined because the Chilean destroyer *Tocopilla* was steaming slowly back and forth along a line outside the mouth of the river, marking that limit as if with a rule and chalk. That was a deadly monotonous business, patrolling that line like a sentry pacing his beat and they would be at it till morning. Smith thought the Chilean Captain probably consoled himself with the thought that he would have a grandstand seat when the morning came.

The pinnace plugged on out to sea against the flowing tide, lifting and falling now as it met that sea but the weather of recent days was only a bad memory. True, the sky was totally overcast but the sea was near calm and the pinnace rode it easily.

He picked out the other cruiser, standing a mile or two further out to sea, hove to. Saving her coal. She was running on a short rein that got shorter with every minute. Smith had seen to that when he sank the colliers.

He lowered the glasses and rubbed at his eyes. They were still a threat. They could still get coal after they had settled with *Thunder*. Some. They could coal in the port of a neutral country once in three months. Ringing the changes on the neutral countries that lined this coast, they might survive some little time. And they might, if they were very lucky, capture an Allied collier. But every time they put in for coal their position would be known. They had lost the element of surprise; Smith had wrested that from them, too, with the sinking of the colliers. Now there would be no quick, easy pickings and there would be almost immediate and increasing pursuit, starting with that battle-cruiser.

Theoretically they could well have entered Guaya at *Thunder*'s heels and coaled there. That would have put the Chileans in a dilemma with their refusal to supply Smith. They had not done so because of the twenty-four hours rule.

If the cruisers had entered Guaya, and then *Thunder* had sailed, they would have had to give her twenty-four hours start. That was international law.

So they waited outside, for *Thunder*, and an annihilating victory that would shake the world with the length of the German Navy's arm, and its strength.

Manton said nervously, "Chilean destroyer's signalling, sir."

Smith realised he was glaring sightlessly out to sea and cracked his stiff face in a smile. "No doubt." They were close to *Tocopilla* now and she was heading, still on that rigid line, to pass close across the bow of the pinnace. She was warning them to keep clear, that they were close to leaving the sanctuary of neutral waters.

Smith said, "Hard a'starboard. Copy her course, Mr. Manton. Half ahead."

The pinnace slowed and came around to run parallel with *Tocopilla*. The officers looked down on them curiously from the bridge of the destroyer as she forged past then left them tossing in her wake. Smith lifted the glasses again as the destroyer's smoke rolled away. He could see the nearer cruiser and the gunboat alongside her, clearly now. He watched for a minute then handed the glasses to Manton and took the wheel himself. "Take a look." He waited until Manton lowered the glasses and then asked him, "Well?"

"It looked like ammunition they were loading on the *Leopard*, sir."

Smith said, noncommitally, "Yes." He had been quite certain of what he had seen but it had also been what he expected to see so he had wanted confirmation. Now he had it. It was one more point to be borne in mind, that now the gunboat had teeth.

But she was no threat set beside the cruisers. He turned over the wheel to Manton and reclaimed the glasses. The further cruiser was too far away to be seen in detail, but the nearer – he thought the fore-turret looked very odd, one gun of the pair bent at a angle. He let Manton see. "As Mr. Aitkyne put it, we gave her a bloody nose."

"By Jove, yes, sir!" Manton stared a long time and yielded the glasses only when Smith said, "We'll return to the ship."

They did not return directly. Having run in under the signalling station and its watchful glass, Smith said, "Steer four points to starboard. Slow ahead." The engine of the pinnace slowed until she slipped through the water at a walking pace. They crept into Stillwater Cove and on Smith's order Buckley took station in the bow with the boat lead. They took soundings for the length of the cove and proved deep water, or near as deep as the main channel. They chugged back to the centre of the cove and anchored and the engine expired in a sigh of steam. Smith stood over the compass, checking bearings. The pinnace scarcely moved where she lay, his bearings showed him that, despite the flowing tide that thrust at her, rippling around her bow. She did not swing at all.

Smith stared for a minute or two at the forest wall that climbed sheer from the water of the cove, then across the channel to where the signalling station was just visible around the right-turning curve of the main channel. As he was visible to them. They could not see this stretch of the channel but they could see the cove and himself. Just.

He cast one last look around at the cove, the forest, the channel, then smiled at Manton. "Home, James."

They ran back up the channel.

As they opened up the pool his eyes went first, of course, to *Thunder*, appraising the work done and finding himself well content. She was grimy still but a sight cleaner than that morning. He would have to give some orders on trim. Terribly light with near empty bunkers, she rode high in the water. Then his eyes drifted across to *Kansas*, lying massive, ugly in her menace but lovely in the clean lines of her.

Manton said, "She's enormous."

Smith smiled thinly. The cruisers could set a steel trap across the mouth of the river and he could act out defiance here but the argument was between themselves. There was no argument as to where sea-power on this coast ultimately rested, whenever she chose to take it. *Kansas* seemed to doze in the late afternoon.

Five minutes later he faced Garrick and Bates. A look at Bates's face was enough but he asked, "All well?"

"Took a lot longer getting back, sir, but all well."

Garrick added, "In the cells."

One look at Garrick's unhappy face was also enough but Smith only said, "Very good."

When Bates had gone Smith stood lost in thought, smiling faintly. That was one worry out of the way. As for the rest ... He turned the smile on Garrick. "Now, about this bun-fight. Mr. Wakely will be in charge of the gramophone. All officers, except for watch-keepers, will be present and I want it understood that this *is* a *party*. Anyone who does not enjoy himself will answer to me." He grinned. "And a word to the Paymaster. I have no doubt at all that the recent action will have destroyed some of his canteen stock, notably beer and probably of the order of two bottles per man, and I will expect to sign a certificate to that effect." That he would do with a clear conscience. The canteen stock would be a total loss inside twenty-four hours.

As Garrick knew perfectly well, but he returned Smith's grin; it was infectious.

They discussed the trim of the ship and Smith said what he wanted done. He told Garrick about the *Leopard* and how she had been armed by the cruiser. "*Kondor*, I think." He said how she had been hit. He told him of the soundings in the cove and that he wanted steam for sunset. And then he gave one last order that startled Garrick, that would have to be passed to the Chiefs and Petty Officers and would mean more work for the men – after they had their beer.

188

He had half an hour to sluice himself down, change into clean clothes and then sit quietly in his cabin. Far below in the stokehold they would be starting already on the long job of trimming and getting up steam with the grate and clang of the shovels. They were busy. But most of the other hands were fallen out below, cooks piped to the galley for the evening meal and there would be beer as well. It was quiet.

He could hear the tick of the clock. It was a background to his thoughts as he re-examined his plans. He was not smiling now.

It might have seemed that he had at least a limited number of courses he could pursue. In fact he knew, as he had known from the beginning, that he would have to fight. They had hunted him down though he had gone half across the world and he could see them . . .

The rap at the door snapped his eyes open and the word from him in a savage bark: *"Yes?"*

Vincent's voice came nervously, "Boat putting off from *Ariadne*, sir."

"Thank you."

He thought that when there was only one course you could take it became terribly simple. He was smiling as he went to join his officers where they waited in a well-scrubbed, shining group, neat in their best dress.

The mess-decks were crowded. Mess-decks are always crowded, even on a ship as short-handed as *Thunder*, but this day it was made worse by the damage to the ship, some parts being too badly burned to be inhabited. They stank. So *Thunder's* crew jammed in together in a grousing matiness, sweated, talked, and wondered.

Chalky White ate furiously, nervously, shovelling the food into his mouth. Through it he mumbled, "What can 'e do? What I *ask* yer! Too slow to run away. That's been proved.

They 'aven't got better than a knot or two over us but that's enough. Too much. Either one o' them's got twice the big guns we have. So what can he *do*? I *asks* you!"

Farmer Bates said placidly, "Why don't you shut up?" He had drawn Gibb's beer besides his own; Gibb was in the cells.

"I just want to *know*." Chalky tapped his chest. "I'm on this bleeder same as him. What happens to 'er 'appens ter *me*. I just want to *know*. Blimey, what beats me is what that Gibb came back for." He stood up. "I'm going to draw me beer."

At that moment Daddy Horsfall hobbled through in his best boots that were crippling him and a starched white mess-jacket that threatened to choke him, on his way aft to the wardroom.

Chalky seized on opportunity. "Hey! Daddy!"

Daddy glanced around, saw him.

Farmer Bates said, "Don't ask him."

Chalky whispered, "Not ask him? He's the skipper's servant, right alongside of him. If anybody knows –"

"Don't ask him."

Daddy called, "What d'yer want, Chalky? I'm supposed to be waiting on, man."

Chalky asked, "What's he goin' to do? The skipper, I mean."

"Do?"

"*Do!* About – this! He's got to have a plan, ain't he?"

"Ah! Plan." Daddy nodded, understanding now. "Well, that's simple enough. He's made no secret of it."

"What?"

Daddy said, "Get them to drop one on us."

Chalky gaped at him. "*What?*"

Daddy nodded. "An' when the bloody great cloud of rust goes up we can sneak away through it like it was a smoke screen." He hobbled away through the guffaws.

Farmer said, "I told you not to ask the old bastard." But Chalky went off, muttering.

Burton squeezed in beside Farmer and glanced at the bottles of beer. "You're not going to drink all that at your age?"

Farmer said amiably, "You're a scrounging bastard." He shoved along a bottle.

Burton took it. "Always was."

They drank. Farmer said, "That was a bit of a lark ashore." They grinned. Farmer asked, "What do you think?"

"Smith? Deep, that one. Dunno what he *can* do but he won't back down."

Farmer nodded agreement. "Just have to wait and see."

They had talked to Rattray, who said indifferently, "All right, I'll leave the little bleeder alone if they ever let him out. Don't matter now, does it? Not with what's coming off tomorrow."

Farmer and Burton sat in companionable silence in the midst of the teeming life around them. The moments of comparative peace would not, could not, last much longer. They would not waste them.

No bugle nor pipe sounded but the crew of *Thunder* had finished their brief breathing space, and their beer, and now turned to under the Petty Officers and Chiefs. They swarmed below deck like a disturbed ants' nest, destructive ants, and the din they created built on itself until it came in bedlam waves and went on and on.

In the wardroom the Chilean Admiral and Encalada were stiffly polite but their ladies openly excited. Neither officer mentioned Smith's request for more time but Cherry sought him out and whispered, "They've agreed. You have until six tomorrow morning but not a minute longer."

"Well done!"

"And here!" Cherry handed him a telegram.

It was a signal from Admiralty. Cherry was to inform the *Thunder*'s commander that a sighting of the cruisers had been reported in error, and if the cruisers arrived in the Pacific he was to avoid action until joined by a stronger force.

Cherry said bitterly, "They're a little late."

Smith shrugged. "Thank you, anyway." He put the signal carefully away in his pocket.

Ballard was openly elated by *Thunder*'s performance and Smith's handling of her but after Smith spoke briefly and quietly with him he became preoccupied.

Donoghue and Corrigan, his Flag-Captain, were easy and friendly looking frankly at the damage, appraising it and the work done but saying nothing. The ship was tolerably clean; for a coal-burning ship that had recently passed through heavy weather and hostile action she was remarkably clean. She still stank of burnt cordite and smoke.

The party was complete. It had an air of unreality as Smith had suspected when he issued the invitation but now he was glad that he had done so. It had been issued as an act of bravado, a gesture, but the party was useful for several reasons. For one thing his officers were readily obeying his orders, they were enjoying themselves. For another, Sarah Benson was here.

The white-jacketed stewards served tea, cake and wafer-thin sandwiches. Wakely's gramophone rag-timed away, decorously muted by one of Wakely's socks stuffed down its horn. Wakely himself scurried between his gramophone and the group of officers who surrounded Sarah Benson. She had come aboard with Jim Bradley, who was pale and bandaged and told Smith, "The Doc's allowed me up for one hour. I wasn't going to miss this!"

Sarah looked anything but a survivor now. During the day she had made demands of Mrs. Cherry and that lady had met them nobly so that Sarah's hair was piled and shone and her dress was expensive and – well, fitted. She was polite and quiet with Smith when she came aboard but she had come alive in the wardroom. Bradley watched the officers clustered around her with tolerant amusement.

Smith thought Bradley could grin like a Cheshire cat because he would be taking the girl away.

Smith laboured at small talk. He was a poor hand at it and with the Chileans it was hard work. They all avoided mention of the war and Smith knew little of Chile. He talked a little of London but London was hard to recall.

Encalada finally noticed the racket below deck. "Your men are still working very hard."

Smith nodded. "Yes."

"Below? I understood you were hit fore and aft and your wireless destroyed – but not below."

"That is correct."

That stopped the conversation and Smith could have left it there but he said disarmingly, "It sounds as though someone's trying to steal the engines! In fact we have a small engine repair, not connected with the action. And of course, we are trimming bunkers. But we will sail on time and shift our anchorage to Stillwater Cove tonight."

Encalada nodded, but Ballard blurted out eagerly, "Captain, there's a mist at dawn – " He bit his tongue.

Smith said quickly, "You came aboard in more comfortable style this evening, Miss Benson."

"But no more eagerly."

They all laughed at that.

Smith said wickedly, "It is a pleasure to open our doors to you."

"Now." And her lips twitched.

"Always."

"Distance lending enchantment to the view?"

"I was – preoccupied at that time."

"I know, and understand."

He had apologised and she had accepted. He was pleased at that and he felt like a tight-rope walker, was enjoying it and tried his hand again. "Normally I would hope to see more of you but in the circumstances – "

"More? In the circumstances that would be difficult." And she looked him straight in the eye and laughed.

When the party ended and the guests departed Ballard stood at the head of the ladder, his hand in Smith's, and muttered, "Was that all right?"

"Perfect."

Thunder was left to herself.

Donoghue found orders waiting for him aboard *Kansas*, orders for the Atlantic and he called for steam from midnight onwards.

Commander David Cochrane Smith paced the deck of his ship, his mind busy. Davies had raised steam and the smoke hung low on the still air. Soon, now.

He remembered Sarah Benson going down into the boat and thought that he had seen the last of her and, now that they had made some sort of peace, he would have liked to have seen her again. But the chance was gone.

12

SARAH BENSON HAD not enjoyed the party. She suspected Smith had given it for reasons of his own, one of them probably that it was the last thing anyone would expect him to do. He had succeeded in that; she had seen the Chileans looking about them in baffled perplexity as the scrubbed officers sipped tea and that fat, pink-faced boy with the worshipping eyes had wound away at his gramophone. She had gone to the party as a duty, as an act of thanks and apology and that had been accepted. She had hated it. Tomorrow was in her mind.

She was wondering about Smith. The stories about a man who haunted parties did not ring true now. Smith was obviously a poor hand at parties, and except for the brief exchange with her his conversation had limped. And a devil with the ladies? No. So maybe the stories were only half-truths and there was another side to them?

Did it matter now? *Thunder* would sail out in the dawn, she was certain of that, and the cruisers would be waiting for her. If only *Thunder* could gain more time.

She stood on the deck of *Ariadne* and stared across at *Thunder* as the night came down. *Ariadne's* deck was dotted with little groups of passengers watching as she did but she stood alone, a small, dejected figure. Cherry found her there.

She turned to him with hope. "Any news?"

Cherry shook his head gloomily. "Bad news or good, it depends on how you look at it. No diver. There are two working out of this port but both were hired for a job up the coast and went the day before yesterday. They won't be back for a week. They were hired by Muller, not directly but through a couple of intermediaries and I know 'em both. What makes it look good is they must have gone because Muller doesn't want a diver operating here until he has one he can trust to keep his mouth shut. And *that* means something in the wreck. Before I suspected it but now I'm certain. But without a diver I can't *prove* it."

Sarah asked, "What kind of proof?"

"I've thought about that." Cherry paused. "Smith got a whole lot of stuff from her, log, ship's papers, everything of that sort and it was all in order."

"So . . . ?"

"Wait a minute," Cherry snapped testily, worried and on edge, "I'm *getting* to it. She was a collier for the cruisers and she had a first-class wireless. So – she'd send in code."

"A book!"

"Right! And one of the places they didn't get the chance to search was the wireless office. It's in the superstructure and that's where the book will be. If I only had a *diver –*" He groaned in frustration.

They were silent a moment, then Sarah said quietly, "I'm a good swimmer." She was not boasting, simply stating a fact, staring out across the pool at the stained and battered *Thunder*.

"I daresay young lady, but I'm talking about diving."

"So am I."

Cherry explained shortly, "I don't mean diving *in*. I mean diving *under* to a depth of ten or twenty feet *into* the super-structure!" His patience was stretched thin by the tension that tautened the nerves of both of them as the hours slid away.

It set her snapping at him. "I'm not a damn fool and don't you dare treat me as one."

"I'm not –"

"I know the diving you're talking about and I can do it. I've swum around in that depth of water plenty of times."

Cherry peered at her, upset and not liking the idea at all and his face showed it. He believed her. Once when he'd talked with her father that abrasive little man had said the girl could swim like a bloody fish. Cherry had worried himself sick over Sarah in the past but he'd had to put up with it because he needed her. But this –

Sarah still stared at *Thunder* and she spoke her thoughts aloud. "The Commander and I never got along very well. Maybe I'm partly to blame. But there's a man who can make a decision. We can either sit on our rumps and do nothing; or –"

The sun dropped down behind the overcast in a red glow that faded and died. The town twinkled with lights and *Thunder* lay in a pool of radiance of her own making. Men worked on her decks, seemingly still repairing the ravages of the fighting that were visible to anyone who cared to look. Donoghue stood on *Kansas*'s quarterdeck, Corrigan by his side.

Donoghue said, "So he's hauling up to Stillwater Cove tonight. He's not going to be interned. He's going to make a running fight of it."

Corrigan sniffed. "He can't run. Those cruisers can give that old lady two or three knots. It sounds like he hopes to use the mist that comes up just before dawn, but ..." His voice tailed away and he shook his head.

"That's right. But." Donoghue scowled. "That mist hangs around the river and its mouth and that's all. It'll give him a few minutes of cover, just a little time. He can't evade that gunboat and they'll be out there waiting for him when he comes out of the mist. The light will be behind him and he'll make one hell of a target."

"He's just trying everything he can." Corrigan paused, then said, "They're still working aboard her. Looked pretty good to me, both the ship and the men I saw. She should be ready when she leaves, ready as she'll ever be."

Donoghue said heavily, "God help them."

Cherry's boat took him ashore and then returned to *Ariadne*. Cherry held a diplomatic post and could not be involved. He walked up to the consulate, to wait.

His boatman, Francis, handed Sarah Benson into the boat when she descended the accommodation ladder. He was an expatriate Geordie, squat and barrel-chested. He had not shaved for several days and smelt strongly of the tobacco he chewed. He wore dirty trousers and a singlet that was black-streaked with oil, hair curling through the rents in it. Cherry had told him all about it and he disapproved but he started the engine and swung the boat away from *Ariadne*.

Sarah sat on a thwart and said tonelessly, "I think we can do without the lights in a minute."

Francis shrugged heavy shoulders. "Don't suppose anybody'll take any notice of us; they'll all be watching her." He jerked his head at *Thunder*. "Still, does no harm to be careful." He extinguished the boat's lights.

Francis was mistaken. One pair of eyes noted their progress, blinked as the lights went out then strained to follow the boat as it slid softly across the dark water. The eyes belonged to Friedrich Kaufmann who sat in his own boat below the quay. He was there to watch *Thunder* but now he watched the boat and saw it slow, drift it to the stub of *Gerda*'s funnel that still showed above water, and come to rest there.

Sarah Benson stared at the black water that flickered jewelled reflections from *Thunder*'s distant lights. She sat

198

in pale gloom, the darkness thinned by those lights and shivered.

Francis clambered forward over the thwarts, crouched before her with the light line coiled in his hand and asked uneasily, "You did say you had done a lot of this, miss?"

"I've been swimming since I was able to walk, I can swim better than most men and that includes under water." She stood up, setting the boat to rocking gently. "Let's get on with it."

She pulled the dress over her head. Under it she wore only drawers and a short chemise that tucked into the waist of the drawers. She took the line from Francis and knotted it around her waist while he muttered, "Remember, I keep it pretty taut so it won't foul your legs. And if you get into any trouble – "

"I tug and keep tugging."

"Right."

Sarah wondered what he could do about it if she ran into trouble down there. She knew that Francis, like many another fisherman, could not swim at all. Now he was muttering, "Remember what Mr. Cherry told you about the wireless cabin, the layout; it should be something like that."

"I remember."

"There should be a table, a drawer or two under it."

She nodded. She was shivering uncontrollably now and annoyed with herself because of it. The night air was not cold. She said again, "Let's get on with it."

Francis hesitated. He had an idea of the dangers involved in entering a submerged wreck, without an airline, in pitch blackness. Moreover this was a girl only half his age and half his size, terribly vulnerable now as she stood with pinched face and shivered. This was a job to be done and this girl had volunteered but he did not like it.

He said, "Take care, bonny lass. And good luck."

Sarah lowered herself over the side, gasped as the chill of

the water took her breath, hung on and breathed deeply, then went under. Francis saw her legs kicking, waving pale below the surface, and then they were gone leaving a trail of bubbles.

She had expected blackness but it was far worse than her fears. She worked by touch alone, striking down until one hand scraped on iron and she fumbled her way along the superstructure, passed one door, closed, reached the second that was the wireless office and found it open.

She dared not enter. She kicked up for the surface, broke into the air five yards from the boat and stroked towards it and clung to the side, gasping.

Francis stooped over her, peering closely and she panted, "About over there. But look, when I go down again I'll have to find the thing all over. Take off this line, will you?"

"You've got to have a line!"

"I need it for something else." And as he reluctantly picked at the knot, "The only way I can do it is to use the line as a guide."

"I don't like it."

"Have you got a better idea?"

Francis had: pack the lot in. But he shook his head and she took the end of the line from him. Her breasts rose and fell under the now transparent chemise as she breathed deeply, then she was gone again.

That dive sufficed to mark the wireless office and she tied the line to the handle of the door.

On the third dive she followed the line and entered the office. After long seconds of awkward groping she located the desk and a drawer beneath. It was open and she felt a key in the lock but the drawer was empty. She turned to re-surface and found she had lost her bearings and went bumping around in the steel cell, fumbling for the door. She found it only when her lungs were bursting and lights wheeled across her eyes, kicked clumsily through it and up.

She paddled only feebly to the boat and clung to the side, exhausted. Francis said, "Good God! Here, let's have you in." He reached for her but she flapped at his hands.

"No! Leave me alone! Just give me a minute."

He had to wait while she tried to fight down fear and fixed her mind on *Thunder* and the six hundred men aboard her . . . David Cochrane Smith. She said, "All right. I should have taken the slack of the line in with me. That's what I'll do. I found the desk and a drawer but it was empty. Must be another one."

Francis said, "Wait a minute. The drawer was open?"

"That's right. Key in the lock. Why? What is it?"

Francis said slowly, "If the feller in there had thought the ship was in danger or that somebody might get hold of the book he would have got it out ready to ditch it."

"So it could be kicking around on the deck in there."

Francis thought glumly, 'Or lying at the bottom of the bay.'

Sarah said, "I'll try the office again."

Francis chewed his lip then said grudgingly, "Once more, then that's the finish."

"I'll finish when I'm ready."

He caught her eye and did not waste time on argument, but privily decided that this was the last dive and she would be hauled aboard whether she liked it or not.

He said, "It'll be heavy, weighted so it would sink – "

"I know *that*!" She dived, and he waited.

She entered the office, taking the slack of the line with her in a loop around her wrist, feeling the light strain kept on it by Francis in the boat. She felt below the desk, around the chair bolted there, moved back towards the door . . . She felt rough canvas, a bag, a handle to it. It was weighty and rested on something. The thing moved, touching her arm as she lifted the bag. She felt at it with the hand that trailed the rope, meaning to push it away, but her hand clasped another, fingers groping.

Air exploded from her with shock. She kicked and went hand over hand up the line, banging through the door, iron stripping skin from her shoulders.

On the surface Francis felt her tugging and hauled in on the line, only to be checked as it tautened between him and the door below. Then Sarah burst up scarcely a yard away, threshed wildly one-handed, spat and took a whooping breath.

Francis thrust the boat away from the funnel and as it moved to her he reached over, grabbed her and manhandled her in over the side to lie gasping, shuddering. She still held the bag and Francis took it from her. "What happened?"

He had an arm around her, lifting her. With his free hand he reached to his hip pocket and pulled out a flat bottle. She accepted the bottle, gagged on the rum but felt it burn inside her. She shook her head or it shook despite her. Then: "There was a – that bag was lying on – a man."

Francis said softly, "Oh, my God."

Then the faint light around them was snuffed out. They turned as one to stare across the pool and saw *Thunder*, now a dark bulk except for her navigation lights, moving, slipping gently towards the channel.

Francis said, "She's on her way." He picked up an electric torch and crouched in the bottom of the boat, shading the light with his cupped hand. In the little glow he tugged at the straps of the bag that were water-soaked and stiff, then swore impatiently, took a clasp-knife from his pocket and sliced through the straps. The bag was waterproof and the book was dry. He opened it, riffled through the pages and sighed. His teeth showed as he grinned up at Sarah. "You got it. This is it. Their code-book." He stepped light-footed aft and as he started the engine Sarah stared after *Thunder*, now a blurring shadow and thought, 'This will make a difference, all the difference. This is his justification, this will give him time.'

Kaufmann blinked as *Thunder* slipped away but his eyes

went quickly back to the boat moored over the wreck of the collier. The boat was also moving and there was no stealth about her now. The noise of her engine growled at him across the pool and she ran straight for the quay. His engineer asked, "We go?"

Their orders had been to observe *Thunder* and report but Kaufmann shook his head. He could catch the old cruiser at Stillwater Cove.

"No. You wait here." And he leapt from the boat, ran up the steps to the quay and crossed it quickly to seek the shadows of the buildings. From that sheltering gloom he watched the boat sweep in, lost it as it ran in under the quay but heard the falter and die of the engine. A second or so later a girl climbed on to the quay, her dress clinging to outline the figure. She turned and called down to the boat, "I'm heading straight for the consulate. You follow when you're ready." She hurried across the quay and entered a narrow street.

Kaufmann hesitated only briefly while he reasoned. The girl carried under one arm a bag that still dripped silver drops as she crossed the quay. It had come from *Gerda* and she was hurrying to the British consulate. There was nothing conclusively menacing about that but it suggested – Enough. The mere possibility that they had found proof of *Gerda's* real purpose was enough to merit action and Kaufmann's course was clear. He could not follow the girl up that street but there were other ways to the British consulate. He broke into a run.

His way took him twisting and turning through alleys so narrow that he blundered along in near total darkness. Once he tripped and sprawled his length but rose immediately and ran on, but limping now. He came out into a narrow street that ran on to a wider thoroughfare and there was light ahead of him there. The thoroughfare led to a square. Light spilled out on to the square from the windows of the houses that surrounded it but it did not reach the garden of shrubs and

203

feathery topped trees that laid a dark shadow across the centre of the square. He ran to that darkness and into it, became part of it. He leaned against a tree and panted, wiped at his wet face with a handkerchief. He was a young and active man but the race had stretched him and the fall shaken him. He thrust away the handkerchief and closed his eyes for seconds, trying to regain his calm. That was essential.

The girl came hurrying around the square. As she opened the gate of the consulate and stepped on to the path leading up to the front door that door opened and Cherry came out. The sudden flood of light from the door set Sarah squinting as she approached but she could see Cherry in the act of thrusting something into his jacket pocket. It set Kaufmann to squinting as he stepped from the trees, the revolver held two-handed at arm's length. It was a good shot for a man partly dazzled, whose breathing was still irregular. It was a distance of thirty feet and he missed Sarah by inches, but Cherry spun and fell as the shot crashed out.

Sarah was still for a shocked instant but Francis, trotting around the square, yelled and sprinted. She reacted and threw herself down so that the second shot slammed into the door-post. Kaufmann did not get another chance. Francis piled into him in a flying tackle that crashed Kaufmann's head on the cobbles and sent the revolver leaping and skidding away.

Servants showed at the open door, peering out nervously. Sarah shouted at them from where she knelt on the path over Cherry, "Get a doctor! Quick!"

Cherry had been hit high in the chest and she snatched the handkerchief from his cuff to press on the wound. Then she saw the slip of paper, a corner of it sticking from Cherry's pocket. She opened out its folds and read the telegram. For a moment she held it, taking it in, then crumpled it savagely and cradled Cherry in her arms. Cherry had been leaving to do his duty, reluctant though he might be. Sarah saw her duty differently. She peered down into his unconscious face and whispered, "We got the proof Smith wanted and I'll see the Chileans have it." *Thunder*'s wireless was wrecked but they could send a signal by the station at Punta Negro to *Thunder* where she lay in Stillwater Cove, waiting for the dawn. They could call her back. As for the telegram balled in her fist, she would find it – later.

The telegram was to relieve Smith of his command of *Thunder* and place him under arrest.

13

Aboard *Thunder* the activity below deck bore fruit. As she slipped slowly down-river towards the sea, lights again sprinkled her decks so the men could see as they began to bring up the furniture, the stores. Everything that could be ripped out, somehow, and moved, somehow, was brought up and heaved over the side. She left a slow, thick trail. At the end of twenty minutes, down to coal for twenty-four hours anyway, she was down to stores for that same period and her inside scoured clean as a washed corpse.

Benks and Horsfall and a party of seamen staggered on deck with the wardroom piano and grunting, shoved it jangling into the river.

Benks groaned, "Going too far it is. He's barmy."

"No, he ain't. He knows what he's doing." But to himself, Daddy added, 'I hopes'. Because stripping for action was one thing and this was another.

On the bridge Garrick said, "They've thrown everything overboard but the galley stoves."

So Smith answered laconically, "See to it, Mr. Wakely."

"Aye, aye, sir."

They stripped the galley except for one stove.

Smith left the bridge and made his way down through the men as they worked and talked, joked, laughed. He passed them with his cap in his hand, the fair hair sweat-darkened and set close to his skull from the cap. He was smiling and the blue eyes searched them, but were not cold. He looked very young. They watched him pass and only then realised they had responded and returned the grin of this young Captain.

Smith descended into the bowels of the ship until he came to the marine sentry and the door of the cell where they had put Gibb. The marine snapped to attention, startled. What was the old man doing down here?

"Open up." Smith waited as the marine fumbled with the keys. Through the little barred opening in the door he could see Gibb in the glow from the solitary light. He sat on the edge of the bunk, hands pressed tight between his knees. There was no bedding, nothing in there but a bucket. Gibb looked up and peered uneasily as the key turned in the lock, saw Smith's face striped beyond the bars and rose to his feet. The marine opened the door and Smith's hand lifted to put on the cap, then he decided against it and walked in.

Gibb stood to attention, too rigid, too taut so that he wavered. His face was black with stubble and shiny with sweat. The knuckles of his clenched fists were bruised and the skin split.

Smith said, "You were in a fight with someone before you – left the ship?"

Gibb noted the hesitation and the choice of words and licked his lips. "Aye, sir." He knew Rattray was alive and working at that moment.

Smith stared at him for a long minute, not a trick to screw the man's nerves tight, but trying to sort out what to say and how to say it. He could preach or bully, sneer or appeal. No, he couldn't. He was not that type of man, not a man for speeches let alone emotional oratory. Anyway, he did not have the time.

So he said flatly, "We will shortly be in action. Would you rather be aloft doing your duty or down here?"

Gibb stared, swallowed and whispered, "Aloft, sir."

"Shave and shift into clean rig." And to the marine: "Give me the keys and report for your normal duties." The marine looked at him oddly then, but handed over the keys and left.

Ten minutes later the cells were empty and Smith returned to the bridge. He had sent two men back to duty. No superfluous weight.

Thunder slipped down between the dark shadows of the forest towards the sea. Then fine on the starboard bow opened a black void, a tunnel thrust into the forest, but to port lay Stillwater Cove.

Smith ordered, "Steer a point to port." *Thunder* edged over and into the cove, dead slow now, barely making headway against the tide that was beginning to flow. A cluster of lights crept into view over the starboard bow, set high on a low hill beyond the black void; they marked the signalling station. *Thunder*, lit up as she was, would be clear to the watchers there. Her anchor roared out, her engines stopped and she hung at the end of her cable as the pinnace had done.

Then the deck lights went out and there were only the riding lights to mark her position.

A lamp blinked a question from the signalling station. They had known she was coming but they put the formal question: "What ship is that?"

Thunder replied.

Voices called softly along the boat-deck and Garrick reported, "Whaler's away, sir." And then: "Gig's away, sir." The boats had been lowered by hand in near silence.

Smith nodded and looked at his watch.

One minute. Two . . . Ten minutes.

He was watching the shore to port and saw the blink of light there that was come and gone in the wink of an eye but a score of eyes had watched for it, marked it. That was

Midshipman Thorne who had taken the whaler and a dozen men, reporting that he was ready.

Now they waited for Kennedy, who had gone off in the gig.

Smith's eyes turned to starboard and he waited again in the night that enfolded them. There was no mist; that would come with the last of the night. The lights of the signalling station were clear but the station itself was not, though it stood on the crest of the hill. The night was overcast, without moon or stars, black dark here under the hanging wall of the forest.

Smith asked, "Who has Thorne got with him?"

Garrick answered, "Leading-Seaman Bates."

Smith nodded approval. Mention of Bates summoned up thoughts of the fore-turret and the men who manned it: Gibb, Rattray – he had been the victim of an 'accident', Albrecht had mentioned it acidly to Smith and Garrick.

Smith said absently, softly so only Garrick could hear, "I think young Gibb had a lot to do with Rattray's 'accident'!"

"Gibb?" Garrick's whisper could not hide incredulity.

But Smith was definite. "Yes. We must make other arrangements, split them up, after this." Then he realised what he had said and what kind of 'arrangements' they might be making in twelve hours' time. If any.

Garrick remembered the words of Fletcher, that he suspected Rattray was slyly picking on Gibb. Garrick thought that belatedly he agreed with Smith on this but that it was a bloody funny time to bring it up.

There came another blink of light where they watched for it, seeming right under the lights of the signalling station but down at water level.

Garrick said, "Kennedy."

"Seen." Smith ordered, "Slow ahead both. Douse the lights."

The riding lights went out. As they did so fresh lights blinked on, duplicates, where Thorne and his men had tied up their lanterns in the forest. *Thunder*, in total darkness now, eased up on her cable until Fletcher forward rasped, "Up 'n down!" And the blacksmith knocked out the pin from the shackle and that length of the cable fell to join the anchor on the bed of the cove.

"Hard astarboard!" The wheel went over and *Thunder* swung out of Stillwater Cove and cut across the main channel. Thorne and his men tumbled into the whaler and chased after her.

Kennedy stood on the shore, at his back the lift of the hill that hid him and the side channel from the signalling station. The water of that channel lapped at his boots and nudged the stern of the gig where it was drawn bows onto the sand. He could not see the two seamen on the opposite bank. He could not even see the seaman high above his head in the tree, nor those strung out, kneeling in a half-circle behind him. They were his sentries, armed with nothing more lethal than thick ropes' ends; his orders were not to be seen, let alone taken.

He saw *Thunder*'s looming, barely drifting bulk lift huge out of the dark and inch into the side channel. She moved past him with the only sound the slow beating swash of her turning screws. Not a voice, not a whisper, not a chink of light. She passed before him and into the darkness of the side-channel and was gone.

"Right," Kennedy said huskily, "it's time we were out of this. Recover that wire."

The two seamen with him on the bank began hauling in on the telephone wire that those in the trees had earlier lowered so that it lay on the bed of the channel. *Thunder* had passed over it. One of them ceased hauling at Kennedy's word and with Kennedy ran out the gig and rowed to the centre of the channel. The men on either bank, perched in the trees, were hauling on the lines attached to the telephone wire so that it emerged from the channel. It hung, not in a sagging loop, but in a sharp V because of the weights Kennedy had made fast to it to make sure it sank and was not cut. He cut the weights free and the wire rose into the night sky and was lost. By the time he reached the shore again the seaman was down from the tree. "All secure, sir."

Kennedy pulled in his sentries and they manned the gig. Halfway across the side-channel on their way back from picking up the two seamen on the far bank Kennedy leaned forward, gestured, and the rowers were still, mouths open. They heard the creak of oars then a boat came at them out of the dark and Kennedy called edgily, "Gig!"

Thorne's voice quivered back at them: "Whaler!" And she slid across their bow, the men in her pulling strongly, little Thorne in the stern, a white face turned to Kennedy, and disappeared after *Thunder*.

Kennedy took a deep breath. "Give way."

Almost at once *Thunder* grew out of the dark where she lay, just enough way on her to hold her against the still flowing tide. She was lowering her boats, all of them, again by hand and the men were swarming out along the booms and down into them. Kennedy thought, quoting Smith's orders, 'No superfluous weight'. Every man aboard who was not absolutely essential to the running of the ship at this time, went down into the boats. Butchers, bakers, stokers, seamen, marines. Albrecht and his little staff. All went into the boats. Enough stokers and engine-room staff remained to move *Thunder*, and men for her bridge and look-outs. Two cooks laboured in the almost denuded galley, sweating in rivers with every scuttle tight closed.

Near five hundred men went down into the boats, going over the side in the same way that every removable part of the inside of the ship, from stoves to stores to partitions to beds to the wardroom piano and Wakely's gramophone, in the same way and for the same reason as the boats themselves. Weight, taken out of *Thunder* for this one passage. The men and the boats might make a difference of a half-inch or more to *Thunder*'s draught. It might be vital.

The picket-boat crept up past *Thunder*'s length and took

station ahead of her, Manton at the wheel, Buckley with the lead already swinging from one fist as he balanced in the bow, getting the feel of it. Wakely stood in the stern to relay orders and reports. *Thunder* inched into the side-channel and the blackness of the night seemed to change in texture into a tangible thing through which they moved yet which seemed to move with them. Mist was here already, wisping pale across the surface of the channel, and through those trailing grey draperies and beyond, on either hand, they could make out the shore where the forest grew out of the water. *Thunder* seemed to stand still, only the slow heart-beat of her screws and the faintest wash from her bow showed that she moved against the tide. The forest and the mist and the night had reached out to wrap them round.

The hail came softly from the bow, repeated from the pinnace: "By the mark, five!" And Phizackerly stepped onto the bridge.

When Smith had let him out of the cell as *Thunder* ran down to Stillwater Cove Phizackerly went straight to the galley. Now he nursed a mug of cocoa as he said with hollow cheer, "'Evening, gennlemen."

Smith said, "Five fathoms. Do you know where you are?"

Phizackerly peered out at the night, to port, to starboard, ahead, his head thrust out on its scrawny neck, questing. "Aye. Five fathom as I remember right."

"You'd better remember right."

"Aye. Starboard a point." The night was chill. Phizackerly buttoned his jacket around him and shivered. He was like to catch his death of this. Lucky he hadn't died of fright already. The bastards had shanghaied him! *Him!* The expert! If they ever found out ashore – but they wouldn't. Smith wouldn't split and Phizackerly would never admit it. They had shoved him in a cell but they'd fed him like a fighting cock, wine with his meal an' all. But Lord! He'd been worried. And when Smith finally opened his cell and told

Phizackerly what he wanted he hadn't felt any better. It had been a long time.

"You said she would draw less'n twenty-five feet, Captain?"

"She's drawing twenty-four feet three inches."

"Fore and aft?"

"Fore and aft." Smith did not add that thirty tons of coal had been moved from forward to aft at cost of sweat and cursing on the part of the stokers to achieve that trim.

"Ta." Phizackerly was only slightly encouraged. He thought that it was one thing to stand safe in the sun full of wind and piss, and boast. It was another matter to prove that boast. He glanced furtively at Smith then quickly back to their heading. Smith seemed cool but that had to be an act, Phizackerly knew it. No master, no seaman could take his ship into this sort of trap without a sickening apprehension. Or rather no ordinary seaman could. Smith was a long way from ordinary and he would not want excuses. But then he thought that if he, Phizackerly, made a balls of this, Smith would not condemn. All at once he knew that and he had nothing to fear from Smith but it brought him no comfort at all. Now Phizackerly had no use for excuses either and felt he would die rather than offer them.

"Ease her a point to port." His voice was husky but there was a new note in it that brought a quick, curious glance from Smith. The whine was gone and the authority lost for fifteen years was back. He was the pilot and this ship was his charge. "Steady."

"And a half, five!" The hail came back, the voice disembodied, its owner unseen in the bow. Phizackerly nodded. That was right.

Thunder crept on through the channel that seemed narrow in any event between the cliffs of forest, was in fact desperately narrow where the deep water lay, where it counted. She seemed suspended, unmoving, in a small world of darkness and mist where even the clock was slowed to tick leadenly away the seconds of the night. The night went on for ever. Fractional changes of course, minute adjustments, with the bridge sparsely staffed by rock-still figures and the only sounds the slow-turning screws and the regular muted hail from forward, "By the mark, five!" . . . "And a half, five!" . . . "A quarter less five!"

They touched, the barest tremor rubbing gently at the skin of the ship beneath them and away. Touched again. And again. But always *Thunder* slid on.

They passed a village on the bank, the pin-point dull red glow of a fire's embers there and a dog that howled and barked, startling the hand in the bow so his call came: "By the mark – *Bloody hell!* – by the mark, five!"

And Smith said, "By the bark, five." Nobody laughed. They grinned nervously in response to his tight grin, teeth white momentarily against pale blurs of faces. Garrick wondered how he could find a joke, however weak, at this moment, because Garrick, like all of them, was aware of the risk that Smith ran.

As also was Smith. If he failed in this then at best he would somehow have to try to take *Thunder* astern into the main channel and to the fate that awaited her there. At worst *Thunder* could be stranded and interned, probably to lie for ever in this swamp to rot.

But they were better than halfway through and with time in hand. He had taken one more calculated risk and it was going right. In three hours or less it would be dawn but by then –

"*And a half, four!*" There was an urgency about that hail and the figures were sufficient to invest it with that urgency. *Thunder* was running into shoal water.

Phizackerly said, " 'Ere!" And: "*Stop her!*"

Smith snapped, "Call back the picket-boat!" And to Phizackerly: "Silted?"

Phizackerly scowled. "Sounds like it. Should be deeper than that."

The screws were still, *Thunder* drifted with the little way on her, stopped. The pinnace slid alongside and Smith called down, "You're certain about that last sounding?"

Buckley's voice came up, "Dead sure, sir. Straight up an' down. And we got another after: four an' a half fathoms."

The tide was at the full, slack water. Soon it would start to ebb and *Thunder*'s chance of running the channel would drain away with that ebbing.

Phizackerly said heavily, "She's silted. Never did afore, though it was always a chance, like, cause the channel forks here. Straight ahead there – see that light?" And as Smith nodded, "Another village on the right hand bank where the channel goes on, that's what that light is, but the true channel turns to port near ninety degrees and she's silted out from that *left* hand bank. So there just ain't the *room* to make that turn. Aw, hell! Of all the bleeding luck – "

Smith cut him off. "We'll take a look at it."

They went down into the pinnace and Manton took it creeping away from *Thunder*'s inert bulk to sound the channel. Phizackerly's forecast was proved depressingly correct. Over the years a bar had built up, maybe it had been building in Phizackerly's day, grain upon grain, running out from the left hand bank and cutting into the channel. The deep water was still there, just. If *Thunder*'s length had been less by fifty feet she might, just, have worked around that tight turn. As it was, she could not. They explored the channel where it ran straight ahead, the false channel, and proved it to be just that. The water was deep for about forty yards but then shelved rapidly. Phizackerly thought exploring it was a waste of time anyway. "It peters out. Another three, four hundred yards and you can walk across."

The village on the bank had its dog. It barked, howled, paced restlessly on the bank opposite them, barked again.

Smith said, "Back to the ship, Mr. Manton."

It meant feverish activity, furious work. Smith's carefully

hoarded time was being eaten away by this check, even if this check did not prove final and fatal, as it boded.

They cast off the boats that they had towed thus far and *Thunder* ran slowly ahead into the blind channel. So slowly. Her progress before had been creeping; now she barely moved. As she approached, lights blinked on in the village, and as she nosed into the channel, eased inching forward with barely a ripple at her bow, the population of the village stood on the bank, shrouded in blankets. They clustered together, eyes wide, fists to their teeth as *Thunder* grew on them out of the mist, first heralded by the distant, muffled slow drum-beat of her engines that came to them more as vibration than sound, felt rather than heard. Then a looming but unsubstantial spectral shape that became finally too real, black and huge, towering over them. Miles in the bow stared down at them and wondered what they made of it. Even the dog crouched, silent now, kicked into silence.

Thunder ran gently aground. Labouring they took a heavy cable aboard the pinnace, dragged its sagging unwieldy length to the right bank of the true channel and made it fast to a rock outcrop. *Thunder* went astern on both engines till she slid her bow off the oozing bottom, then slow astern on the starboard engine and dead slow ahead on the port while the capstan aft hauled in on the cable. It tautened, straightened and as *Thunder* came out of the blind channel her stern started to edge around towards the true channel.

Smith gave all his orders from the port wing of the bridge where he could see the channel and the slow-swinging stern and the pinnace anchored at the point of the spit that ran out from the far bank. The ship was still in darkness because any inordinate display of light might still be reflected and seen from Punta Negro, but he could see the water of the channel, slack water still – or was it ebbing now, pushing gently at the pinnace? He could see all he needed and they watched him. He saw the critical point and ordered, "Stop engines!"

Thunder was not clear of the blind channel. She still drifted astern with the way on her, still turning and with the cable dragging her around in an even tighter arc than before. Yet the stern edged across the channel until it hung over the pinnace and Manton broke out his anchor and shifted from under with Buckley sweating and swearing. The stern touched, dragged with that shiver through the ship and as the stern swung so did the bow as the capstan hauled her around and now the bow stroked sand, and stopped. The stern hesitated in its arc and the Chief at the capstan chewed his lip and Phizackerly's lips moved. The cable was bar-taut and the rock groaning out of the earth. *Thunder* was aground fore and aft across the channel.

The stern shivered again, moved, moved on as the cable groaned, coming around. The rock tore out of the bank like a tooth and the cable sagged and the capstan stopped. But *Thunder*'s stern pointed towards the sea and she floated.

Phizackerly breathed, "Gawd amighty!" He voiced the sentiments of many and one of them Garrick. Phizackerly thought there would be many a tale told about this lot. He would tell a few himself and he wouldn't need to lie.

A party in the whaler recovered the cable and the boats were taken in tow again. The pinnace took station ahead and *Thunder* headed once more towards the open sea – stern first.

The channel ran straight. Only once she struck, hesitated for a second on a bar right under her until the engines went full astern and dragged her, grating, over into deep water beyond. Smith thought he could see the faintest wash of phosphorescence where the sea broke at the mouth of the channel and Phizackerly leaned wearily on the rail. "There she is, then. She's yours, Mister." He felt washed out, limp, drained by nervous tension. He thought that Smith and his men had laboured like madmen for the privilege of having their heads blown off.

The dinghy was hauled alongside. Smith scribbled in his notebook, ripped out the page and tucked it in the pocket of Phizackerly's jacket. "A note for Mr. Cherry to say that you've done us all an enormous service tonight. Thank you." He held out his hand and Phizackerly shook it. "The dinghy is yours. Away you go."

"Thank you, sir." Phizackerly sniffed and cleared his throat. "God bless you, sir. Good luck to all of yez." He was properly embarrassed so that it came out in an awkward mumble as he headed for the ladder but they heard it and his sincerity. He was their last tie with the land. He went down into the dinghy and the seaman holding it there thrust it clear and climbed the ladder as the dinghy and Phizackerly bobbed away astern of them and was gone.

The boats came alongside and the men poured aboard and went straight to their action stations. Smith snarled at Kennedy, "Get 'em aboard! Quick as you can! *Quicker!*" Kennedy ran and Smith shouted after him, "And cast off the boats!" Garrick's head jerked around although he knew the order would come. Smith knew Garrick believed they would need those boats, and he was right, but they could not waste a second now let alone the time needed to recover the boats.

The pinnace they towed.

In the fore-turret the 9.2 was cleared away. Farmer and Chalky White shipped the circuits for lighting the layer's and trainer's telescopes and Gibb the circuit for lighting the dials. Communications were tested.

Gibb's heart thumped but he was watching the others and seeing the tension in their faces. Farmer turned his head and winked. Gibb licked his lips and grinned, feeling the muscles move stiffly. But they accepted him. He was back and one of the team; they needed him. Farmer had said, "Just do your job and hold on like the rest of us."

He would.

A minute later they were clear of the widening channel. For minutes more *Thunder* steamed out to sea as they strained

218

their eyes against the darkness, but there was no challenge, no sudden salvo smashed out of the dark.

There was a gradual stretching, an easing as the tension ran out of them, so that for the first time they were aware of the chill of the night, of weariness, thick mouths and gummy eyes. There was no sense of achievement, only disbelief that they had done it, that they had forced the channel. Only slowly did it come to them that they had slipped through the net.

Thunder was free.

14

CHERRY WAS SHOT on the stroke of midnight. The German consulate was only minutes away but Muller was long abed, preparing to be out at Punta Negro when the dawn came. It was nearly an hour before his staff, after hearing of the shooting and then dithering, finally woke him. When they did he smelt a rat but his cautious, surreptitious enquiries took time and when he found out the police held Kaufmann he could not believe it. That fool was under orders to watch *Thunder*!

So it was three in the morning when he went hurrying through the dark alleys down to Kaufmann's boat and got the story from the yawning engineer. Despite Muller's efforts the British had found a diver and dragged up from the *Gerda* – what? He did not know. He could make a guess but it did not matter. They had been satisfied with what they had found and gone running with it to their Consul. That was enough. The British would demand more time for *Thunder* and would probably get it, though he would fight them. But he was in a bad position now.

One thing was clear: the cruisers must be informed.

Kaufmann's boat cast off, surged away from the quay and headed for the channel. Muller was gratefully aware that he was leaving a hornets' nest behind him; the Chileans would be hammering on his door soon and demanding explanations from him. He was grimly aware that he must return sometime and face them, but he had time. He needed time to think.

When they sighted the signalling station at Punta Negro they also sighted the lights that marked *Thunder* where she lay in Stillwater Cove and as they came abreast of the cove Muller glared in, then stared.

15

Thunder WAS FREE, the Pacific open before her.

Free? It was an illusion. Smith said, "One man from each gun or department to the galley to draw. At the double!" And as the pipes squealed, "Slow ahead both."

He left the bridge to Garrick and went down to give Manton his orders. The boy looked tired, strained, as also did Wakely who was now on duty on the bridge. Both had worked continuously through a long night. It was still night but the day was not far off and Smith thought it would not be a long one. He gave Manton the orders for the pinnace. "You'll be running north along the coast, full speed ahead and you must not attempt to conceal it. No stoking restrictions now. You will maintain course and speed until you are recalled. Is that understood? Repeat the orders."

Manton repeated them, stumbling on a word but correctly. Smith asked, "Any questions?" And when Manton hesitated, Smith told him why.

A messenger trotted up with a paper-wrapped, greasy bundle of sandwiches in one hand, a kettle of tea in the other and lowered them down to the pinnace. The two cooks had prepared a mountain of bacon sandwiches as *Thunder* had crept through the channel. A low cheer came up from the pinnace.

Smith held out his hand to Manton. "Good luck."

"Thank you, sir. And to you, sir."

Smith watched him climb down into the pinnace. He was sending Manton away with only Buckley and Quinn, the signalman, Rudkin the engineer and Jenner the stoker. He heard Manton give the course, saw the pinnace sheer off and heard Buckley's pained, outraged protest: "Bloody *'ell!* We'll be seen for *miles!*"

Smith smiled bleakly and returned to the bridge. He stooped over the chart with Aitkyne and then ordered, "Steer three-four-oh." He went to the voice-pipe and spoke to Davies in the engineroom. "Chief, I'm going to want full speed ahead in a hurry."

"Not now?" Davies knew they were clear of the channel, had slipped through the net.

"No. Revolutions for eight knots." Smith turned away and far below in the clanging, roaring cavern of the stokehold the black gang spat on their hands and hefted their shovels.

He stood on the starboard wing of the bridge as *Thunder* headed out into the Pacific. Davies had thought they would be running full pelt for the north and safety but it was too soon for that. They had forced the channel and slipped the cruisers, but got clean away? That was too much to dare to hope for.

Smith swept the sea astern of *Thunder* once more with his glasses then lowered them and rubbed at his eyes. There was light astern but it was the glow against the cloud base that came from the lights of Guaya. And to starboard? He stared at the light between *Thunder* and the coast and Kennedy said, "That's Manton, sir."

Smith knew it. The pinnace was invisible at that distance but through his glasses Smith saw the light as a trail of sparks and a recurrent whiff of flame that pointed to her funnel and her position as plain as any pointing finger. It was a sign of appalling, careless stoking. Or a craft sacrificing any attempt at concealment for speed in flight.

Kennedy said involuntarily, "A bleating lamb." And bit his lip.

Smith only said quietly, "Yes." It was true enough. He had staked out the lamb. He would have to live with that decision. If any of them lived.

He ordered, "Starboard two points. Steer three-five-oh."

Thunder came around until she was running north at eight knots, parallel to the coast and to the course that Manton steered; he could still see the pinnace, just, a pricking, blinking red light.

Smith asked, "Bearing and range to the pinnace?"

Kennedy reported, "Bearing green one-five!"

"Range eight-four-double oh!" came down from the rangetaker.

The figures coincided with Smith's rough estimate. That estimate would have been good enough but the confirmation was useful and anyway, it did the rangetaker good to get his eye in. Smith worked out a little triangular problem in his head and got another rough answer: Manton led them by about eight thousand yards on a parallel course two thousand yards from that of *Thunder*. As Smith wanted him, and wanted *Thunder*.

He turned aft once more.

The ship was quiet now, closed up at action stations. Garrick had gone to the fore-top, and Smith held the bridge with Aitkyne, Kennedy, Knight and Wakely. Action stations. He was coldly aware once again that this ship, preparing to fight for her life, had not been intended to fight any such action. So her complement had been reduced. Now the eight guns on the main-deck were manned by scratch crews of off-watch stokers and others, though they had fired under Garrick, exercised under Smith. And the effective range of the six-inch guns was only six thousand yards.

He snapped irritably at Aitkyne, "Keep a good look-out astern!" And hid behind the glasses. Searching. Searching.

Was there a first faint lightening of the sky in the east? The sun rising now but still hidden behind the mountains of this mountainous coast?

They had been running for nearly fifty minutes.

Smith stood still, waiting, outwardly calm. Inwardly he was cherishing a wild hope, now. He had planned for one eventuality but now another, too ambitious to hope for, seemed a bare possibility: they might have got clean away. He still could not believe it. The chances of the decoy lights remaining undiscovered in Stillwater Cove dwindled as the night wore away and it was incredible they should not be discovered. *Thunder* was only matching the eight knots of the pinnace, she could run faster than this if she was going to run and now it looked as if the chance was there.

He had coal, just enough, to steam hard for a port in Peru to the north. There was a chance to escape annihilation, to coal and wait for the Japanese battle-cruiser, *Kunashiri,* and then sail south again with her ...

It was time to commit himself but he still waited though no longer able to contain that familiar restlessness of his, forced to pace out along the bridge and return, sensing the tension that prickled between Kennedy and Wakely, Aitkyne, that seemed to still all life on the ship.

The voice cracked urgent from the masthead: "Smoke bearing green one-six-oh!"

The still figures on the bridge jerked to life. Smith croaked, nerves slurring his voice, "Full speed ahead!" His glasses swept an arc on the approximate bearing and found first the faintest blink of funnel flame that marked the smoke that climbed black against the glow of Guaya.

Aitkyne quietly reported, "Smoke bears green one-five-nine. Range six thousaind."

The smoke lay five-and-a-half thousand yards astern of *Thunder*, was on the same course as the pinnace and maybe thirteen thousand yards astern of *her*. He was sure the ship, whoever she was, would not see the pinnace – yet. He swept the glasses from right to left, from the smoke astern through a blur of darkness to settle on the funnel flame of the pinnace, fine on the starboard bow. He stared at her then lowered the glasses.

His voice sounded harsh to himself as he ordered, "Get that man down from the masthead!"

"Aye, aye, sir!"

The minutes ticked away and the softly called bearings and ranges marked the minutes like the hand of a clock as the bearing ticked around the compass as the cruisers made up on the pinnace and crept up more slowly on the accelerating *Thunder* and edged out to sea towards her.

"Bearing green one-five-five ... Green one-five-oh ... Green on-four-five, range three-thousand.

Ten minutes. Fifteen. Twenty. All the time *Thunder* was working up to her full speed so the cruisers came up more slowly, and all the time he watched their smoke. His eyes were not playing tricks now. There was a lightening in the sky to the east so that the mountains now stood vague but black against the background of the coming dawn.

It would be a fine day.

He caught the flickering white of broken water that was bow-wave and wash below the pall of funnel smoke and the ships came up.

They were there. Two of them. *Leopard*, with less than half the cruisers' speed, would be trailing far behind. He could make out their silhouettes, or rather one long, blurred silhouette because they were in line abreast, the farther a fraction astern of the closer, seaward vessel. So that both of them could see the chase ahead and both could fire. They *had* to see the pinnace now; they were about five thousand yards astern of her –

They fired! The long tongues of flame ripped the night and Smith snapped his eyes shut against that glare. "Starboard ten!" He opened his eyes and the flames had died and out of the dark came the slamming bellow of the cruisers' guns. *Thunder* was heeling under him as he strained his eyes, peering for the cruisers and saw them take shape again off the starboard beam.

"Midships!"

Thunder was near her full speed and driving down on a course that would intersect that of the cruisers and take her across their bows, if held.

"Bearing green seven-oh! Range two thousand!"

The cruisers fired again, lighting up the dying night and this time he saw them lit in that split-second of brilliance, surging along at full speed, swift, powerful, deadly. They were still astern of *Thunder* but edging up to draw level with her. Unaware of her; intent on the target ahead. They could not see that target to identify it but were firing at the distant funnel flame, banking on the million-to-one chance that it could be no ship other than *Thunder*, a certainty.

The target. Smith remembered the target was the boy Manton and his little crew in their tiny cockleshell. A near-miss from one of those massive shells would swamp them and sink them, a hit would leave only splinters for flotsam. And another ghost to haunt him.

Wakely reported, "Picket-boat's still in sight, sir."

"Thank you." Of course Wakely would be watching out for the pinnace, for Manton. But that last salvo had not landed yet and if they survived it they would have to survive another.

"Range one-seven-double-oh!"

"Port ten! ... Midships!"

"Midships, sir!"

Thunder heeled then straightened and Smith swayed to it, eyes fixed on the shadows of the cruisers. Close! *Thunder* ran dead straight, paralleling the cruisers' course but leading them, on their port bow. It seemed they *must* see *Thunder*, but while they stood against that first faint light *Thunder* was out in the black void, and they were not looking for her there, eyes locked on the prey ahead.

"Bearing green one-three-oh! ... Range one-five-double-oh!"

The cruisers fired and now the crash of discharge followed only a blink after the flash. They were that close.

Through the shadows Wakely's voice came clear, edgy, "Picket-boat still in sight, sir."

So they had survived the second salvo but there was still the third, hurtling towards them now.

He could, *must* forget them.

This was the time.

"Open fire!"

There was an instant when he checked his breathing as if he was physically firing a rifle, then *Thunder* heaved as she fired her broadside. Simultaneously the searchlights crackled as their carbons struck arc to create the point of intense white light that was reflected by the big dished mirrors in the searchlights, beams flooding across the thousand yards of dark sea to swallow the dying flames of the guns and bathe the nearer cruiser in light – as the broadside struck her.

This was 'Smith's game', that they had played so many times with the pinnace and they had learnt the rules by heart.

The broadside could not fail to hit, fired at point-blank range, the trajectory virtually nil and the time of flight of the shells less than two seconds. Their impact was seen as the echoes of the guns' firing hung and their smoke still whipped on the wind.

It was *Wolf*. The ships were twins but Smith was certain that it was *Wolf* that took the broadside from the two turrets and the six starboard six-inch guns that fired as one seemed to take them all with leaping orange flash of burst, spurting grey smoke and explosion of impact that came rolling back across the black water.

He shouted, *"Douse!"* The searchlights expired and the

darkness rushed in to smother *Thunder* but he could still see *Wolf*. She was afire in three places, one aft and two amidships. Flame painted her black and yellow and shivering but very clear, very close. She would be closer yet.

"Hard astarboard!" *Thunder* heeled as the helm went over. "Port torpedo tube stand by!" The forward-turret was grinding around. The after-turret would not bear as *Thunder*'s bow came around to intersect *Wolf*'s course again. The forward of the starboard six-inch still bore but pointed at the sea in that tight turn. The rangetaker's chanting came down the voice pipe: "Eight-five-oh! . . . Eight-hundred! . . . Seven-five-oh! . . ." *Thunder* pounded along, still heeling in the turn. The 9.2 fired from the forward-turret, the searchlights slashed once more across the dark sea but were beaten this time by the impact as the range closed. They stabbed probing white fingers that showed *Wolf* leaping at them broadside out of the dark, fresh columns of yellow flame soaring and smoke balling up. She was rushing at them but *Thunder*'s helm was still hard over.

Kennedy shouted, "Torpedo running, sir!"

Smith lifted one hand in acknowledgment and shouted in his turn, "Midships!" *Thunder* hurtled down past *Wolf* at an acute angle, passing at their combined speeds of forty knots. In the swift-flying seconds as *Thunder* began to respond to the change of helm he saw on *Wolf*, lit now by a dozen fires, that her forward turret had swung to meet *Thunder*'s attack but too late. As searchlights shot their beams from her to chase *Thunder* a thumping explosion came from forward on *Wolf*. Then one more leaping flame.

Wakely screamed, "Torpedo hit, sir!"

They were barely a cable's length apart. *Wolf* seemed to stumble in her headlong career as the torpedo struck. Orange flames spurted but this time it was her guns firing and there came a crashing impact as a shot hit *Thunder*. But now they were charging right past *Wolf*'s stern and the after 9.2 and port side six-inch guns fired right into her.

Smith did not see the result of that. As they cleared *Wolf's* stern he ordered, "Hard astarboard!" So just as *Thunder* had settled to an even keel she heeled again into that swinging circle.

Wakely yelped, *"Jesus!"*

Kondor was also heading to cross *Wolf's* stern, seeking for a sight of the attacker who had burst from the night and was masked from her by *Wolf. Kondor* and *Thunder* were on a collision course. All of them on the bridge grabbed hold and hung on like grim death, instinctively preparing for that collision. There was nothing they could do. But they missed *Kondor*, it seemed by only feet, and swept past her in the blinking of an eye but in that blinking the forward-turret hurled a shell into her. And Smith saw that already *Kondor's* forward-turret had a gun pointing drunkenly; *Thunder* had done that thirty-six hours before. Guns fired on *Kondor* but they fired at a ship already storming away into the night, fired blind into that night.

Thunder still canted in the turn. Smith swallowed. "Midships!" He clawed his way out to the starboard wing of the bridge. They had been at it only minutes but mad, hell-filled minutes. *Thunder* had been hit, one of the port six-inch being put out of action and the after-bridge wrecked but she had come off relatively unscathed compared to the damage she had inflicted on *Wolf.* He could see her now, lit by flames from end to end and in that light she looked down by the head and scarcely moving. He could see *Kondor* too, clear of *Wolf* now and heading out to sea in pursuit of *Thunder.* He could see her against the growing light in the east but they would have their work cut out to see *Thunder* in the outer dark.

"Starboard ten . . . Midships!" *Thunder* steadied on the new course and the starboard six-inch battery and the after-turret bore on *Kondor.* The guns recoiled and bellowed. "Hard aport . . . Midships!" *Thunder* headed out to sea again.

"Port ten ... Midships!" It was the turn of the after-turret again but this time with the port six-inch battery.

Thunder dog-legged erratically out to sea and she was scoring. Smith could see *Kondor* and he could see the hits. He could also see that she was firing hard and steaming hard after him, but she was firing at a dimly-seen, jinking target. He saw the water-spouts of the falling salvoes and some were close but none of them hit. *Kondor*'s course was diverging from that of *Thunder*, not making a stern chase of it but trying to claw her way out of that stretch of sea that lay between *Thunder* and the growing light, light that she knew marked her in sharp silhouette for *Thunder*'s rangefinder and layers.

That diverging course meant that despite *Thunder*'s swerving the range was opening.

"Range five thousand!"

They were nearing the extreme effective range of *Thunder*'s old six-inch guns.

She fired her starboard broadside and he ordered, "Hard astarboard!" And this time she kept on turning through sixteen points and headed back into the light, and towards *Wolf*.

Smith could see all of his ship now in that grey light and the faces of Aitkyne and Kennedy and Wakely, all the bridge staff, all their faces strained but excited. *Thunder* was fighting a good fight and they knew it.

He had a bleak moment in that dawn. He conned his ship, keeping her jinking to confuse *Kondor*'s guns, but he looked ahead with cold certainty. The element of surprise was gone, the advantage of the dark was going and *Thunder* was still badly out-gunned. And *Kondor* was shooting well, very well indeed. A salvo plummeted into the sea close alongside, emphasising the point as the hurled water lashed across the bridge.

Finally, *Kondor* would have the edge in speed.

And *Wolf*? He thrust off the mood as *Wolf* took shape again. *Thunder* was racing down on her and she was still burning and she was not moving at all. He thought he could have left *Wolf* to her fate, would have wished to, but he needed her. Away to port *Kondor* had also turned and was roaring back towards her consort.

He said, "We'll shift to the conning-tower," and himself passed the word to Garrick before leaving the bridge. From the circular conning-tower below it, with its eleven inches of armour, their view was restricted to what they could see through the observation slits. It would have to serve. In the darkness he had risked fighting his ship from the bridge because he had to see. But now the day was upon them, from the conning-tower he would see enough and it was senseless to stay on the bridge.

They were under fire from both *Kondor* and *Wolf* now though the latter's firing was ragged. *Thunder* scored hits but was hit herself. And again. A starboard six-inch gun was reported out of action with the loss of its crew of ten men.

Smith warned, "Pass the word to look out for torpedoes!" *Wolf* still had teeth.

They ran down across her stern and a mile away and at Smith's order Garrick shifted the target from *Kondor* to *Wolf* and fired a broadside, raking her. *Thunder* turned to port and ran down past *Wolf*, pounding her. She was shrouded in smoke and the sun was above the mountains now so that *Wolf*'s rangefinders and layers had to peer through that smoke and squint against that low early morning glare, but she fired and, as *Thunder* pounded her, was pounded in return across two miles of sea.

They left *Wolf* astern and came under fire from *Kondor*. Smith ordered the target changed to her and, as the guns roared out, the change of course that pulled *Thunder* right around again in a sixteen-point turn to pass once more the blazing hulk of *Wolf*.

She was not only down by the head but listing to port now. Fires sprouted all along her hull and they saw her through rolling clouds of smoke. *Thunder* fired into her twice more and Smith thought he saw a solitary gun flash in reply but it might have been the flash of a burst.

He turned from her because they were done with *Wolf* but she had served her purpose. *Kondor* was driving inshore of her to chase *Thunder*. *Kondor* had not finished with them. She was chasing and firing hard, Smith could see the salvoes as the flashes rippled along her hull in awful beauty. But she, too, had been hurt, her second funnel leaned crazily against the next astern and –

Aitkyne drawled, he had to shout but being Aitkyne it still seemed a drawl, "I don't reckon she's making up on us, sir."

It was hard to tell but the feeling was there. And if she was making up on them it was so slowly as not to matter. She should have the legs of them but she had been punished. Smith grunted.

And then the salvo hit them.

Aitkyne was thinking that because of Smith they had still not felt the weight of *Kondor*'s fire.

Then the salvo struck. They had left *Wolf* astern and Smith's mouth was open to order yet another change of course when the salvo roared in like a train. It skittled them all except the Coxswain at the wheel and he staggered, recovered, picked up the course again. Smith pawed his way to his feet and felt *Thunder* listing. From the rear of the conning-tower he saw the cause of that list, the after funnel a battered cylinder of wreckage hanging over the starboard side. It slipped and the ship heeled further, slipped again and then ground over the side with wire stays parting and flailing and *Thunder* righted herself.

She steamed on and Smith croaked, "Starboard ten!" And: "Midships!" *Thunder* headed out to sea once more, the smoke-wrapped hulk of *Wolf* came between them and *Kondor* – and the guns fell silent. He called up the voice-pipe to Garrick: "Engage the ship astern of us!"

Garrick's voice came back, rusty and metallic, "Port an' starboard batteries don't bear on this course, sir, and the after-turret is out of action. No contact with them and I can't see much because of this damn smoke – " *Thunder*'s three remaining funnels still rolled it out – "but I think they took a direct hit. Can't see the other cruiser."

Yet. Smith said, "You will. You're doing very well!"

He found Kennedy at his elbow, who said, "After-turret a total loss, sir. We've a fire aft – " Smith could see that, flames leaping pale in the sun and bending on the wind – "and damage in the after boiler-room."

Thunder's speed had fallen away.

Smith ordered, "Port ten! Steer one-seven-oh!" He stepped to the voice-pipe and called the engineroom. The Chief's voice was strained. In the background a man was screaming and another shouted, "Put the poor sod out of his agony or get him *out*!"

Smith asked, "What speed can you give us, Chief?"

A second's hesitation, then Davies began: "I think – " He stopped, knowing Smith would not like that woolly answer. He said definitely, "I can maintain revolutions for fourteen knots."

"Thank you!" Smith called to Garrick. "Engage the enemy when sighted."

"Sir!" And Garrick added: "This light is hell."

It would be lancing into Garrick's eyes as he strained them towards the rising sun. Smith said, "Do your best." He had *Kondor* where he wanted her, where he had to have her and the bad light was a price they would have to pay for that. They would pay far more before they were done.

Kondor thrust out from behind *Wolf*, pointing at *Thunder* who steamed broadside to her on the new course, and opened fire as *Thunder* heeled again to her broadside. The battle closed down around them.

They entered, and existed in, a world of thunderous discharge and shuddering impact as hits ripped into the old ship's frame. Damage reports came in by voice-pipe or gasping, staring messengers. Smith conned his ship, swerving her to try to unsight the enemy, listening to the endless reports of damage and death, to the ranges called: "Double-five-double-oh! ... five-six-double-oh! ..."

The range was opening. "Port four points!" Smith set to closing it again. The enemy was edging away, trying to open the range and make it a big gun battle. *Thunder* had only one big gun now.

Minutes later *Kondor* opened the range again, and again Smith ordered a closing course. The message he sent was clear: If *Kondor* edged away he would follow her until she ran aground. But he knew the Captain of *Kondor* would not just accept that.

When Wakely shrieked, *"Torpedo! Red-four-oh!"* Smith leapt to his side and peered at the tell-tale track.

"Hard aport!" *Thunder* turned towards the enemy and the torpedo. The alternative was to turn away but Smith would not open the range, would not show *Thunder*'s stern with her after-turret incapable of firing, still smoking. The torpedo ran down *Thunder*'s side, well clear of her and clear away. Smith stared at *Kondor* as *Thunder* held the turn. *Kondor* was already turning, intent on running back along her wake and then clawing out to sea where she could dictate the course of the fight. Smith held the turn, then: "Midships!"

So they were running again on parallel courses five thousand yards apart and *Thunder* a steel door between *Kondor* and the open sea. *Kondor* hammered at the door; the nerve-battering, brutal slogging match went on.

In the conning-tower, thrown about, deafened, bruised, Smith took the reports as they came in. They came baldly, without lurid description that would only have understated the horror of a ship and a crew being torn apart.

The twin after six-inch casemate on the port side took a

direct hit from an 8.2-inch shell that wrecked the main-deck-gun, the upper-deck gun above and decimated the crew of the latter. Only Daddy Horsfall walked out of it and clear around the splinter-swept chaos of the upper-deck before consciousness crept in slowly from his body to his mind. He felt for the carefully sock-wrapped bottle that held his illegally hoarded tots and found that as miraculously intact as himself. He drank as if it was water then looked for a way off that exposed upper-deck and for work for his hands. He ducked below and headed forward. Behind him, a minute later the after starboard casemate was mangled beyond recognition.

The port forward casemate took a freak hit on the muzzle of the gun that left its crew tossed about like dolls but still alive. That was Nobby Clark's gun. He bellowed at them, dazed and deaf, "All right! Don't lie there idling an' scratching your arses!" He started to shove them out of the smoking wreckage like a dog herding sheep. His intention was to aid any short-handed gun; there would be gaps from casualties now. Before he got them out another shattering hit sent them all flying again. But once more he rounded them up. One of the port side midship casemates had ceased to exist, blasted clear out of the ship into the sea, leaving a smoking hole.

The upper-deck was an obstacle course from a nightmare, unrecognisable, a strange place of ripped, curled plates, jagged-edged; piled wreckage and tangled rigging; sprouting fires fought by ghosts that came hoarse-voiced, haggard and filthy out of the smoke, trailing hoses, and were lost in it again; over all rolled the smoke, from the fires, the clanging guns, and *Thunder*'s belching funnels. Clark fought his way through and hauled and herded his crew along by willpower and discipline. He lost his layer to a hit somewhere forward that filled the flaming hell with screaming splinters and threw them all to the deck. Clark would mourn for the layer as a friend but later. He led the rest below to a starboard six-inch with a dead crew they dragged aside.

They manned the gun moving like automata. The shell

and the charge came up after Clark talked on the voice-pipe with Sergeant Burton who now seemed to be running some of the magazines. It was a miracle that repeated itself while they laboured unaware that fighting had run the magazines low and some were lost and locked under water in flooded compartments. The ammunition that came up the hoist, which was worked manually because the power had failed, had travelled half the length of the ship from a port side magazine. The few men of the ammunition parties that were left carried those shells and charges along narrow ammunition passages. These were in almost total darkness, smoke-filled, blocked in places by wreckage they had to climb around or over and the projectile a huge deadweight.

Elsewhere in the 'tweendecks men toiled in the smoke and frying heat, hauling at canvas hoses as they choked, with weeping eyes but fighting the fires. They saw the horror around them, the littered dead in the bloody, smoking wreck that *Thunder* had become but they kept on. Duty was something to hold on to in a world gone mad and being blasted apart around them.

Clark in the layer's seat squeezed the trigger and the gun slammed into action.

Down in the forward 9.2 magazine Benks continued the praying he had begun before the action, with only a break for the catch of his breath. He knew nothing of the progress of the battle, down there below the waterline in his hushed little monk's cell with the charges. He only knew the turret still fired rapidly and he was kept hard at it filling the demanding hoist. And that *Thunder* had been hit and hit again more times than he could count but he had felt them all, shuddered to them. He had commended his soul to God and now prayed for the men in the turret above him. He had not expected they would all live this long.

In the conning-tower the reports came in. "Hit forward, sir! Torpedo flat and prison flat flooded!"

Smith acknowledged the report, it was just one more blow,

and altered course again in that continual erratic weave trying to outguess the enemy guns. Occasionally he saw *Kondor* through the drifting smoke that surrounded her and saw she was badly mauled. As a raider she was finished; she needed a dockyard and that meant internment. *Wolf* was in at least as bad a case and probably worse, lying crippled, miles away.

But as *Thunder* fired her remaining guns, there were only three now, and as Smith strove to evade the salvoes that rained down in reply, it was evident that *Kondor* had the whip hand. She was firing more guns, four or five, in regular salvoes, the flashes rippling down her side.

The beating went on. An explosion right over the conning-tower sent them sprawling for the twentieth time, there was a rending crash and as Smith dragged to his feet with blood running from his nose he saw that the mast had gone, fallen back along the length of *Thunder*'s deck, thrusting the tilted, riddled funnels to an even crazier angle.

Garrick's voice, hoarse and urgent, no longer echoed down the voice-pipe because the fore-top was now just part of the wreckage heaped in the waist.

The beating went on.

Thunder swerved under Smith's orders and twice salvoes fell alongside, while he saw that *Kondor* was hit and that she had fires of her own, flames licking yellow through the smoke, but her firing did not falter.

Thunder had only one six-inch gun still in action besides the forward-turret. She took a direct hit on the turret. The orange flash split the smoke-filled drum of the conning-tower. As the flame blinded them, the blast rattled them around the drum but Smith held on and kept his feet as did the Coxswain at the wheel. As Wakely rolled to his knees Smith grabbed at him and hauled him upright, croaked, "Get a fire party on that turret!" And thrust him, staggering, on his way. That was the most Smith could do. The turret and the men in it he must now forget. He looked again for the enemy.

Thunder's speed was falling away. *Kondor* was head-reaching on her and he saw she was starting to turn, slowly, to creep across ahead of *Thunder* and so out to sea. She was trying again to make it a big gun battle and *Thunder* did not have a big gun. She would haul out of range of the lone six-inch and then smash *Thunder* to pieces. Smith could not stop it.

"Steer four points to port!"

Thunder started to turn so that at least that one six-inch would bear.

Reports had built on themselves to tell him of a ship so battered that it seemed not an inch of her but had been torn by high-explosive, ripped by splinters or scourged by fire, a ship that still fought with a solitary gun, that still functioned only by the courage and the dogged discipline of the men who manned her. He did not need reports. He could see some of the havoc from the conning-tower, feel the sluggish response with the ship's speed down below ten knots and falling still.

She was dying beneath his feet.

16

WHEN THE HIT smashed the mast below Garrick it threw him up in the air to fall on his back in the fore-top, that was itself already falling. For a second it hung as stays parted, then it fell and Garrick fell with it. He clung on with arms wrapped around the mast as the fore-top smashed against the funnel and then on to the boat-deck. He was hurled loose to roll and almost plunge the ten feet to the upper deck but he grabbed half-dazed for handhold, found one and held and checked that rolling as he hung on the edge.

He was winded, bruised, disorientated. His left arm *hurt* and he could not move it. He collected his scattered thoughts slowly but with instinctive sense of priority realised his danger out there on the boat-deck where splinters whined with every hit that *Thunder* took. So he rolled over the edge, this time of his own volition and at his own speed, lowered to the length of his good arm and dropped to the deck. His legs gave under him and he collapsed in that illusion of shelter as *Thunder* was hit forward.

Flame reached back a long tongue to lick at the conning-tower, blinding him. When he opened his eyes he was staring down at the deck below his face, clinging to it. His legs felt numb, useless. He rolled over and rubbed at them, flexed them, until he felt the numbness running away and instead the pain of a huge bruise across the backs of his knees. He tried to stand and succeeded at the third attempt. He had to reach the Captain. He took a step and *Thunder* was hit aft and he skidded once more across the deck. He climbed to his feet blaspheming, sobbing at the pain in his arm then stopped and stood with breath held. Then he turned and started to stumble aft, felt the shock and slam of a six-inch firing and thought that there was one gun still firing, and then somehow broke into a shambling trot.

The engines . . .

Albrecht's little party consisted of Gabriel, the sick-berth Petty Officer, and Purkiss, with half-a-dozen cooks detailed as assistants and gruesomely, the butcher. Through the first few minutes of the action they waited scattered around the sick-bay. The ventilation was still working then and the air was tolerably clean but they sweated. The scuttles were closed so they could see nothing of the dark world outside. They rocked and braced themselves as *Thunder* heeled and rolled in those tight turns and shuddered as her guns fired and jerked at the nerves of all of them.

They waited, Albrecht with hands resting on the operating table, shirt sleeves rolled up above the elbows. His eyes checked once again the knives and saws, the gag and the drop-bottles of chloroform and ether.

Until *Thunder* shook to shock that was not recoil and a crash that was no discharge. She had been hit.

The horror began. The casualties came down; vicious splinter wounds, the flesh cloven to the bone; hideous burns. Albrecht saw the shock on the faces of his raw amateurs and even, carefully concealed but obvious in its stiff-faced absence, on Gabriel and Purkiss. This was new to all of them. Albrecht seized on his expression of professional detachment and stamped it on his face and on his mind. Feeling he would banish until later when it would hurt no one but himself. From now until it was over he would not feel. It was a determination hardly held.

The trickle of casualties became a stream, the wounds more terrible, the task impossible. The sick-bay filled as Albrecht operated with Gabriel's assistance, Purkiss stitched and treated and the amateurs wound on dressings. As the ship rocked and lurched around them the light flickered and returned, went out and gave way to the emergency lighting. The ventilator sucked down smoke and fumes now, and vomit added to the stench. The stream of shattered men became a river, overflowing the cots and carpeting the deck with their bodies.

Then the firing ceased. Albrecht thought, 'Maybe he's surrendered. He must have surrendered.' But he did not believe it. Or was Smith dead? Were all of them dead up there – it was incredible that they should survive – were all the survivors here, around him in this abattoir?

Looking up for an instant he saw Daddy Horsfall and a stoker black with coal dust stumble in, a body between them. They found a space and carefully, gently laid him down and Purkiss went to them.

Albrecht called, "Horsfall!"

He came over, looked once, quickly, at the thing on the table then up at Albrecht. Who asked, "Has the action ended?"

"Dunno, sir."

"If it has I want to move out of this. Find out what you can. I want a place with light and air –" *Thunder* came out of a turn and the smoke and opened fire. The ship shook. Albrecht finished: " – as soon as it's over."

"Aye, aye, sir." Daddy went away, thinking: 'You'll be bloody lucky, old cock. D'yer suppose some referee'll blow fer time? More like the first you'll know'll be the water round your balls.'

242

Albrecht worked on. The hit just forward sent him to the deck and Gabriel sprawling, clawing over the table to hold the latest victim from following the surgeon. The emergency lighting failed totally. Gabriel produced a torch then others flicked on and bobbed around them. The ship still shook but Albrecht knew his shaking came from inside now and clamped down on that weakness to keep his hands steady until the job was done. And the next one. And the next . . .

Until he stopped. Everything stopped. He stared across at Gabriel, similarly frozen, as the sick light of the torches made greasy yellow masks of their faces.

Gabriel said dully, "Stopped, sir." And: "Engines have stopped, sir."

Gibb had worked lost to the world outside the clanging, reeking turret. Fletcher, and the trainer and the layer through their telescopes, saw something: smoke, spray, a blurred and lurching, distant target that was lost, seen and lost again. Everyone else sweated in ignorance of how the battle went. Until they were hit.

Gibb returned to hazy half-consciousness to realise numbly that a great weight lay across his legs, pinning him to the deck. He had been hurled against the side of the turret and lay there. Now besides fumes, smoke rolled in the turret and flame danced. Hit in the instant of loading, the shell lay on the deck below the open breech and the charge was scattered around the turret and blazed in a dozen places. It blazed around Gibb. The crew, like the charge, were tossed about the turret. Through weeping eyes he saw that the weight on his legs was Farmer Bates.

He had to move. He shoved feebly at Farmer's bulk but could not shift it. He choked on fumes and then he saw the figure that blundered through the smoke and stooped over him. He recognised him by the bandage. Rattray glared at him. He carried a bucket of sand and he dumped it on a flaming fragment of charge. Then he knelt and rolled Farmer Bates away, worked a hand into Gibb's collar and dragged him across the turret.

Gibb's legs hurt him. They screamed with pain at the slightest movement and he almost fainted again on the rough passage across the turret. At the door Rattray let him down. The door was jammed and Rattray had to kick at it until it swung heavily open. He fell out on to the deck, scrambled around on hands and knees and hauled Gibb out after him. Still on all fours he dragged him clear of the turret to lay him down by the conning-tower, then collapsed beside him.

Rattray lay for a full minute, chest heaving, coughing, eyes narrowed on Gibb, then he pushed up on his hands and crawled back to the turret and in. Gibb saw him standing, a bucket in his hands, and saw another flame doused. When Rattray came out again he brought Bates with him.

After another minute of retching and coughing Rattray went to the turret again and Gibb watched him, vague in the smoke, before his eyes closed. He slumped against the conning-tower and sucked in the air that was tainted with smoke on the deck of this smoke-wreathed ship, but sweet compared to the murderous reek in the turret. When he opened his eyes again smoke still oozed from the turret but there was no longer the flicker of flame. Rattray did not come out.

He looked beyond the turret and saw the enemy cruiser and the flashes along her hull and he knew that another salvo had been fired at *Thunder*, at him.

He tried to get away from it, dragging his body around the conning-tower and somehow dragging Farmer Bates as well. He cried at the pain in his legs but strove frantically for shelter. As he went the random thought flicked through his mind that *Thunder* had not fired a gun for a minute or more, but when he reached the dubious shelter to port of the conning-tower, and slumped there with Farmer beside him, he felt and heard the thump and bang of a six-inch firing and thought, 'We're not finished yet.'

But he knew he was finished.

He should try, somehow, to reach the sick-bay but he was just too tired. Somebody might find him and Farmer and take them there. He doubted it but he could do nothing about it.

He wondered if there *was* a sick-bay any longer. He could see no one forward of the conning-tower. No fire party. Young Mr. Wakely lay not far away, scalp bloody and eyes closed. He still breathed. Gibb could see the rise and fall of his chest, would have liked to help him but he just could not move.

Thunder was hit as the salvo fell, the deck lifted beneath him and splinters whanged and whined around the conning-tower. As he started to breathe again a seaman's sense warned him that something was amiss. He groped for it, woolly-minded and then it came to him: the engines had stopped.

Just feet way, Smith felt the heart stop, as they all did. Now *Thunder* lay inert to be destroyed at will.

Another salvo shrieked in.

Nobby Clark, eye glued to the layer's telescope, squeezed the trigger and the gun recoiled and spat flame, the smoke blew back and fumes swirled. The gun's crew at his back rocked to the recoil, recovered then fell yet again as *Thunder* was hit.

Nobby rubbed at his forehead where it had slammed against the telescope and snarled back at them, "Come on, you lot! The've just dropped another brick on us. Let's 'ave another one for them!" And under his breath: Bastard's *too* bloody good!

He held that breath, feeling the heart-stop, and the sight-setter croaked, "Engines have stopped."

Nobby sighed. Oh, Christ. He bellowed, "Where's that

flaming round?" He half-fell from the layer's seat, stumbled back to the hoist and bawled down into the darkness, "Where's the ammunition? What're you doing down there, for Gawd's sake?"

There was silence, only the ringing in his sound-battered ears, then he heard movement in the passage below and saw at the bottom of the hoist a face turned up to him, just a smudge, unrecognisable under the filth and in the gloom but the voice was unmistakable. It came up, gravelly, calm, "Noisy bastard, ain't you." Burton the indestructible.

"Just give us the round."

The hoist creaked and the round came up, was rammed.

The charge was inserted. As the breech clanged shut Nobby slipped back into his seat, rubbed at blood-shot eyes and peered through the telescope again. This was one of the main deck guns, close to the waterline, and unthinking he muttered another old jest of _Thunder_'s crew: "Like being in a submarine!"

He could see the cruiser as a ghost ship almost hidden by the smoke she made and trailed; he could see she was burning, great gouts of flame leaping through holes in her hull. He thought that _Thunder_ was sinking but she had savaged the cruiser. Or Smith had. Got the first one in and a few more. Like he laid for them down some dark alley and turned them over afore they could help themselves.

He laid the gun. The way had fallen off _Thunder_ and she was still in the water so that he was firing from a rock-steady platform. He squeezed the trigger.

Recoil. Flame and smoke and fumes.

With his eye glued again to the telescope, watching, he ordered automatically, "Load!"

"No bloody round to load."

He heard them shouting huskily down the black steel well of the hoist.

It was now too terribly easy to watch. _Thunder_ lay still, dead still, so that he and the trainer kept the ship in the scopes easily, hardly touching the wheels. *Thunder* was a sitting target and they both knew it.

He saw the flash on the hull of the distant ship and thought, 'Hit her –'

Blinded, he recoiled from the telescope, hands to his eyes. A flash like a great burning sun had blotted out the cruiser. He rubbed at his eyes, blinked at the wheeling lights. The explosion came rocking across the sea in great shock waves and he clawed at the telescope, pulled his watery eye to it, spun the wheel till the gun was laid and he glared at the cruiser. A ball of smoke climbed up from the cruiser, rolled up and up, shot with sparks and debris soared in that smoke, soared and then fell.

He whispered, "She's blown up."

Kondor sank.

SUNLIGHT SPARKED ON a quiet sea. Smith stood forward of the conning-tower, clear of the twisted wreckage of the bridge. He was numbed. The deck on which he stood was unrecognisable as that of any ship let alone his. Forward of him the turret smoked thinly, the barrel of the gun askew; the fore part of the ship was a moonscape of craters. Aft was a scene of tangled wreckage laced with licking pools of flame fought by men who stumbled over and around the wreckage, weaving like drunken men. It was a cat's-cradle of twisted steel, riven plates. Of the three funnels remaining to *Thunder* only one stood, riddled. The two aftermost had fallen in on each other, joined by the mast and the whole steel mountain sagged over the port side, canting the deck. She was down by the stern.

Garrick was alive. His face was streaked with black blood from his scalp, one arm hung limp and his face was drawn with pain but he had reported and returned to his duty. So had Davies, his boiler-suit half-burned from him, his grizzled hair singed. And the long Miles, who seemed to bear the mark of every fire aboard.

And Smith had gone to see for himself. The steering compartment was wrecked and flooded; she was flooded right forward to the engineroom bulkhead. She was also flooded in several compartments forward. There was no power at all.

Davies summed it up, hugely understated the obvious: "It's a dockyard job."

That meant a tow. No doubt a tug would come, hurrying, a vulture. It meant internment. For the ship and her crew, for Smith himself.

But the fires were under control and *Thunder* was not sinking.

Wolf was sinking.

They could see her by squinting red-weary eyes against that sun that was still low, across the miles of sea. Smith, with his glasses, could see her better. He looked again and again during the swift-flying minutes of his tour of inspection. A man here and there would lift his head to pause and breathe and stare before working again. Watching as she sank. They were all still, watching, when her stern lifted and her bow went under and she slid down. A rush of steam, and smoke from the funnels hung in a spreading pall like a shroud.

It covered the men in the water. Smith could not see them with the glasses but they would be there. There were no boats to be seen and Smith had none to send. The pinnace had crabbed alongside to weak cheers, Manton at the wheel and all hands bailing. When Manton stood swaying before Smith he had explained, "One dropped rather close, sir." She leaked in a dozen places and now she hung in the water, not floating, where they had made her fast at *Thunder*'s side. She was no more seaworthy than a colander.

Smith came on Gibb where he sprawled blank-eyed and gasping by the conning-tower, Bates at his side. He had them carried to the upper-deck abaft the bridge where Albrecht had contrived to clear a space to which he was evacuating his wounded. They carried them up, coughing, from below.

Albrecht glanced at him coldly. Albrecht was devoid of emotion; professionally he had no time for it but in any event he was drained of it. He had seen too many men die, was glutted with pain. "I'm setting up here. The sick-bay is impossible. Everything smashed. A hit – "

"I know. Do what you can."

"I've blankets, bandages and cold water for one-hundred-and-forty-seven cases of everything from concussion to amputation, to severe scalding, to burns. The burns – " He shook his head. "There are more. They're still coming in, they're still finding them. Young Thorne has a broken leg, young Vincent is dead. Knight is dead."

He stopped at sight of Smith's face, who knew that Lieutenant Day was dead. He had commanded in the after-turret which was a total loss. Lieutenants Knight and Day, who had been the coster and his missus at the ship's concerts. No longer a comic turn. He knew that *Thunder* had seventy-three dead – so far.

Albrecht sighed and went on wearily, "I'm not blaming you. I know that if you hadn't fought those cruisers they'd have run wild all along this coast, and all the rest of it. I know. It had to be done. You did it and still saved most of us and the ship though only God knows how. I still can't believe it. The surgeon's knife. I only wish my surgery was as successful as yours, but we both have to live with it."

Smith knew that; he had laid one ghost only to raise another. He said, "Anything you want, anything I can do . . ."

"I know. If you have time, later, you ought to come and talk to the men." Albrecht smiled wryly. "They call you all kinds of a tough, mad bastard, but they love you, all of them."

That silenced Smith, daunted him while he simply could not understand it. But he looked at the men where they lay uncomplaining, silent or weakly joking on the deck and beyond them to the others who laboured like filthy spectres, and beyond them in his mind's eye to the others below, out of his sight in the smoke-filled reeking darkness. And he wondered for the thousandth time or more in his life how he could deserve men like this.

Albrecht cleared his throat. "And I'd like to see that boy Wakely. One of my lads put a dressing on him but I want him as soon as you can spare him." Smith had seen him working on the deck below, the once plump and pink Wakely now haggard and grey, skull wrapped in a bloody bandage.

Albrecht started to turn away and the shell shrieked in and landed aft in the centre of a working-party. Smith winced against the flash, rocked by the burst and saw men tossed like bloody dolls. He stared stupidly then his eyes searched as he cursed himself for forgetting, knowing what he would find.

The *Leopard* was coming in from the sea. *Thunder* had left her behind guarding the mouth of the river, a cork in an empty bottle, but she had followed the cruisers. He had forgotten her. She was coming in from the sea because she would have set that course while *Kondor* still fought, not risking going inshore of the bigger ships. Now she was left with nothing but vengeance and she would take it. She must know *Thunder* hadn't a gun that would fire seaward. She only had two four-inch guns herself and they would not sink *Thunder* quickly but they would steadily tear her to pieces.

There was nothing to stop her. Garrick was trying with a party to clear a midships twelve-pounder that looked as if it *might* have survived. If he succeeded that pop-gun would not stop *Leopard*. The men were ready to fight again but they stumbled with fatigue. Near one-hundred-and-fifty wounded and not a boat.

He saw Benks standing among the wounded where they lay in rows on the deck. "Benks!" He spoke briefly, tonelessly, to the hollow-eyed steward and Benks disappeared below and Smith climbed to the fore-deck to stand by the conning-tower, eyes fixed on the gunboat. Like a rich man's yacht. He flinched as her forward gun fired again. The round burst close alongside.

Smith had thrown himself to the deck but he scrambled up as Benks called to him and he took the bundle from the steward. He jammed it inside his jacket to leave his hands free and started to climb painfully slowly, wearily up through the tangle of wreckage to the top of the conning-tower. A shell burst on the useless fore-turret and blast plucked at him, splinters droned and snarled through the wreckage. He hung on, looked down and saw Garrick standing by the twelve-pounder that was abandoned, unworkable, staring dumbly up at him, agony in his face. Smith turned away from him and climbed again. The gunboat was only nine hundred tons, not a tenth of *Thunder*'s bulk. She had only ten knots of speed and was manned by a rusty, unhandy crew but she carried *Thunder*'s certain death in that gun.

He stood up on top of the conning-tower, blinking at the gunboat as he fumbled at the big, white tablecloth tucked inside his jacket. Garrick's face showed agony but Garrick knew as well as he that Smith had no choice. The gunboat came on. She would turn soon so that she could fire both the fore and aft guns, and then . . .

The water-spouts rose in white towers, a line of them that hid the *Leopard* behind a curtain of water that hung for seeming seconds as the sound of that salvo came rumbling across the sea. As the water fell and the spray blew away he could see her turning on her heel, but turning away from that sudden enormous salvo from out of the blue. The sound-wave rumbled in bass over the sea and staring aft he saw *Kansas*, unmistakable, huge, roaring up from the south.

Aboard *Kansas* the messenger from the wireless-room said, "Signal, sir."

Donoghue took it, read it and handed it to Corrigan who muttered the words as he read: ". . . 'commence hostilities' . . . Came just a trifle late."

Donoghue growled, "I didn't commence hostilities. I said we would come out in case survivors needed assistance but once here I wasn't going to sit on my butt and watch murder done. However. Order that gunboat to heave to or we'll sink her. And make to *Thunder*: United States at war with Germany. Where are the enemy cruisers?"

On the signal bridge a yeoman with a telescope to his eye drawled, "Feller on top of – the bridge – I think. Signalling with a couple of white flags. He's hellish slow, even for a limey."

Smith was rusty.

The answer came to Donoghue. *"Thunder* replies, sir: 'Sunk. Can you tow me?' "

Corrigan said quietly, "Jesus Christ."

Donoghue groped for some noble phrase, some stirring reply but this was an exercise alien to him and he remembered the slight, filthy, lonely figure on the quay naming himself simply, "Smith."

And Donoghue said, "Affirmative."

Smith fought off the lassitude of reaction and started the climb down to the deck. There was work for him to do but there would be help for all of them now, for Garrick, for Davies, for Albrecht and the men. For the ship. His mind already worked on the details of the tow, of the bulkheads that needed to be shored up. *Kansas* could lend them divers ...

He found himself wondering about Sarah Benson and the destruction wrought this day. There was a good reason for that destruction, for him at least. When she had raised the pistol at arm's length and fired – what was the reason? He had never asked her ...

The battered hulk that was *Thunder* wallowed in the seaway. "One long roll ..." On *Kansas* as she swept down on her every man who could find a spot where he was able to stare at that hulk, in silence.

The guns were silent.

Arnold Phizackerly stood in the stern of the dinghy at the mouth of the channel. He had waited there listening to the rumble of the distant guns and peering out at the far flaming that marked them. Now with the sun warm on his back he stared at the smoke on the horizon, unable to make out any ship, and wondered.

Sarah Benson listened to that silence, cold. And waited.

EDWARD L. BEACH

DUST ON THE SEA

From the depths of the Yellow Sea a wolfpack wages its savage war on the Japanese. Three American subs must destroy vital reinforcements bound for Okinawa. Their orders are to harass, attack and sink the enemy.

But the sea is a vicious battlefield. In its depths hunters become the hunted, submarines sink and men die. And once the brave men have gone only the dust on the sea is left to mark their grave.

DUST ON THE SEA may well be the last great novel of World War II to come from one who knew and fought in it.

CORONET BOOKS

MORE WAR BOOKS FROM CORONET

ROBERT LITTELL
☐ 21313 2 Sweet Reason   75p

EDWARD BEACH
☐ 19868 0 Dust On The Sea   £1.25

HENRI FRENAY
☐   The Night Will End   £1.00

AIREY NEAVE
☐ 10524 0 They Have Their Exits   75p

CORNELIUS RYAN
☐ 19941 5 A Bridge Too Far   £1.25

ELVET WILLIAMS
☐ 22010 4 Arbeitskommando   95p

All these books are available at your local bookshop or newsagent, or can be ordered direct from the publisher. Just tick the titles you want and fill in the form below.

Prices and availability subject to change without notice.

CORONET BOOKS, P.O. Box 11, Falmouth, Cornwall.

Please send cheque or postal order, and allow the following for postage and packing:

U.K. — One book 25p plus 10p per copy for each additional book ordered, up to a maximum of £1.05.

B.F.P.O. and EIRE — 25p for the first book plus 10p per copy for the next 8 books, thereafter 5p per book.

OTHER OVERSEAS CUSTOMERS — 40p for the first book and 12p per copy for each additional book.

Name ....

Address ....

....